KNOX'S STAND

JAMIE BEGLEY

Knox's Stand

ISBN-13: 978-0615916521
ISBN-10: 061591652X

PROLOGUE

He pounded into the woman underneath him hard, knowing that was exactly how she liked to be fucked. Her loud moan bugged the hell out of him as it reminded him of who he was fucking and the bed banged against the wall while he gave her every bit of his cock. She had always been one of the few women that could take his length comfortably without bitching that he was too big.

Hell, he was a big man. Why they always thought that he would have an average dick was beyond his understanding.

Gripping her under her knees he spread her thighs wider, thrusting high within her hot pussy. Letting himself go, he pounded his condom covered cock inside her.

Knox jerked away when she tried to draw his head down to kiss her. That shit wasn't going to happen. He never kissed, and he certainly wasn't about to put his tongue in this bitch's mouth.

She arched her hips, taking all of his cock while she gripped his ass, pulling him closer. His lust rising, he took a nipple into his mouth, sucking hard as he felt the first spasms of her orgasm.

"Fuck me!" she screamed. "Fuck me!" Knox put his

hand over her mouth when she started screaming like a bitch in heat, which was what she was, but Knox knew the thin walls of the cheap motel wouldn't prevent the other guests in the connecting room from hearing.

He didn't want anyone to know that he was fucking the bitch. His brothers from The Last Riders would be furious he had taken a dip in this particular hole. Hell, he was furious at himself for giving into her wanton enticement.

"Dammit, Sam. Quit biting my fucking hand!" Knox jerked his hand away from her vicious teeth.

"Then move it." Her face stared up at him in triumph.

"Quit screaming then. Someone's going to call the fucking cops."

"Worried someone will find out your fucking me, Knox?"

There wasn't a chance of that, he thought. She would make sure she spread the news of his lapse in judgment all over town. Dammit, he was mad as hell at himself. If he hadn't swerved to miss an animal on the ride through Treepoint, he wouldn't have crashed his bike into a fucking tree. The brothers were never going to let him live it down. His bike had been trashed. He had called Viper, however it had gone to voicemail. Therefore, when Sam had pulled up in her fancy car that he knew better than to get into, he'd climbed in anyway to wait for Viper's call.

It had taken her all of five minutes to have his cock in her mouth. He'd called himself a dumb fuck as her tongue played with his dick, yet she had been able to convince him to go back to her hotel room. Now he simply wanted to finish and get the hell out before Viper and his brothers found out and he got an ass reaming.

Sam's moans grew louder and Knox decided to bring an end to this clusterfuck. Biting down on her nipple, he used his teeth to give her that bite of pain she needed to bring her over. Thrusting even harder, he adjusted himself so that the piercing on his cock would rub the inside of her pussy with each stroke. The maneuver gave him the bite of pain he needed.

If she wasn't such a bitch, they would have made the perfect match. Both of them enjoyed sex that held an edge of pain. Nothing drastic, he wasn't into sadism, however he did enjoy something that made him feel the pain. That was why he had the piercings, which he'd had long enough now to know how to use to their best advantage, both for the women he was fucking and himself.

His tightening balls were warning him that he wasn't going to last much longer. Jerking her legs up until they were folded by her ribs with her feet dug into the mattress, giving him the leverage he needed, he stroked inside her until he felt her climax against his cock. When he could tell she was almost finished riding it out, he finally allowed himself to come, his cock jerking inside of her as it brought her into another screaming climax.

Could the bitch get any louder? Knox questioned himself again on his stupidity.

He didn't allow himself to relax as soon as his climax played out. He was climbing off the now content woman he despised. Pulling off the used condom, he threw it into the trashcan conveniently by the bed then jerked on his jeans, shoving his traitorous dick inside before buttoning it closed.

"What's the rush?" Knox looked up to see her lying still sprawled on the bed.

"I have to get my bike taken care of before the cops come by and tow it off."

His cell phone rang. Picking it up, Knox saw it was Viper returning his call. *Now he calls*, Knox thought in self-disgust.

"What's up?" Viper's cool voice on the phone made Knox even more furious at himself for betraying the club's decision not to have any contact with Samantha.

When the president of The Last Rider's found out who he had spent the last few hours fucking, Knox was going to get his ass kicked. Sam was responsible for attacking

Viper's fiancée and almost getting two other women raped, who also belonged to two of The Last Riders. Sam was lucky she was still breathing.

The only reason she had been left untouched was because the men didn't want to hurt a woman. They had left that side of things to the women in the club. Evie, the leader among the women, was waiting for the opportunity to deal with the lying woman. Sam had tried to blackmail Viper by telling him the child she had was his murdered brother's child. Winter, Viper's fiancée, had found out that his brother had never touched the underage, lying bitch.

"Crashed my bike on Maple. I need the trailer and a ride," Knox answered his President.

"I'll send Rider. Give him twenty. You okay?"

"Yeah, I'm cool."

"Good, see you when you get back to the house." Viper disconnected the call.

Knox put the phone back in his pocket before sitting down on the side of the bed to put on his boots. Sam came up behind him, circling his neck with her arms.

"Come on, Knox. When is one time ever enough for you?"

Knox stood up, shrugging her arms off him. Picking up his t-shirt off the floor, he put it on before turning back to Sam.

"Why are you staying here, Sam?"

A hateful look came over her face. "Since Slot and Tank have disappeared, I don't have anywhere to stay. The Blue Horsemen don't want me near them because they don't want trouble with Viper. The Last Riders won't let me crash there so I don't have many choices left. The courts have seized all my dad's properties because of the money he's stolen."

"Your grandmother would let you stay with her. You have a choice, Sam," Knox said, not feeling any sympathy for the woman.

"Stay with her? Hell, I'd rather stay here. I'd give the

4

old bitch a heart attack if I brought someone home to fuck."

Knox stared at the hard-hearted woman. How she could call her sweet grandmother a bitch beat the hell out of him.

"Gotta go; Rider will be waiting."

"Don't you want me to drive you?" Samantha asked, though she made no effort to get out of the messed up bed.

Let Rider see he had screwed up before he could tell Viper? Hell no. "It's not far. I can walk. No sense in you getting out." Knox walked to the door.

"See you around," Sam called out as he opened the door.

Knox turned around, about to say something nasty, but controlled his tongue. He had just fucked her. His dick hadn't cared that everyone in the club hated the woman; it was his own fault he had screwed up. He didn't have a right to open his mouth now.

Shutting the door behind him, he walked through the empty parking lot. It had become dark since he and Sam had come to the motel. He thought he saw a movement to his left, pausing momentarily and seeing nothing, he continued. Rider was going to be pissed if he kept him waiting too much longer.

When he arrived back to where he'd left his bike, Rider was already there waiting.

"Where in the fuck have you been?"

"You don't want to know," Knox said, moving forward to help Rider load his bike onto the trailer. "You going to be able to fix it?" he asked after the bike was loaded and they stood back surveying the damage.

"The front wheel is a mess, but I can bang it out." They both climbed into the truck to head back to the clubhouse. Rider cast him a sharp look as he pulled out.

"So where were you?" Rider asked.

Knox leaned back against the seat.

"Making the biggest mistake of my life," Knox said.

CHAPTER ONE

"Case dismissed" Judge Creech slammed down the gavel and the crowded courtroom began to empty.

"Thanks, Ms. Richards." Diamond turned to the spoiled man standing by her side.

"Don't thank me. If you get caught driving drunk again, lose my number. My bill will be in the mail." Diamond began putting her papers back into her briefcase, angry at herself for taking Luke Baxter's case in the first place. Her brief foray into criminal justice was as bad as she had feared it would be. She hated defending clients that were guilty as hell but had the money to afford her fee.

Sighing, Diamond put her regrets behind her, knowing this case would take care of several outstanding bills and give her some breathing room for a couple of weeks. Treepoint might be small, however it had an abundance of lawyers, each competing for clients.

When her bills came due, she had a choice of either beginning to take cases like Luke's or become an ambulance chaser. She had picked the lesser of two evils, but she was beginning to doubt herself when she saw Luke cockily leave the courtroom. *The dumbass is probably heading to the closest watering hole to celebrate.*

"Want to grab some lunch?" Diamond smiled as Caleb Green came to stand next to her as she snapped her briefcase closed.

"Consorting with the enemy?" she asked the assistant Commonwealth's Attorney.

"We could never be enemies, Di." Although he had been flirting with her the last couple of months, she had yet to accept one of the many dinner invitations he had issued. Caleb was good looking, always impeccably dressed and he was a constant gentleman, opening and closing doors for her.

She didn't know why she wasn't attracted to him, but she wasn't. He had the same attitude as several of the men she had dated in the past; perhaps she was simply saving herself the inevitable heartbreak in becoming involved in yet another relationship that had the same markings of failure.

"So, do you want to grab some lunch?" Caleb asked again, holding the door to the courtroom open as they walked through it into the busy hallway.

"Sounds good, I'm starved." Diamond felt his eyes running over her body, but refused to let it bother her. She was tall at five-nine and wasn't model thin. She had learned long ago that she was never going to be skinny with her love of cooking and food. Diamond liked to think of herself as curvy, not fat, and from the way Caleb was eyeing her breasts under the demur blouse she was wearing, she thought he would agree with that assessment.

Walking across the street once they were outside, they entered the diner to find it packed. It was the lunch hour and the diner had good food, therefore it took several minutes before Caleb managed to snag them a table.

Taking their seats, they sat down across from each other. Diamond picked up the menu to study it while Caleb ordered drinks for both of them.

Trying to decide between the fried chicken or a healthy

salad, she wasn't paying attention to the other customers in the restaurant when Caleb's low voice drew her eyes away from the menu, "I see one of your former clients is here."

"Who?" Diamond asked, looking up from the menu.

"Winter Simmons. She's sitting over there in the corner with that biker gang she runs around with now."

"It's not a gang, it's a motorcycle club," Diamond corrected.

"There's a difference?" Caleb asked snidely.

Diamond gave him a sharp look. "Yes, there a difference." Diamond made herself take a deep breath, calming herself against Caleb's prejudice.

It was exactly because of the same ill-informed prejudices that her childhood had been made miserable. As she had grown older, she had placed distance between herself and her parents' club. Her parents had been together for almost thirty-five years, and while she did not agree with their lifestyle, neither did she call it something it wasn't. She had been raised with the motorcycle club, learning the hard way of the contempt that people viewed them with.

When she had graduated college she had moved back home, but grew tired of the judgmental attitude of everyone who was aware of her parents' connection to the Destructors. Especially since the club made regular use of her services without paying for them, and becoming a regular pain in her ass, Diamond had decided to move to Treepoint. She had wanted a fresh start, yet still be close enough to visit her mother.

Caleb gave her an inquiring look as the waitress arrived to take their order, diverting his attention from questioning her any further. Aware of Caleb's judgmental personality, she ordered the chicken salad and sat back in her chair, unhappily staring at the nearby diner's plates of fried chicken and biscuits, not surprised when he ordered a salad for himself. *She was a better judge of character than he was,* Diamond thought.

Her eyes surveyed the room, going to Winter Simmons' table, who had been a client of Diamond's only two months ago. Her fiancé, Viper, the president of The Last Riders, was sitting next to her at the largest table in the diner. Diamond also recognized Evie and Bliss, who had been at the school board meeting where she had represented Winter to regain her job as a high school principal.

Winter was very attractive and her face glowed with happiness. The two other women at the table were knockouts as well. Evie was a brunette who carried sexy easily while Bliss was neither too large nor too small. She was perfect from her sultry face to her short, spiked blond hair in a large over-sized t-shirt that said 'bite me'. The t-shirt was low cut and displayed the curves of her firm breasts. Both women were sitting on each side of the huge, completely bald man sitting at the table. She had seen him the day she had met Winter at the clubhouse of The Last Riders for the first time.

He had come down the steps from the upper floor, entering the huge living room of the clubhouse with two women. He hadn't been wearing a shirt, showing his huge, muscular chest. The two women he had entered the room with had been scantily clad, just wearing t-shirts. It had been obvious to her what the three had been doing upstairs. It had been like stepping back in time to her childhood, seeing the same crap that had been going on in her parents' motorcycle club.

Diamond started to turn her eyes away when they were caught and held by the large man sandwiched between the two women. A spark of desire struck her; she had always been attracted to large men since she herself was so tall. Unfortunately, they always were drawn to the little delicate ones that were sitting next to him. Self-disgust with herself had her giving the staring man a look of contempt. A lot like the one she had worn when she had been angry with Caleb moments before.

Angry at her knee-jerk reaction to an unwanted attraction, she shifted her gaze back to Caleb, trying to divert herself from the scrutiny she still felt on her. She began discussing the case they had just fought over while putting the large group out of her mind. It wasn't easy; they were a boisterous group and Diamond was relieved when they stood up to leave the restaurant.

Her relief was short lived as the group made their way to her table. She could tell from Caleb's expression he wasn't pleased when they stopped at their table.

"Hello, Ms. Richards. How are you doing?" Winter asked curiously, looking at Caleb.

Diamond gave Winter her patented, lukewarm smile. "I'm fine, and you?"

"I'm doing well. I'm enjoying my new school." Winter gave her a smile in return, however Diamond could tell that the intelligent woman hadn't missed the snub of not being introduced to Caleb. Hell, Diamond was doing her a favor, but Winter had probably taken it as an insult.

"I'm glad you were able to work things out with the school board." Diamond had been relieved that both Winter and the school board managed to work out an agreement. Winter had fought the school system to keep her job, and while not retaining her position as the principal of the local high school, the school board had agreed she would be acceptable to replace the one that needed to retire at the alternative school.

"It's good seeing you again." Diamond gave her another cool smile. This time, The Last Riders got the message. They all stiffened while Viper gave her a hard look at her snub of his fiancée. Winter didn't let it faze her, merely ignoring their angry glares.

"You'll have to come to lunch with Sex Piston, Killyama and Crazy Bitch sometime. It was good to see you again, Diamond." With that parting shot, Winter and The Last Riders moved to leave the restaurant. Barely managing to keep her face from showing her embarrassment, Diamond met the angry glare of the large man as he threw a contemptuous look at both her and Caleb.

"Who's Sex Piston, Killyama and Crazy Bitch?"

Diamond skillfully evaded the question. "We better finish; we have to be back in court in thirty minutes."

Caleb looked as if he was about to ask the question again, but she quickly took a bite of her salad and Caleb began eating his lunch while he threw her several inquiring looks. Afterwards, they each paid for their own lunch before returning to the courthouse.

Diamond's next case was another DUI. This time her client received a stint with rehab and a device placed in his car that he would have to breathe into for the ignition to start. She wasn't upset about getting those requirements; he hadn't been given jail time and he would get some help with his drinking problem. That was what she called a win-win situation.

Diamond drove home afterwards, tired after the long day. Her mind kept wandering back to the episode in the diner. Winter had witnessed her rocky relationship with her sister, Sex Piston. Diamond was the first to admit she deserved the set down for her behavior, yet she had felt uncomfortable with the large group surrounding the table. She had been well aware that the judgmental townspeople as well as Caleb were eavesdropping on their conversation.

As she passed the local motel, she saw the local sheriff and the coroner's car. Wondering what had happened, she almost pulled over, but didn't. She was sure she would read about it in the local paper tomorrow.

CHAPTER TWO

Knox woke to someone shaking his shoulder hard. "Leave me alone." He felt Evie raise up on an elbow next to him.

"Knox, wake up. Something's going on downstairs. Viper just called and wants you to come down."

Groggily sliding out of the bed, he stood up and grabbed his jeans from the floor before pulling them on. Turning back to the bed, he saw Evie going back to sleep. She always ended up sleeping in his bed with one or more of the other women members. His bed was the largest in the house and he liked waking up in the middle of the night with a woman available.

"Don't get too comfortable. I'll be back in a few minutes." Evie merely gave a mumbled reply to that.

Already wide-awake by the time he pulled on his boots and t-shirt, he left the room and headed towards the downstairs when he heard loud voices from the top of the stairs. Looking down, he saw Viper and Shade arguing with the Sheriff.

"This is bullshit. Knox didn't touch that bitch!" Viper was yelling at the Sheriff.

"Calm down, Viper. Let's hear him out," Knox heard

Shade's calm voice.

Knox went down the steps and everyone turned to watch his approach. Knox began getting a bad feeling in his gut when he saw the grim looks on his friends' faces.

"What's up?" Knox asked the Sheriff.

"Samantha Bedford's body was found this afternoon at the motel," The sheriff replied while watching his reaction to the news.

Knox stiffened, already sensing where this was going.

"Knox has had nothing to do with that bitch since she attacked Beth; none of us have. She wasn't allowed back here at the clubhouse, and after the stunt she pulled with Winter, Beth and Lily at the diner, we haven't seen her."

The sheriff didn't say anything, just continued staring at Knox.

Knox could tell by the sheriff's reaction that he already knew that Knox had spent some time with Samantha the day before.

"I saw her yesterday. She stopped her car after I crashed my bike." The silence in the room became tangible.

"What happened then?" The sheriff probed.

Knox debated keeping his mouth shut, but by the look in the sheriff's eyes, he already knew that Sam and Knox had been in the motel room.

"We went back to her hotel room and fucked. When Viper called, I left. She was breathing just fine when I walked out that door." Knox stared back at the sheriff.

"Damn it, Knox," Viper said angrily.

"You're not going to say anything I didn't say to myself." Knox felt the anger of his brothers directed towards him.

"There are enough women here that you didn't need that bitch. What were you thinking?" Viper asked the question on everyone's mind.

"I wasn't. She pulled out my dick and went down on me," Knox said wryly.

"I have to take you in for questioning, Knox. There's no way around it; the newspaper is involved. A witness saw you leaving her room and told the reporter." *Of course someone saw him*, Knox thought wryly. Treepoint was full of busybodies.

Knox nodded, stepping forward. "Let's go."

Viper took his arm. "Don't answer any more questions. I'll get you a lawyer." Knox nodded his head and went out the door with the sheriff following him closely.

As the approached the squad car, the sheriff held the passenger door to the front seat open for Knox. He ignored it, and instead he opened the door to the backseat, getting in. "No sense in giving anyone the chance to say that you didn't do everything by the book."

Sighing, the sheriff closed both doors before getting in the car. Knox stared out the car window as the sheriff pulled out of the club's parking lot. As he leaned his head back against the seat, he had a sick feeling in his stomach that things were about to change, and not for the better.

* * *

Diamond poured herself a cup of coffee as she opened her newspaper, barely managing not to burn herself when she saw the headline. *Murdered woman found at the motel.* She read further on to discover that Samantha Bedford, a local woman that Diamond had never met, had been found by the maid sent in to clean the room.

Diamond moved to sit behind her desk as she read. It didn't say how she had died, however it did mention that a local resident had seen a man leave the room hours before her body had been discovered. Although it didn't state the man's name, the article did say he had been brought in for questioning. Diamond was sure she wouldn't know him anyway; she hadn't lived in Treepoint long and hadn't met many of the residents yet.

She heard the phone ring, but didn't move to answer it. She had hired a secretary part-time to answer her phone and mail. She really couldn't afford the added expense right now, yet with the new criminal cases she was taking, the secretary helped ease her workload.

"You're due in court in twenty minutes," a soft voice said from the doorway.

"Thanks, Holly. I'll be leaving in a few minutes." Diamond looked up at the young woman in the doorway. They had met when she had applied for the job she had posted in the want ads. They had liked each other on sight. Both were new to Treepoint and had become friends in the short time they had known each other.

They both were quiet and liked to keep to themselves. Holly was a dainty little brunette that had abundant curves. Whenever they had lunch together, Diamond felt men's eyes going to the woman next to her, but she wasn't jealous, she felt sympathy for her when she felt the woman's embarrassment at the way men looked at her. She had even confided in Diamond she had once considered breast reduction surgery, however the expense was out of her financial means.

She waved to Holly as she left the office, heading to the courthouse. Diamond was only a block away from the courthouse, which made it an easy walk. The back of the Church was across the street from her office, a building over from the courthouse. She would often cut across the Church parking lot. Today she wanted the walk and went the longer route, cutting down another side street. She turned the corner of the street to the courthouse and saw several motorcycles parked in front of the sheriff's office next door to the Courthouse.

"Hey Di."

Caleb greeted her from the top of the steps.

"Hi Caleb. You ready for court?"

"Always." He gave her his 'game on' smile, nodding towards the sheriff's office. "Did you hear the news?"

"What news?" she asked as they walked through the large doorway.

"They arrested one of The Last Rider's for the murder of Samantha Bedford," he answered her question as they walked into the crowded courtroom, each going to their respective tables, bringing their short conversation to an end.

Diamond opened her briefcase as the deputy brought in her client. Greer Porter had been caught selling a small amount of pot. The cocky, young man sat down next to Diamond at the table.

"You going to get me out of here today?" he asked as soon as his butt hit the chair.

"I'm going to try," was all Diamond could get out before the Judge entered the room.

"All Rise," the bailiff called from the front of the courtroom.

The case didn't last long with Greer being given a stern warning and a huge fine. He was lucky it had been such a small amount or it could have gone much harder on the young man.

"Thanks, Ms. Richards," he said as soon as the judge left the courtroom.

"If you get caught again, Greer, you won't get off so lightly."

The young man smiled back. "I don't intend on getting caught again. I should have known better than to sell to someone I didn't know. How was I supposed to know the sheriff hired a new deputy from out of town? Tate is going to kick my ass for being such a dumbass, but at least I was smart enough to start him off with a small enough quantity that I wouldn't get in too much trouble." Diamond could only stare back at Greer who was obviously proud of himself.

Diamond wanted to kick his ass herself.

"You're done here. I paid your fine." Tate Porter walked up behind Greer. The tall, lean man was older than the one that she had represented. He was the opposite of his brother as Diamond had found out when he had hired her to represent Greer. Greer had told her Tate had raised his brothers and sister after his parents were killed in a boating accident the year after Tate had graduated high school.

Diamond stared as the youngest brother, Dustin, and the sister, Rachel, came to stand by their brother. Dustin had a head full of jet black hair unlike his brothers and sister who also had dark hair, but it wasn't as curly nor did they have Dustin's grey eyes. The effect was a handsome man that Diamond was sure kept the local girls busy.

"Thanks, Ms. Richard." Rachel reached out to shake Diamond's hand. Her hand was rough unlike most women. She had learned that Rachel was a popular herbalist in the area, actually around the country. People traveled from all over to purchase her homemade medicines and have her perform a healing touch on them. Diamond thought it was ridiculous herself, but had found that the people in Treepoint took it very seriously.

The work-roughened hand that touched hers inspired nothing except wanting to end the uncomfortable contact.

Rachel eyed her curiously as their hands separated. Diamond avoided her eyes as she picked up the papers on the desk, shoving them into her briefcase.

"I'll send you my final bill in the mail," Diamond stated, turning to face the family with her briefcase in hand.

"That will be fine. As soon as I get it, I'll stop by your office and take care of it. You never know when we might need your services again," Tate said, looking at his unconcerned brother with censure. Diamond didn't envy him trying to take care of his strange family.

She walked outside with them, saying her goodbyes in front of the courthouse. She was turning to walk towards her office when The Last Riders walked outside the sheriff's office with an angry Marc Harris, the town's best criminal lawyer. The older lawyer looked ready to have a heart attack.

"I won't be talked to that way by anyone! Did you hear what he told me to do?" Marc was practically screaming at Viper and Winter.

"Mr. Harris, Knox didn't mean for you to take it so literally. He's just—" Winter tried to placate the older man.

"I don't care. You can find another lawyer, one that can deal with that asshole." Diamond was shocked that the established attorney had lost his composure to the extent she was witnessing.

"But—" again Winter tried to intercede, yet before she could continue, Harris stormed across the lot to his car.

All of them were still staring when he pulled out with a screech of tires. Diamond closed her mouth when she realized The Last Riders were all staring at her. Seeing the speculation in Viper's eyes, she could almost see the wheels turning in his mind.

Hell no, Diamond thought to herself. Swiveling in her high heels, she took off down the street at a brisk walk, trying to avoid what she saw coming.

"Ms. Richard." Diamond heard Winter's voice, but kept booking it down the street.

Suddenly, a man stepped out in front of her, bringing her to a sudden stop. She hadn't seen him before, but there was no doubt in her mind that he was a part of the motorcycle club. He was covered in tattoos, wearing dark jeans and a t-shirt. The sunglasses on his face hid his eyes, but he was good looking in a harsh kind of way. He gave Diamond the chills down her back. She didn't even try to move past him as Winter, Viper and two other members surrounded her on the sidewalk.

"Ms. Richard, we need your help," Winter began.

"I'm not taking on any new cases," Diamond said, turning to look at Winter instead of the one that was giving her the willies.

"That isn't what your sister said. She said you're having a hard time finding clients, and that was why you moved to Treepoint from Jamestown. Please can we just go somewhere to talk for a few minutes?" Winter pleaded.

Diamond grudgingly gave in. "My office is just around the corner." Her heart sank at Winter's relieved smile. She had every intention of convincing her to accept her friend's case, but Diamond had every intention of refusing. Nothing on earth could convince her to take the case. It would mean having more contact with the motorcycle club. She hadn't managed to get away from her parents' club to find herself entangled in another club's problems. No way in hell.

CHAPTER THREE

Diamond went into her office, followed closely by The Last Riders. Holly was filing papers in the cabinet when she turned to see who came in. Diamond wasn't surprised when the woman's mouth fell open as the office filled with several of the bikers.

"Holly, I'll be in my office if you need me." A nod was the only response the woman could manage besides the look that begged her not to leave her alone with the dangerous looking men that were taking a seat on the few chairs and small couch she had available for seating.

Winter, Viper and the heavily tattooed biker followed her inside her private office. Diamond went behind her desk, placing her briefcase on the neat surface before taking a seat.

"What's going on, Winter?" Diamond decided not to beat around the bush; the faster she found out what they wanted, the faster she could get rid of them.

"One of our members has been arrested in the murder of Samantha Bedford," Viper answered her question. Diamond blew out a breath of air. She had been expecting that, thanks to the brief information that Caleb had told her before court. Drug possession, assault, DUI; those were what she had dealt with since moving to Treepoint. She had never thought to represent a case for a client with the seriousness of a murder charge.

"I am going to save us both some time. I don't have the experience to defend a murder case." Diamond started to rise to her feet.

"The best criminal defense lawyer in the state of Kentucky just walked out on us. That asshole will defend anyone for the right amount of money. Knox pisses everyone off. There's not a lawyer that won't become angry and quit with his attitude. I don't want to be looking for a new lawyer everyday, we need someone that isn't going to run away the first time that Knox gets angry and scares the shit out of them."

"I'm sorry." *Actually she wasn't*, Diamond thought again, rising to show them the door.

"I'll pay whatever fee you want," Viper stated, looking around her office. Diamond sat back down.

"If money is no object, then you can afford any lawyer you want," Diamond protested, but then paused, rethinking whether she really wanted to talk them out of hiring her.

"Money didn't prevent Harris from walking out on us," Viper said in disgust.

Diamond just bet. Lawyers were notoriously uptight, leaving the men like Knox to the lower lawyers to deal with. Diamond swallowed. She was one of the lower lawyers hungry enough to need the money and the exposure the case would bring.

"How much money are we talking about?" Diamond asked.

The gleam in Viper's eyes said he knew he had her. Diamond forced down her anger and mentally added another figure on for his being an asshole.

"Let's cut to the chase. You prove Knox is innocent, I'll give you five hundred thousand dollars."

Diamond's figure went out her open door, liking his

much better.

"I take it you believe Knox is innocent?" Diamond queried.

"I know he is," Viper stated without pausing.

"You can't be so sure. Everyone has a breaking point, and from what you're telling me, Knox isn't the sweetest man in the county. Perhaps they got in an argument—"

"If he had killed her, Ms. Richards, no one would have found the body."

Diamond's eyes widened at Viper's calm reply while Winter winced, but didn't speak up, which led her to believe that she felt the same way. She stared out into her outer office at the men who were listening and saw the agreement on their faces.

Damn. Diamond knew she shouldn't touch this case, however the money was too much to resist. Even if she bailed, they would still have to pay her for the hours she billed.

As if reading her thoughts, Viper stated, "Of course, if you quit on us, I won't pay you one fucking dime."

Diamond started to protest, but she could see that this part was nonnegotiable.

"All right, you have a deal." Diamond heard herself agree while at the same time she wanted to smack herself silly. Her eyes saw one of The Last Riders get up from his chair in the lobby and go to Holly's desk, leaning against it as he spoke casually to her. She could tell from the seductive smile on the man's face he was making a play for her quiet secretary.

She was right. The sound of a chair hitting the wall sounded in the outside room and Holly all but ran into the room, coming to stand behind Diamond's chair with her face flaming red. The man gave a smile and came to stand in the doorway, watching with a predatory gleam in his eyes.

"Ms. Richards, your next appointment is due in ten minutes." Holly's voice was surprisingly firm, but she remained behind her desk. The Last Riders didn't try to hide their amusement at Holly's reaction.

"Stop it, Rider. Go on outside," Winter snapped at the man who then turned and walked away with a final wink at Holly.

"Thanks, Holly." Diamond stared hard at Viper. "After I'm finished with my next client, I'll go down to the sheriff's office and see what they have on him. I'll keep in touch. Get a bail bondsman ready for a call. I'll see what I can do about getting him out. Is he going to be a flight risk?"

"Knox wouldn't run if you pointed a gun at him. It's not in him; he is a soldier. He stands and fights."

"Good to know because, if he takes off, I'll still expect my money, and you can find yourself another lawyer."

"Deal," Viper said, walking out her door and taking his men with him.

Winter paused before leaving. "Thank you, Ms. Richards."

Diamond nodded her head, watching as her office emptied and Holly came to stand next to her.

"You took a case involving one of them?" she questioned.

"Yes," Diamond said grimly. "I did."

"What did he do?"

"They arrested him for killing Samantha Bedford." Diamond kept staring out of her office, seriously thinking about running after them and telling them to find another lawyer.

"Can I quit?" Holly asked her boss, gripping the desk.

"No."

* * *

Diamond took a deep breath to steady her nerves before going into the sheriff's office. The small office wasn't very busy as the dispatcher sat behind the front desk and watched curiously while Diamond approached.

"Hello, is the sheriff in?" Diamond requested.

"He sure is, honey. You wanting to see him?"

"Yes, thank you." Expecting the woman to pick up the phone, Diamond jumped when the woman yelled.

"Sheriff! You have someone here wantin' to talk to you." The office door at the end of the hall opened showing the sheriff.

"Come on back." His loud voice filled the office. Diamond hid her wince at the lack of decorum.

"Sheriff." Diamond extended her hand towards the large man who everyone in town respected. Diamond had met him before, several times, at the courthouse.

"What can I do for you, Ms. Richards?"

"I'd like to talk to my client, Knox Bates. I've scheduled a hearing in the morning to set bail."

Diamond didn't see surprise on his face when she told him she was representing Knox.

"Have you met Knox before?"

"No, but I know he must be a little difficult if his other lawyer quit," Diamond answered.

"Little doesn't describe anything about Knox. Prepare yourself." Diamond ignored his warning. Thanks to her parents' lifestyle, she had been exposed to some hardass bikers and she had held her own. She wasn't worried about dealing with Knox.

The sheriff went into his office again before coming back with the keys and then walked down the short hallway, Diamond following behind. The steel door was unlocked and pushed opened.

Diamond walked into a large, grey room containing a small window and long table with several chairs placed around the table.

"Have a seat. I'll bring him out."

Diamond sat down, opening her briefcase and pulling out her writing pad as well as a pen. She looked up when the sheriff returned with a huge man that Diamond recognized instantly. It wasn't like you could forget something that big and bald.

The huge biker was wearing faded jeans and a blue t-shirt that covered a muscled chest that she had seen the day that she had gone to The Last Riders clubhouse to interview Winter. He had been wearing only jeans then and his muscled chest had been bare, showing the tats on his chest and arm. He had also had his hands on two very attractive women who had obviously just been very intimate with the biker.

Diamond was more than familiar with the loose sexual atmosphere of a biker club, but from the way the trio acted, Diamond suspected it went beyond what even she had been exposed to.

Observing the man as he came across the room, Diamond was struck by his sexual aura. His cleanly shaven head and fierce expression were intimidating. He wasn't ugly by a long shot, however he wasn't handsome, either. The huge body, she was sure, had caused more than one man to back down from the threatening looking biker.

Diamond stood to her feet. "Hello, my name is Ms. Richards…"

"I know who you are." Knox took a seat at the table across from where she was standing, ignoring her outstretched hand.

Diamond's eyes narrowed at his interruption. "Then you know that Viper hired me to represent you in court."

"Viper told me. When you getting me out of here?" Knox asked bluntly.

"You have a hearing in the morning. If they set bail and your friends come up with the bond, you can be released afterward," Diamond explained.

"They'll have the money; just get me out of here."

"I intend to. Now, I looked over the case and I would like to ask you several questions. Sheriff, if you don't mind, I'd like to be alone with my client."

The sheriff gave her an amused look. "Certainly, if you need anything, just yell," he said, leaving with a warning look towards Knox who gave him a stubborn one in return.

Opening the file that Holly had put together for her, Diamond tried to ignore his hard stare.

"How well did you know Samantha Bedford?" Diamond started her questions.

"If you needed to know how she fucked, I could tell you anything you want to know. Personally, not a damn thing," Knox answered crudely. Diamond looked up at him from her papers to show him he wasn't going to get anywhere by trying to shock her.

"Okay. How long had you been fuck buddies?" she rephrased her question.

"Not buddies, we just fucked. You have to like each other to be buddies. I hated the bitch."

"I see. How did she feel about you?"

"Nothing. Sam didn't feel emotion other than the need to fuck. Had to have it all the time, didn't care who gave it to her or where as long as she got off," Knox said, leaning back in his chair and crossing his arms across his massive chest.

"Can you give me some names of other men she had a sexual relationship with?"

"No."

"Can't or won't?" Diamond tried to clarify his answer.

"Sam wasn't allowed to hang with The Last Riders anymore. Since she quit being a hang around, I don't know who she's been fucking. I didn't care enough to ask."

"You had sex with a woman and didn't inquire about her sexual history?" Diamond couldn't believe that a man could be so stupid in this day and age not to check out a partner's health status.

Knox shrugged, unconcerned. "I used a condom. Didn't let her have my mouth. She was safe enough to fuck."

Diamond's fingers tightened on her pen. This man was a living,-breathing jerk. Taking a deep breath, her mind kept going over and over how much she needed the money that defending Knox would bring.

"Let's move along. When did you meet Sam on Friday?"

"I didn't meet her. I crashed my bike and she was driving by and offered me a ride about four o'clock," Knox estimated.

"She offered you a ride?" Diamond looked up at him. "So how did her giving you a ride end up with both of you at the hotel? Are you sure you didn't have plans to meet her?"

"I'm sure," Knox stated.

"Okay, so she gave you a ride and you both decided to go to the motel?" Diamond asked. Trying to get the chain of events straight was like pulling teeth.

Knox sighed. "I called for a lift. While I was waiting for Viper to call me back, we sat in her car. She made a move, I didn't say no, so we went back to her hotel where we fucked for an hour. Viper returned my call, so I left to meet Rider. End of story."

"Do you have any witness to that fact? Did she come to the door and someone see her?" Diamond asked hopefully.

"No, she was still lying on the bed when I left." Damn. Diamond should have known it wouldn't be that easy.

"Was she breathing?"

Knox's eyes narrowed at her caustic reply. "Yeah, she was breathing." Knox leaned forward. "If I was going to kill the bitch, I wouldn't have left my condom in the trash can. They wouldn't have found my fingerprints and they fucking would have never found her body."

Diamond shivered at his harsh answer. She was definitely understanding why the rest of his club had no doubt that he spoke the truth. This man would cover his tracks.

Diamond again looked down at her paperwork. "She had bruising around her mouth and vagina. Were you aware of that?" Keeping a professional appearance was hard when she was fighting the embarrassment of her question.

"Sam and I both enjoy sex that gets a little rough. " Knox shrugged.

"You have bite marks on your hand that are consistent with the bruising around her mouth."

"When Sam comes, she likes to scream; the walls at that motel are paper thin." This time Diamond wasn't able to prevent herself from blushing.

"I see."

"I doubt it," Knox said sarcastically.

Diamond looked up at his reply, meeting his mocking gaze. She smothered her irritation once again, thinking about the money she would earn defending him.

"How often have you and Sam seen each other since she was no longer allowed at the clubhouse?"

"Friday was the first time."

"Can I ask why, if you disliked this woman so much, did you have sex with her?" Diamond didn't think he seemed the type to be swept away with passion.

A look of self-disgust flashed across his face. "Not many men would turn her down. Sam was not only good at sex, she enjoyed it. She was one of the few women that could give it to me the way I like it."

Diamond wasn't going to touch that answer. Gathering her paperwork, she began putting it back in her briefcase.

"The hearing is first thing in the morning. If you think of anything else that's important, ask the sheriff to contact me. I'll see you tomorrow." Hastily Diamond stood up without looking at him directly.

Diamond went to the door and yelled for the sheriff to let her out. He rushed out of his office, looking at her in surprise.

"Finished?" he asked, looking over her shoulder at Knox still seated at the table with an amused expression on his face.

"Yes, I have what I need." As soon as the sheriff

opened the door, Diamond rushed through it, well aware she was making an ass of herself.

"Thank you, Sheriff." Without waiting for a reply, Diamond walked through the office, ignoring the receptionist's curious eyes. Once outside, she took a deep breath, trying to gather her composure. As she stood there, several people passing by gave her inquiring glances, which she ignored. When Knox had described Sam, he hadn't been trying to embarrass her. He had merely been stating a fact.

She hadn't really been all that embarrassed, either. No, she had left quickly to escape the feeling of arousal that had stormed her body at his blunt revelation. Diamond had only known a few lovers in her life. One, her high school sweetheart, who she had mistakenly thought would be with her forever; another when she had graduated college and began law school; and the last, who'd thought he saw a meal ticket on her forehead. Diamond enjoyed sex with each of them, but she had a feeling that what Knox participated in was something she had never experienced and had no intention of introducing in her life.

Walking back to her office, she went to her car parked in the lot. Shakily opening her car door, she was finally able to regain control of her wayward body; now angry for making a fool of herself. The next time she was around Knox she would be able to manage her composure and keep her traitorous body under control.

One thing her parents' life had provided was an insight into the life Knox led and she wasn't about to find herself attracted to a man involved in a lifestyle she hated.

CHAPTER FOUR

Diamond waited patiently as the clerk signed the release papers. The older woman kept glancing up at Knox, finally handing her the paperwork she needed. Once they were in her hands, she turned to Knox.

"You're free to go." Diamond kept her tone completely business-like.

Knox nodded, turning on his heel to leave, while Diamond followed along, rushing to keep up with his long strides. Outside, Diamond came to a stop at seeing her client swallowed up in the crowd of The Last Riders waiting for their friend's release.

Diamond ignored a pretty blond wrapping herself around Knox and instead moved toward Viper and Winter standing on the edge of the crowd.

"Keep him out of sight, and whatever you do, don't let him get into any trouble. The Commonwealth's Attorney won't hesitate to throw him back in jail."

"I'll make him stay at the clubhouse," Viper promised.

"What's next?" Winter asked Diamond.

"A trial date will be set. I'm going to look into the case and hopefully find something to prove his innocence before then. It's our best hope." Diamond knew a jury would convict him on sight alone. The Commonwealth's Attorney had already pulled a fast one, bringing evidence the day before to the grand jury— in which Knox's previous lawyer had represented him—to get him indicted.

"Is that safe?" Winter asked.

"Yes. If Knox didn't kill her, then we have to cast some doubt. The best way to do that is to prove someone else had a motive. I'm mainly going to be talking to Sam's friends."

"Good luck with that; she didn't have any." Evie was once again easily recognizable to Diamond.

"There has to be someone in town who knew Sam well. I'll find them." Determination to earn her money had her bracing for the work ahead. "I need to get back to my office. Like I said, keep him out of sight." Diamond cast a last look at Knox, who now had a dark haired woman locked to his side.

"No problem." Diamond cast Viper a doubtful glance and then turned on her heel, leaving the large crowd that was drawing attention. She heard the loud roar of the motorcycles pass as she turned down the side street to her office. Unable to help herself, Diamond watched as they passed. Knox was easily noticeable as he was the largest in the group. Evie was sitting behind him with her arms wrapped tightly around his waist. Diamond felt his gaze on her and dropped hers to the ground then kept on walking.

* * *

Knox let himself into his room. Alone, he went into the bathroom and took a shower. Viper had immediately taken him into the huge room off the kitchen where club meetings often took place where he had been given an ass reaming in front of all the brothers for making the mistake of fucking Sam. He had deserved it and had made no excuses for himself. Apologizing for his mistake had eased the tension in the room. Finally, seeing his friend's exhaustion, Viper had told him to grab some sleep. Knox hadn't argued; weary from sleeping on the small cot in the jail, he wanted nothing other than his big bed and a few hours sleep.

After washing and shampooing his scalp, he let the clean water slice over his flesh, thinking about the stuck-up lawyer representing him. His cock hardened thinking about her large frame and how she would fit underneath him without him worrying about crushing her. Grabbing a clean towel when he got out of the shower, he hung the towel up on a hook on his bathroom door.

Going back into his bedroom, he opened the door that led to the hallway.

"Jewell!" His bellow sounded throughout the house. Minutes later, Jewell sauntered down the hallway with a smile on her face.

"Need anything?" she asked, already unbuttoning her top.

"Get your ass in here."

Jewell smiled as she went into his bedroom, surprised when the door closed. Seeing her surprised look, Knox explained. "I'm tired. Take off your pants."

Jewell immediately started taking off her pants. As soon as she was undressed, Knox lifted her, tossing her onto the bed.

Jewell was just what he needed right now to burn off his frustration of being stupid enough to touch Sam, for being caught up in her murder, and just now, having to take shit in front of everyone when he knew he was a fuck-up. She immediately went into the position she knew he preferred, climbing onto the bed on her knees.

Knox thrust his cock high inside her with one lunge of his hips and she released a small scream at his entry.

"Be quiet." Knox gave her his command and Jewell obeyed, going silent; the only sound in the room was the sound of their bodies as they slapped together while he rode out his passion on her willing body.

Jewell, other than Sam, was the only woman he had found who could take his sexual drive. The other women he had discovered each and everyone's turn on and none had been into his way of rough and ready. It didn't make them less attractive to him; he would just pick the one to suit the mood he was in. He was in the mood now to burn out some frustration and Jewell was the best choice for that.

Smacking her ass, he let himself thrust higher within her, hearing her moans of pleasure. Smacking her ass again, he ground his cock into her, making sure his piercing rubbed against her g-spot. She went off like a rocket and Knox had to hold her up by her hips while he continued thrusting. Feeling his own orgasm approaching, he thrust faster to bring his own self over, spilling into the condom he had put on before entering her.

"Damn, Knox." Jewell lay against his chest, breathing hard. "I missed you."

Knox smiled, rolling her to his side. "You mean you missed my cock." He lay on his side, pulling her to the curve of his body, grasping her breast and playing with her nipple.

"You want me to leave so you can get some sleep?" Jewell offered.

Jewell and Evie usually ended up sleeping most nights in either his or Rider's bed.

"No, stay. I'm only going to take a cat nap. When I wake up, I plan to fuck you again."

"Okay." Knox dozed off with Jewel's naked body close.

When he woke up, he would wake her for another round; this one more intense because he wouldn't be tired. Jewel knew, which was why she hadn't wanted to leave.

* * *

Diamond let herself into her apartment. Taking off her heels at the doorway, her feet sunk into the plush white carpet as she dropped her briefcase onto the table beside the door. Sighing, she went into her living room and plopped down onto her leather couch. The soft material felt good against her skin.

Thinking about Knox's case, she put up her feet, relaxing as her mind played back the events that had led up to Samantha Bedford's murder. Knox had said that she had driven by and seen his crashed bike. He was in a neighborhood that wasn't well traveled, but it was used as a shortcut to a road that led out of town towards The Last Riders' clubhouse. It explained why Knox was there, but why Sam?

Standing up to get her briefcase, she returned to the couch and began going through the information she had already gathered on Samantha.

That neighborhood had houses that were in the older part of town; cross-referencing her notes, she noticed Samantha's grandmother, Mrs. Langley, lived not far from where Knox had crashed; her home was only a block away. Diamond got to her feet, fixing herself a quick meal which she ate while planning her next course of action. Making several phone calls, she sat up quite a few appointments for the next day.

Finally with her plans in motion, she went to her bedroom. Gathering her nightclothes she went into the bathroom, filled up her tub with hot water and then sank into the deep warmth, letting her remaining tension evaporate. This was the perfect ending to her long day. Diamond had no doubt in her mind how Knox would be celebrating his release, the only question was with who and how many.

Turning her thoughts away from him, she thought about stopping by her mother's house in the next few days. It had been a while since she'd visited, and taking this case had caused her to think more and more about her family. Sex Piston would invariably show up at some time during the visit, though; no matter how hard Diamond tried to dodge her. It would always piss of Diamond because she was an irritant. She would consistently start an argument and her mother always took Sex Piston's side, which never made for an easy visit.

Sex Piston thought Diamond was a stuck-up bitch, and Diamond thought Sex Piston was a slut. From the time they were children, they had always fought. They were the complete opposites; where Diamond hated the biker lifestyle they had been raised in, Sex Piston loved the freedom and don't-give-a-shit attitude that was so much a part of the Destructors that their father had been President over until he had recently stepped down.

It disgusted Diamond that her sister took sex as casually as their father did. Sex Piston and her boyfriend, Ace, had continuously had an on-and-off relationship for years. They would break up when they had an itch to scratch with someone else then, when that lust-fest was over, they would end up back together. It was the same stunt their father would pull when they were growing up except he hadn't broken up with their mother, he had simply cheated on her behind her back.

At one time Diamond had worshiped her father as much as Sex Piston, if not more. She had loved both of her parents and was close to her mother, but her father had been her hero. No one could beat him; he was a strong, silent man, but when he took action, everyone watched themselves. She would run to him when he would come home from work; Diamond still remembered him lifting her from her feet and tossing her up in the air to be caught. Laughing, she would hug his thick neck. "I love you, Daddy," she would say.

That had come to an end the day she had been beaten up at school from someone mad at Sex Piston. Instead of walking the two blocks to her home as she was supposed to, she had run off before Sex Piston could appear and gone to her father's clubhouse to cry on his shoulder.

It had taken over an hour to walk there. She still remembered how tired she had been and how sore she was from the other girl's fists when she had reached the clubhouse. A new probate was outside watching the door and she had known he wouldn't let her in to see her father. Not wanting to embarrass him by showing up in front of his friends with a black eye, she had sneaked around back and climbed in through a window that was broken. She had heard her father telling someone to get it fixed, thankfully they hadn't and Diamond managed to wiggle through.

She had searched the house that had appeared mainly empty, but she had seen her father's bike out front, therefore she knew he was there somewhere. Hearing sounds from the front room, Diamond went down the hallway and peeked around the corner. There she had found two other men in the room with her father as well as a woman lying on the pool table. One of the men was slamming his thing into her as another man sucked on her breasts. Her father had merely watched without touching the woman.

Diamond turned away, embarrassed, yet she hesitated as the man who was having sex with the woman groaned and pulled out of her. That was when Diamond had gotten her first glance at a man's penis, watching as he pulled something off it and threw it into a trashcan. With her eyes on the startling first look, she had missed her father unzipping his own jeans and placing a condom on. Diamond's attention was drawn back when the woman moaned.

"Can you handle another one?" The woman widened her legs as her father stepped between them. He plunged his penis into the withering woman who wrapped her legs around his waist and began moving with him.

"Fuck me." The woman arched into the mouth of the man still sucking on her breast.

Diamond had sneaked back down the hallway and climbed back out the broken window and walked home.

That evening, when her father had arrived home she had not rushed down the steps to greet him nor had she gone down to dinner. Her mother had come in to check on her and had consoled her about the beating, however Diamond found a huge barrier now in place between her mother and herself. She had been unable to meet her mother's eyes and tell her what she had witnessed.

Her father had come to her room as soon as her mother had told him about the fight at school. Diamond still remembered when he had reached out to touch her face. She had jerked away from this touch, stepping away. She had then pretended an interest in her homework until he had left.

Diamond had never told any of her family about what she had seen, and the disillusionment had created a wedge between her and her father. After that, she'd no longer gone to the biker get-togethers unless forced by her parents, emotionally withdrawing to spend more and more time alone in her room.

Sex Piston's sexual antics brought out the revulsion she'd felt when she had found their dad with the other woman. It was a painful reminder and often made her act out towards her sister.

Diamond would have long ago broken off contact with her family if not for her mother. She alone was the reason Diamond didn't cut the final tie to her family, yet it was becoming harder to maintain a relationship with her as her mother was determined that her daughters get along. Diamond knew it was never going to happen.

Getting out of the bathtub she dried herself off and dressed for bed. Diamond lay down on her bed, turning out her bedside lamp, then for some odd reason, missing her mother. Tomorrow, when she finished the interviews, she would stop by her mother's house early enough that she should be able to avoid her father and Sex Piston.

CHAPTER FIVE

Early the next day, Mrs. Langley answered her door when she heard Diamond's knock.

"Mrs. Langley, I'm Diamond Richards. Thank you for seeing me."

"Please come in. I'm anxious to be of any help I can." The older woman's face was grief-stricken. Samantha, Diamond had come to find out, was Mrs. Langley's only relative. With her death, she no longer had any family left.

The woman showed her into a formal living room that was very well taken care of with several family photos and expensive knick-knacks placed around the room.

Sitting on the couch, she accepted the cup of coffee the woman had waiting for her.

Diamond didn't want to upset the woman further, but she needed answers. "I am sorry for your loss, but do you mind me asking if Sam had stopped by the day of her death?"

Mrs. Langley nodded, placing her shaking cup back down on the ornate coffee table. "Yes, she came by for a few minutes then left. She didn't stay thirty minutes." Her voice cracked.

"Did she come by for any particular reason?" Samantha

carefully probed.

"She needed some money." Mrs. Langley answered, a tear running down her cheek.

"Did you give it to her?"

"Yes, but it wasn't much. I'm not wealthy, but I have enough to live on. Sam wanted several thousand dollars. She was upset with me when I couldn't give it to her."

"So she left when you told her no?" Diamond asked gently.

"No, she asked me for some of my jewelry to sell."

"Did you give it to her?" Diamond disliked the woman she was investigating. The more she learned, the more her dislike grew. Seeing the woman in front of her, Diamond wished Samantha was alive so she could kick her ass.

"Yes, I gave her two rings and a necklace. She took them and left. Do you think that the jewelry could have drawn the killer to her?" The thought had her hands shaking.

"No, I'm sure it didn't, Mrs. Langley." Diamond felt angry with herself because it could be a false assurance, however she couldn't help wanting to make her feel better.

Diamond finished drinking her coffee and sat with the woman a few more minutes. She was about to leave, but then brought up a subject that she knew would further upset the woman. "I understand the sheriff is currently investigating the whereabouts of your great-grandchild?"

"Yes, Samantha had the baby in Jamestown. From there, they can't find a trace of the child. She tried to claim that Gavin James was the father, but I put a stop to that."

"Do you know who the father is?"

"No, I can't help you there. Samantha always kept that part of her life secret from me. She knew I wouldn't approve."

"Thank you for your time, Mrs. Langley. I know this is a very difficult time for you," Diamond apologized and meant it; the woman seemed really sweet and didn't deserve the ungrateful granddaughter fate had given her.

Mrs. Langley nodded and then showed Diamond to the door. She hated leaving the woman alone in her grief, but having no other option, she reached into her purse to find one of her cards, giving it to the woman.

"Take my card. If you need anything I can help you with, please call, Mrs. Langley."

"Thank you, Ms. Richards." Mrs. Langley managed a weak smile.

"Call me Di," Diamond said, waiting until Mrs. Langley nodded her head and then closed the door before she returned to her car. When the car started, Diamond put it in gear, then backed out of the driveway, thinking of Samantha. The sheriff hadn't mentioned the jewels, which meant the only one who knew about them had to be the murderer. If she found the jewels, she would find Samantha's murderer.

* * *

On the way back to her office, Diamond passed the diner as several bikers were going inside. She caught a quick glance at one of the men's jackets. Coming to a sudden decision, she braked sharply and turned into the diner's parking lot.

Leaving her briefcase in the car, she grabbed her purse then braced herself to go inside the busy diner.

Inside, she saw the men she was looking for sitting at a large table. Searching the group, she found the one she thought might be the leader.

Diamond assumed her professional mantle as she strode forward confidently. As she approached, the men noticed her and quit talking to see if she would be brave enough to talk to them.

"Hello. May I talk to you gentlemen for a few moments?" Diamond addressed her request to the man with the long blond hair. His moustache and beard covered a good portion of his face, but Diamond could still see he was an attractive man. He appeared to be in his late thirties; however the dead look in his eyes spoke of a man much older. For some reason Diamond couldn't explain, she felt sympathy for this man who had been through something that had marked him to such an extent.

"Sure, sweet thing. Will my lap do?" One of the men slid his chair back and motioned for Diamond to have a seat.

Diamond moved to the side and pulled out an empty chair, sitting down. The waitress came to take her order, giving Diamond a worried glance. She ordered herself a glass of water; she couldn't handle another cup of coffee. After the waitress left, Diamond faced the table of men who were staring at her with astonishment.

"I was wondering if it would be possible to ask a few questions." Diamond felt the atmosphere at the table change with her request.

"Unless you want to ask me how long my dick is, then no," the man who had offered her his lap to sit on said sharply.

Ignoring him she asked the question to the man she now was sure was the leader.

"It won't take long."

"You a cop?" His eyes brushed over Diamond's designer dress.

"No, I'm a lawyer. I'm investigating the murder of Samantha Bedford."

Everyone's face closed off and Diamond knew that they had been acquainted with the woman.

"Then I'm going to repeat, the answer is no. Now get the fuck out of here," he said.

It took all her years of dealing with badass bikers to keep her seat as the waitress sat down her water and retreated with another worried glance.

"I just need to talk to the three men that Sam was friends with in your club. Warrants have been taken out for their arrests since they missed their last court appearance and I know you won't break a confidence and tell me where they are, but if you had a way to contact them, perhaps you could give them my number?" Diamond reached into her purse and pulled out her card, handing it to the blond biker.

He took it from her and tore it into pieces.

"I told you to fucking go. Next time, I won't be so nice." His glare went from detached interest to a threat that she had no doubt he would see carried out.

Just after that, the door to the restaurant opened and several of The Last Riders entered. Diamond recognized Knox, Viper, Razor and Rider—the one that had all the tats—brought up the rear.

They came to stand behind Diamond. "You having problems?" Viper asked Diamond.

Before she could answer, the leader spoke. "She doesn't have a problem, we do. We've asked her twice to leave, she's ignored us both times."

"That true?" Viper turned to her.

Diamond looked at Viper. "I need to find the men who were with Sam that day outside in the parking lot. They belong to the Blue Horsemen. You want me to clear Knox?" Diamond stared pointedly at Knox.

The blond man leaned toward Diamond, losing his casual appearance. "I don't know where the fuck they are, and I don't know a damn thing about their families. They aren't horsemen anymore and they weren't when they pulled that stunt with Sam."

"Stud. I think she got your message," Knox said, taking a step forward.

"Good. Then maybe she'll get her ass away from our table," Stud snapped.

"Ms. Richards. Let's go," Viper ordered.

"Ms. Richards? When the hell did you become so polite?" The men around the table laughed at the sarcastic reply from the man who had offered her his lap.

"You laughing at Viper being polite, Bear?" Knox came back with his own smart-ass remark. The tension filled the restaurant this time as the men from the rival bike clubs began to escalate. Diamond rose to her feet.

Ash looked at Knox. "No."

Diamond didn't blame him from backing down; Knox looked furious.

"I'm finished. Sorry for the interruption." Diamond left the men and then left the diner without looking back, however she was brought to a stop outside when she was grabbed by her arm.

"What in the hell were you thinking?" Knox angrily asked her.

"I thought I might try to find out who killed Samantha. It's what Viper hired me to do," Diamond answered, jerking her arm out of his grasp.

"I didn't tell you to take on a motorcycle club. You should have called me or the sheriff who could have found out the information you needed," Viper said as he came outside, hearing her answer to Knox's question.

"I didn't need your help. I was safe. What were they going to do in a restaurant across from the sheriff's office?"

"Were you planning on staying in there? They would have followed you home." Knox stared at her like she was stupid.

"It doesn't matter; it's over." Turning on her heels, she strode to her car.

"It isn't fucking over. You're on their radar now. They're going to watch and make sure that you don't drag their club into being investigated," Knox said, striding after her.

"How do you know that?" Diamond snapped at the big lug following behind her with the rest of The Last Riders following.

"Because it's what we would do," Knox answered, slamming his hand on her car door when she would have jerked it open.

"Back off, Knox," Viper stated calmly. Knox stepped away, removing his hand from her car door.

Diamond swung around to face Viper and the rest of The Last Riders.

"If you want me to find out who killed Samantha, I'm going to have to step on some toes. Are you going to give me shit every time?" Diamond asked bluntly.

"We're not giving you shit. The men that Samantha associated with were dangerous, and those are the ones we know about. Obviously someone killed her, so eventually, you're going to come into contact with the person who did. The best way to handle this situation is to keep someone with you who can keep an eye on the situation so that you won't get hurt," Viper cautioned her.

"I don't need someone to watch my back. I can take care of myself," Diamond said, becoming angry.

"I'm sure you can. We'll merely provide you with back-up if you need our help," Viper reasoned.

"I can't find out what I need to know with you guys following me around," Diamond argued back.

"You won't need all of us, one will do. Knox and Rider can take turns keeping an eye on you." Viper crossed his arms over his chest, giving Diamond the impression that the decision had been made.

"Hell, no." Diamond refused to have either of the men following her.

"Why not?" This time it was Knox who answered. "I should be helping. It's my ass that will be back in jail if we don't find out who killed her."

Diamond couldn't argue with that reasoning. The stubborn male faces staring at her weren't going to give in unless she agreed to have one of them watching her.

"Fine, the next time I want to talk to someone that is in a motorcycle club, I'll give you a call." Diamond opened her car door, slid in and slammed the door closed. The men moved out of the way as she reversed and pulled out of the parking lot.

"Knox," Viper ordered.

Knox nodded and headed to his bike to follow the

stubborn attorney. Whether she liked it or not, he had just become her shadow.

CHAPTER SIX

Diamond pulled into her office parking lot and got out of her car. Seeing Knox pull in behind her, she didn't stop. She merely ignored his presence and opened her office door.

Holly was sitting behind her desk on the computer when she entered the room.

"I put your messages on your desk. You had a couple of calls from potential clients; One a DUI another an assault."

"I'll call them back." Diamond stopped briefly at her desk. Opening her briefcase, she pulled out the notebook she had used to take notes of her conversation with Mrs. Langley. "Could you type this up and place them in Knox's folder."

"I'll take care of it."

"Thanks, Holly."

Holly smiled. "No problem."

Diamond went into her office and made several calls. She returned the phone calls to the two potential clients, turned down the DUI and accepted the assault case, scheduling an appointment for the client to come in the next day. After she disconnected the call, she pulled up a list of pawn shops online and called, seeing if anyone had pawned jewelry fitting the description Mrs. Langley had provided.

It was a long shot, and Diamond wasn't surprised when nothing turned up. Leaning back in her chair, she stared up at the ceiling, contemplating her next move. Deciding to call it a day, Diamond shut down her computer and placed her papers back into her briefcase.

"I'm leaving early today, Holly. Finish up what you're working on and you can leave." Diamond paused in front of her secretary's desk.

"Thanks, Ms. Richards. I'm not feeling well, so an early day sounds good."

"Are you all right?"

She noticed then, for the first time, that her secretary was pale. "I'm fine, probably a virus."

Diamond tried to discreetly take a step away from her desk without causing offense. When Holly gave her a faint smile she knew she had been unsuccessful.

"If you don't feel better, don't bother coming in tomorrow. I'll handle the office," Diamond offered.

"I'm sure I'll feel better," Holly protested.

Diamond left her secretary finishing up her work. When she opened the door, she came to a full stop. Knox was sitting casually on his motorcycle with a couple of secretaries from the building talking to him. His eyes met hers as she walked up to him.

"Do your bosses know you're out here on their dime?" Diamond said to the two women.

"We're on break," the model thin blond stated, giving Diamond a hard glare.

"Well, breaks over," Diamond snapped.

Diamond's lips tightened at Knox's raised brow.

"I don't need you to sit in my parking lot. I told Viper I'd call when I need assistance, and I will." Diamond spun on her heel before he could answer then turned back in case he hadn't listened. "I'm off for the day anyway, so you can head home to the women waiting for you there," she said disdainfully.

Diamond got into her car and then drove out of the lot without a backward glance.

* * *

Knox watched the stone-faced bitch pull out of the parking lot. "Fuck it." Starting his bike, he followed her through town. He made sure to stay far enough back that he didn't draw her attention and was surprised when she headed out of town. He trailed behind her as she drove, surprised when she drove through Jamestown twenty minutes later. Sure this didn't have anything to do with his case, he almost turned around, but his curiosity had him continuing to follow.

When she drove through a neighborhood that had seen better days, he hung back further, not wanting to alert her to his presence. Ten minutes later, she pulled in front of an older home that was in better condition than most. She then got out of her car, going inside. Knox sat watching the house she entered, curious as to who she was visiting. She had an apartment in Treepoint, Viper had told him, so this must be family or friend.

An hour past before Knox picked up the sound of another bike, which was coming from the opposite direction he was sitting. Knox watched as a biker swung familiarly into the driveway. From the jacket he spotted on the biker's back, he recognized the man belong to the Destructors. The man's long, grey ponytail reached down his back, yet Knox could tell from the way he moved that he was still in good shape. As the biker climbed off his motorcycle, Knox saw him eye Diamond's car before he went inside.

Knox was surprised to see the door open minutes later and Diamond rush outside, followed by an older woman that resembled her. Knox instantly knew he was looking at Diamond's mother. Her hair was a brighter shade of red than Diamond's and she was pretty; dressed in tight jeans as well as a tight top that would have younger women envious of the sultry curves she possessed.

He watched as the two women argued while the biker came to the doorway to watch. The biker's face was unguarded with Diamond's back to him; Knox easily read the man's hurt. Diamond shook off her mother's restraining arm then headed straight to her car and drove away.

Knox watched the mother turn back to the house with anguish on her face while the biker left the doorway, taking the woman in his arms. Knox figured there was some heavy shit going down in that family for there to be such pain on her parents' faces. The stuck up bitch probably figured she was too good for them now that she was a lawyer.

That realization had Knox liking the lawyer even less than he had before. Starting his bike, he went back through the neighborhood, not surprised when he came back to the main road and Diamond was a few cars ahead. He maintained his distance as she drove back to Treepoint without stopping until she parked at her apartment.

When she got out of the car, she took her briefcase, letting him know that this time she was in for the night. Continuing on, he headed back to the clubhouse where he parked his bike then went inside the house.

The large house had initially been intended to be a bed and breakfast when Viper's brother had come to town to explore the possibility of opening the business The Last Riders owned. The living room, where they held their parties, was easily the size of four normal living rooms with a bar in the corner while the kitchen was a chef's dream. It was more than able to cook the large quantities of food that they needed. The attached dining room was also large, as was the meeting room off to the other side. The many bedrooms upstairs provided all the brothers with their own rooms as well as several of the women, though they were more than likely to end up spending the night in whichever bed they wanted.

As he entered, Knox spotted Viper sitting on the couch with Winter close to his side. "What are you doing back so early?" he questioned.

"She's in for the day," Knox answered his president. "I'm going to grab a shower then I'm going to Rosie's."

"I'm in for that," Rider said, coming into the room.

By the time he was showered and changed, several others had decided to tag along.

"Stay out of trouble," Viper warned.

Knox gave him the finger as he walked out the door. What trouble could he get into at Rosie's? It was The Last Riders favorite bar. The only fight he had ever gotten into there had been with Viper's father, Ton.

Knox, Rider, Train, Cash and Shade all headed to the bar with several of the women riding at their backs. As they pulled into the lot, Knox recognized Diamond's car in the lot. The woman actually surprised Knox. Not only had she not stayed in for the night, but she had not called Viper to tell him she would be going to Rosie's. The woman had no fear.

Knox was about to show her just how much she had to fear.

CHAPTER SEVEN

Diamond had showered and changed into more comfortable clothes when a thought occurred to her. Looking at her watch, she knew it was early enough that it shouldn't be too busy at Rosie's. Deciding not to call Viper, she put on her tennis shoes, not wanting to take the time to change back into her other clothes.

The drive to the bar on the outskirts of town, halfway up the mountain, was a short one. Diamond was happy to see the empty parking lot. After the day she'd had, she would have broken and called Viper if there had been too many bikes around.

Once inside, it took Diamond's eyes a few minutes to adjust to the dim lighting. The bar was old and looked it, however it was clean with tables and a dance floor. In the middle of the dance floor was a pole that Diamond was sure had been taken advantage of after a few drinks.

The bartender was watching her from behind the bar, so Diamond pasted a smile on her face as she went to the counter and climbed onto one of the stools.

"Hi." Diamond tried her most disarming smile.

"Hey." The bartender didn't return her smile. "What can I get you?"

"A beer would be great."

The bartender reached into the cooler and brought out a beer and a frosted mug, placing both in front of her.

"Thanks." Diamond reached into her pocket, pulling out some cash then placing it on the counter.

She then watched as the bartender went back to cleaning his glasses before she cleared her throat. "I was wondering if you could help me. I was trying to find out some information on a woman."

"Don't know nothin'." He didn't stop what he was doing.

"You don't even know who it is."

"I don't want to know. Finish your beer and get out. You want information, go to the computer. It knows everything about everyone now."

"It doesn't know who's fucking around, but I bet you do," Diamond snapped.

The man stopped cleaning his glasses, his lips twitching. "Who's the woman?"

"Samantha Bedford." She watched for a reaction.

"She ain't fucking no one anymore." He moved to stand in front of her. "Why do you want to know about that slut?"

Diamond thought that was kind of harsh considering she was dead, but she kept that opinion to herself. "I'm representing Knox."

The bartender's whole attitude changed. "What do you want to know?" he asked with a friendly smile.

"Did Sam come in here often?"

"A lot when she hung out with The Last Riders. Not so much after she tried to hurt their women. She came in here a couple of times with a couple of Blue Horsemen. After they got arrested, I haven't seen them since. Heard they skipped bail and disappeared."

Diamond took a drink of her beer. "Anyone else since then?"

He shook his head.

"How about before she was involved with The Last Riders? She come in here then?"

"A few times, always trying to pick someone up and go home with them, but I can't remember anyone in particular." He started wiping the bar top down with a cloth. Something bothered Diamond and she couldn't place what it was. She thought he might not be telling the truth with the way he avoided her eyes.

"I can be very discreet; no one needs to know how I found anything out," Diamond said.

"I've told you what I know. If I remember anyone in particular, I'll give you a call."

Diamond sighed. She had pushed hard enough. Reaching into her pocket, she pulled out her card, which she placed there before leaving for her apartment.

"My name is Di Richards. If you think of anything, let me know. I'm trying to help Knox. Anything could be of help and you may not realize it."

"Names Mick. If I remember, I'll call."

As she turned to leave, the door to the bar slammed open and The Last Riders filed in. Diamond could tell by the look on Knox's face he was angry. He was an imposing figure dressed in his dark jeans and black t-shirt with his boots swallowing up the floor as he strode across the room.

"What the fuck are you doing here?" Knox asked angrily.

Diamond's back stiffened. "Drinking a beer. What business is it of yours?"

"Since when do you hang out in biker bars?" Knox inquired.

"Is this a biker bar? I wasn't aware of that. There weren't any motorcycles out front. Nor were there any signs saying 'Assholes only'," Diamond mocked him.

"She was asking about Sam," Mick interrupted. Diamond threw a look at the traitorous man for disclosing why she was there.

"What did Viper tell you about letting us know when you were going to be snooping around?"

"*You* might have to bow down and kiss Viper's ass, but I'm not one of your members that actually give a damn what he wants."

"He the one that pays you?" Knox asked, already knowing the answer.

Diamond knew she had stepped on a landmine. "Yes."

"Then you better be worried about what he wants."

"It doesn't matter; I'm done here." Diamond knew when a strategic retreat was in order.

"Since you're here, you might as well stay and have another beer." He turned to the bartender. "Mick get her another beer on me."

Mick turned around, reaching for another beer.

"I don't want one." Diamond started to slide off the seat when she found an arm around her waist and her ass planted back on the barstool.

"But I want you to stay. At least then I'll know where you are." His body blocked her from getting off the stool.

Reluctantly giving in for the moment, Diamond took a drink of her beer, aware that the dumbass was trying to frighten her. Two could play at that game. She relaxed. Turning her face toward him, she then gave him a venomous smile.

"You think your macho attitude is going to send me running? You're just pissing me off, Knox. I'm trying to find out who killed the woman you're going to go to jail for murdering unless I catch a break and find out who did."

"What did you think you would find out here?" He reached for his own beer, his chest brushing against her shoulder.

"I thought I would find out if there was someone else in town that she was sleeping with that might have a motive. Until I can find the men who were with her that day at the diner and find out if they could be responsible, then your ass is still the best suspect the jury will have."

"They weren't responsible for Sam's death, so if that's your only lead, you need to start searching somewhere else." Diamond watched as a group of The Last Riders sat at the tables while others went to the dance floor.

"How can you know that for sure?" Diamond questioned.

"Because they're not in town. If they were, the sheriff would have them locked up. Find someone else."

"It's not that easy," Diamond snapped.

"If it was going to be easy, Viper wouldn't have hired you." His brown eyes stared down into hers, making her aware that she wasn't wearing her suit. She had on soft blue jeans and a low-scooped, blue top that hugged her breasts, showing the generous swells of her breasts. She felt his eyes brush them each time she leaned forward.

"Let's dance." The abrupt change in topic had her speechless as Knox, not waiting for her answer, took her hand and led her to the dance floor. She tried to pull back, but he didn't loosen his hold.

On the dance floor, he turned her into his body, pulling her hips close.

"Let me go. I don't want to dance with you. This is unprofessional."

"Move your ass." Knox took her hips in his huge hands. She felt like an idiot for arguing with someone who was dancing against her seductively while she stood still, however Diamond was stumped as to how to react.

"One dance won't kill you," Knox answered, as if he read her thoughts.

Gradually, Diamond began moving to the music. She couldn't remember the last time she had actually danced; probably as a freshman in college, but she wasn't sure.

The music wound through her body, relaxing her and Knox used the opportunity to move her body closer to his, swamping her senses with his masculinity. Her eyes escaped his to watch the other dancers. Bliss was grinding against Rider while Evie was dancing seductively with a man that she hadn't seen before. Two other women in seductive clothes were dancing together.

As soon as the music ended, Diamond moved away and Knox released her hips before catching her hand and leading her back to the bar. He picked her up and placed her back on her stool.

"I need to be going." Diamond finished her beer so it wouldn't appear as if she was running away.

Knox moved closer to her side. "Want another beer? I can give you a ride home."

Diamond saw where this way headed and put a stop to it. "No, thanks, I've had enough."

When she would have jumped down from the stool, Knox leaned forward, placing his hand on the stool between her thighs. Diamond froze in place. If she moved forward an inch, her mound would be up against his hand.

"I think you should stay and party with us. We can show you a good time." His finger slid forward and she felt Knox trace the cleft of her pussy underneath her jeans. Shocked at his blatant move, she was unable to stop the shudder which shook her body.

His eyes narrowed on her and his tongue came out to moisten his lips, which caused Diamond's eyes to fall onto the metal ball on his tongue. Her hands then reached out to clasp his wrist and jerk it away from between her thighs.

"If you don't move your hand, I'm going to drop your case and keep the half million that Viper owes me without giving a damn that your ass will be sitting in jail for a crime you didn't commit."

Knox removed his hand, standing back up straight to lean back against the bar. He picked up his beer and took another drink. "How do you know I didn't kill Sam?"

Diamond was aware that Rider had come to stand on her other side, motioning to Mick for a drink. When Mick gave him his beer, Rider remained, obviously listening to their conversation.

Diamond planned to get her revenge on his touchy feely moment.

"I drove through the neighborhood you crashed your bike in before I came here today. It's a shortcut to the road that leads out here then to the clubhouse, so I know why you were on the road."

"So I was taking a shortcut? What the fuck does that have to do with me killing Sam?"

"I couldn't understand how you wrecked your bike on such a little road with barely any traffic. I saw by the skid marks you obviously crashed to avoid hitting something."

Knox shrugged. "So, a car pulled out in front of me."

"Nope. There was no parking where you wrecked and it's a one lane road. As I sat, trying to think how such an experienced rider had wrecked, I saw several interesting things."

Knox stiffened, throwing Rider a dirty look. "Don't you have something better to do?"

"Not right now. This sounds too good to miss. You never did tell me how you busted up your bike."

"Fuck off," Knox said, taking a drink of his beer while glaring at Diamond.

Rider's grin widened as he took a seat on the stool next to her.

"I saw a beautiful neighborhood filled with older homes that had an abundance of trees. The yards also had several squirrels. I think you swerved to miss a squirrel. You couldn't kill Sam if you wrecked your bike to prevent killing a squirrel."

"I didn't wreck my bike to keep from hitting a fucking squirrel." His red face showed he was lying.

Diamond burst out laughing. "You're a marshmallow."

"You actually wrecked your bike to keep from killing a squirrel?" Rider said in disbelief.

"No, I didn't," Knox barked back sharply.

"You fucking did." Rider burst into laughter.

"Marshmallow." Diamond nodded her head at Rider.

"I am not a fucking marshmallow!" Knox yelled as he slammed his beer down on the bar.

"You better go; the marshmallow is about to explode," Rider joked.

Diamond grinned back. "I'm going." Siding off the stool, this time Knox didn't stop her leaving as Rider continued antagonizing Knox.

She got in her car, her laughter dying as soon as the door slammed, incasing her in safety.

Her body was in turmoil from Knox's brief touch. How he had managed to excite her from a brief stroke defied her imagination. He was the typical biker, which she despised, yet her body hadn't cared, wanting more. Diamond had to be very careful. She had seen the recognition in his eye at her response. Knox wasn't as stupid as she'd thought. He wasn't such a marshmallow that he wouldn't take advantage of her attraction then leave her wanting more.

CHAPTER EIGHT

Far too early the next morning, her cell phone woke her from a deep sleep.

"Hello?" Diamond said drowsily into the phone.

"Ms. Richards?" Diamond easily recognized the sheriff's voice. Her drowsiness disappeared at the tone in his voice.

"Yes, what's happening?" The sheriff had never called her before; he must have found her number in the contact information on Knox's paperwork when he had been released from jail.

"The state police received a call, giving information about jewelry that was in Samantha Bedford's possession when she was murdered. They are about to serve a search warrant on The Last Riders in thirty minutes. If you hurry, you should make it when they get there."

"Dammit! Thanks, Sheriff."

Diamond threw back her covers and then grabbed a suit out of her closet, scrambling into her clothes. Brushing her hair and putting it up, she slipped on her heels. Grabbing her briefcase, she hightailed it to her car.

Driving as fast as she could without breaking the speed limit, she managed to pull into The Last Riders parking lot just as the state police were getting out of their cars.

David Thurman, the Commonwealth's Attorney that would be prosecuting Knox, waited at the bottom of the steps. "What are you doing here, Di?"

She held her hand out for the search warrant. "To make sure you stick to the areas of the search warrant, of course." Diamond took the copy of the warrant, reading it as fast as she could without missing any details.

"You're limited just to Knox's bedroom, nowhere else. Make sure your men know that."

Thurman threw her an angry look before taking the warrant back from her hand. He was a bigger asshole than Caleb Green. The higher up in rank the attorneys for the state were, the category of how big an asshole increased exponentially.

The large group climbed the steep steps to the porch where the police trooper knocked on the front door. It took several minutes before Viper answered the door with Winter behind him. Thurman handed him the warrant as the police stormed up the steps.

"Second doorway on the left," Thurman said, following behind them.

"This is bullshit, Thurman. How do you even know which room is his?" Diamond followed up the steps as the police motioned Viper and Winter to wait outside on the porch. Diamond motioned for him not to argue. She was at the top of the steps when she heard the police go through a door. Women's squeals could be heard from within the room.

"What in the fuck is going on?" That last voice was definitely Knox's grouchy one. Diamond came to a stop in the doorway. It was everything she could to maintain her professional appearance at the sight that met her eyes.

Knox was getting out of the biggest bed she had ever seen with a sheet barely covering his dick while two women were burrowed under the blanket, screeching for everyone to get out. Rider stood on the other side of the bed, pulling up his jeans, unconcerned that his junk was waving everywhere as he stuffed it inside his pants before zipping them closed.

"I'll be damned. We stepped into a bona fide orgy." One of the troopers laughed. Diamond could tell by the angry expression on Knox's face that he was about to lose it. Hoping to forestall the explosion, Diamond stepped forward so that the occupant could see her in the room, although she didn't enter.

"Knox, you and your friends need to vacate the room. The troopers have a search warrant. Go downstairs and wait with Viper and Winter. It's only your room that they will be able to search." Diamond spoke from the doorway, unable by law to enter further.

Diamond stood against the wall as Knox grabbed his jeans from the floor before pulling them on. She then averted her eyes as he flung the sheet away. Bliss grabbed the sheet, going to her knees on the bed and wrapping it around herself before climbing off the bed. When her eyes met Diamond's, she saw only anger, no embarrassment.

Evie took the blanket once the other woman, Bliss, was wrapped in the sheet, wrapping the blanket around herself. Her eyes met Diamond without any embarrassment evident on her face, either. Each of them strolled out of the bedroom without a care while the troopers' eyes followed them out before they began searching through Knox's things. Diamond cleared her throat and both men got back to work.

"You couldn't stop this?" Knox's harsh voice drew her attention.

"No, someone called in an anonymous tip," Diamond answered without looking at him. "Go downstairs." Her cold voice dripped ice. Knox's eyes narrowed and he hesitated, opening his mouth. "I need to pay attention to what they're doing and you're blocking my view."

Diamond took a step sideways, watching the troopers search through Knox's things.

"Let's go." As Rider took Knox's arm, he shrugged it off, turning on his heel and leaving. Diamond released her breath. The stench of sex still hung heavy in the air that had surrounded them as they left.

Revolted at herself for letting her body react to his last night brought her attention back to the men tossing Knox's things casually throughout the room. His bedside table drawer was pulled open and spilled onto his bed. The men laughed at the sex toys and large number of condoms displayed.

"Gentlemen." Diamond's voice held professional reproof. The men threw her dirty looks. Thurman walked to the bed, glancing down at the mess.

"You've got yourself a hell of a pervert for a client, Di." His sarcastic voice angered her.

"I wonder what I would find in your drawers if I went through them with no notice." Thurman turned red, but didn't say anything else.

"Look at this." One of the troopers had pulled out Knox's chest of drawers. There was a bag taped to the back. The trooper opened the bag, pulling out dozens of pictures.

Caleb took the pictures, going through them one by one before throwing them on the bed. "She has her clothes on and is over age; those are useless."

Diamond could see the pictures from the doorway. There were a least a dozen pictures of a pretty, young woman with blond hair. Knox had obviously not wanted anyone to see them.

"I've got it." One of the troopers had pulled open a bottom draw, holding the jewelry that Mrs. Langley had described to her.

"Take pictures of each one and bag it," Thurman said, smiling smugly. Diamond raised a brow at his unprofessional behavior.

"Don't you think it's strange he takes more trouble to hide innocent pictures than jewelry he took off a murder victim?" Diamond questioned the Commonwealth's Attorney.

"So, he's a dumb fuck; we already knew that." Thurman shrugged at her comment.

"We've found what we're looking for, we can go." He motioned the troopers out of the room. "Take him back into custody." He told the last trooper as he came out of the room.

"Why?" Diamond argued. "He didn't resist."

"With this, the chances of his taking flight increase."

"He's not going to run," Diamond tried to reason with him.

"I'm sure his ass won't be in their long, Di, but he's going back to jail," he said, walking off and leaving her no alternative other than to follow. Hesitating, she went back into Knox's room, opening the drawers she found him a shirt and socks. Picking up his large boots, she hurried down the steps where he was already in handcuffs, being lead down the steps.

"Diamond? Why are they arresting Knox again?" Viper yelled angrily.

"Someone called in a tip last night. They found what they were looking for, that's why they're taking him back in. Don't worry; the court is just going to raise his bail. The quicker you let me get out of here, the sooner I can get him out."

"Go," Viper answered begrudgingly. "When you're done, I expect to see you."

Diamond nodded before going down the steps. All The Last Riders were standing on the porch with Evie and Bliss among them, still wearing their coverings. Diamond avoided eye contact as she carried Knox's clothes down the steps, getting into her car then followed the procession of cars down the mountain.

Holly wouldn't be in the office; she had called last night and told Diamond that she was still ill. She was going to have to wait until she got to town to make the phone calls she needed. The twenty-minute drive was frustrating, but Diamond used the time to organize her thoughts, formulating a plan of action.

As soon as she pulled into the sheriff's office's parking lot, she watched as the troopers pulled Knox from the back of the squad car. Calling in what few favors she had earned in the short time she had been practicing in Treepoint, she managed to get a hearing later that afternoon.

She knew they were going to raise the bond he was on to a huge sum. Calling Viper and confirming the funds would be available, she was hopeful that Knox would be out that day.

Picking up Knox's clothes, she went into the small office. The sheriff was talking to David Thurman so Diamond handed Knox's clothes to the receptionist. The woman rose from her seat and then went through the clothes before handing them to the sheriff. He looked at Diamond while taking the clothes from his secretary then excused himself, going into the rooms where the cells were.

Thurman turned at the sheriff's abrupt departure, seeing Diamond standing by the front desk.

"Quick work, Diamond. I heard you finagled him onto the docket."

"Nothing has changed, David. This shouldn't affect his bond. He hasn't tried to flee and has no intention of doing so."

He laughed at her. "I think you're misjudging your client. I think when he realizes his case just went into the dumpster that he is going to run."

"He won't."

"He's a known member of a motorcycle gang, what makes you think that he's not going to run?"

"Because he didn't kill her, David. Did you even research the man you are trying for murder?" Before he could say anything, Diamond filled him in on the facts that she had learned. "He graduated at the top of his class in high school before going into the Navy at eighteen where he stayed, becoming a navy seal. He has served on several dangerous missions before becoming elite at search and rescue. He has donated his time to several countries after natural disasters to help recover victims. He's also very wealthy; several of the patents that The Last Riders have are his and the products the patents are on sell extremely well. One is a hatchet that turns into a small shovel so that rescuers can use it to help get victims out that are covered in ruble.

"So, no, I don't think a man who is extremely sensitive to others in dire circumstances killed a young woman to steal her jewelry when he could easily buy her the whole jewelry store."

Thurman turned pale at Diamond's information. "Why didn't my investigators find out about his money?"

"They didn't dig deep enough. The business is in The Last Riders' names, but I did a patent search with Knox's name. He keeps his money within the business for his own reasons. I haven't asked, but from what I gather, he could care less about his wealth. His bike isn't even an expensive make."

David shrugged, gathering his wits. Diamond could practically see the wheels turning. "The money just makes him an even bigger flight risk. He has the funds to leave the country. Thanks, Diamond."

"Tell yourself that, Thurman, if it makes you feel better for putting a veteran that has honorably served his country and still volunteers his time in dangerous situations behind bars. I don't happen to think Judge Creech, a veteran himself, will see it the same way." Diamond turned on her heel, running into the sheriff who had come up from behind.

"I agree also. I don't think he's a flight risk, and why would they call that tip into the state police and not the sheriff's office?"

"Probably because the tipster knows the preferential treatment The Last Riders receive from you," Thurman said with rancor.

The Sheriff gave Thurman a look of steel. "I think it's more likely that they thought that someone from this office would recognize their voice. This is all premature bullshit anyway; until the final autopsy report comes back from Frankfort, you're way ahead of yourself." The sheriff didn't back down from Thurman.

"I didn't realize there was a question about the autopsy?" Diamond said. It was the first time she had heard that the autopsy was in question.

"There isn't," Thurman prevaricated.

"There is," The sheriff disagreed.

"David, if you're using your power to railroad an innocent man..." Diamond stared at the man, aghast at the thought of someone with his power trying to push an innocent man into prison.

"He had the jewelry! How innocent could he be?" Thurman retorted nastily.

"That house is never locked during the day when everyone works at the factory next door, and with the influx of new employees, anyone could have planted that jewelry," The Sheriff argued.

"We'll know that once we fingerprint it, won't we, Sheriff? Now, if you two are done fighting about putting a murderer behind bars where he belongs, I need to get back to the office. I have court this afternoon." Thurman left both Diamond and the Sheriff staring after him.

"He's a dumb fuck," The Sheriff said.

"Yes, he is," Diamond confirmed, but he was a dumb fuck that had the power of the State of Kentucky behind him. He was more than able to put Knox away; innocent or not.

CHAPTER NINE

"Thanks for the clothes," Knox grudgingly thanked the lawyer as she handed him the paperwork releasing him from jail for the second time that week.

"You're welcome," Diamond's response was just as begrudging.

His long steps had no trouble keeping up with her strides outside the courtroom where Viper and Rider were waiting.

Before Viper could talk, Diamond cut him off, "The bond wasn't raised, pending the result of the final autopsy. When the autopsy or fingerprints come back, he could be back in, Viper. Whoever called that tip in wants him to take the fall. Any enemies that want him out of the way?" Diamond questioned.

"None. Even the Ohio branch of The Last Riders is calm right now," Viper answered her question with one of his own. "Any idea who could be behind the call?"

"No, but I think the reason they called the state police is they were worried someone would recognize their voice," Diamond stated; after the sheriff had mentioned it, she had become certain that this was the case.

The men all stared at each other.

Diamond shifted on her feet. "If there's nothing else, I'm going home. It's been a long day, Viper."

Their attention turned to her. "Thanks, Ms. Richards," Viper said.

Diamond nodded. "I'll be in touch."

Diamond left the men talking, going to her car which she had left in the sheriff's parking lot. Opening her car door, she noticed The Last Riders had also parked their bikes not far from her car. She put the key in the ignition and it took a second before she realized her car wouldn't start. Turning the key again, silence was the car's only response.

Diamond picked up her cell phone, but a knock on her window had her turning toward the sound to find Knox was staring back at her.

Opening her door, he looked pointedly at the dead instrument panel. "Car won't start?"

"No. I'm calling a tow truck."

"Open the hood; we'll take a look," Knox said, stepping back from her car.

"That's all right; I can call—"Diamond tried to put him off.

"Open the hood." Knox didn't wait for her answer, going to the front of her car with Viper and Rider following. Reluctantly, Diamond pressed the lever, releasing the hood to her car, and then stepped out to stand beside the men who were all staring down at her engine.

Rider examined her engine several minutes before rising from the motor to look at her. "It's the alternator. Leave it here tonight. In the morning I'll go to the auto store and pick you up a new one."

"That's okay. I can handle it." Diamond could already tell she was going to lose the battle, though. Men had an abundance of testosterone on two subjects, women and cars. Giving up, Diamond went to her car and got her briefcase as well as her purse out.

"How much does the alternator cost?" Diamond pulled her wallet out of her purse.

"Don't worry about it," Rider said, closing the hood of her car. "I'll pay for it and you can pay me back."

Diamond nodded her agreement. "All right." Diamond locked her car. Scrolling her phone for taxis, she was about to call one when Knox spoke.

"I'll give you a ride home."

"No thanks, I'm calling a cab," Diamond refused.

"Don't be stupid. I can have you home before you can get someone here." Diamond paused; she was tired and not feeling well. She was beginning to feel nauseous; having a feeling that she was coming down with her secretary's virus. She just wanted to go home and climb into her bed.

"How?"

"Razer brought my bike. Beth picked him up already," Knox answered, pointing to his bike.

She was not enthusiastic about getting on the back of a bike, but Diamond was feeling worse by the moment.

"Let's go," Diamond caved.

All three men looked at her in surprise at her easy capitulation.

"Are you all right?" Knox asked warily.

"I'm fine. It's been a long day," Diamond responded, trying to keep her heaving stomach calm a few more minutes.

"You're telling me," Knox said sarcastically, bringing back the vision of him barely covered in the sheet. Diamond almost changed her mind, but her heaving stomach had her climbing on the back of Knox's bike and taking his helmet as he tied her briefcase onto the back of his bike.

Knox got on then turned on the bike, waving at Rider and Viper as he pulled out. Diamond remembered that she hadn't told him where she lived, but wasn't surprised when he drove in the direction of her apartment. Thankfully for

Diamond's stomach, she was able to make it there. As soon as Knox pulled to a stop in her parking lot, she jumped off his bike.

"Thanks." Diamond took off at a run for her apartment.

When shaking fingers kept her from being able to unlock her door, a hand reached out, taking the keys from her and inserting them in the lock. As soon as the door was opened she took off again, dropping her purse on the floor by the door. She barely managed to slam the bathroom door shut and reach the toilet basin before she lost the contents of her stomach.

It was terrible. Her heaving stomach didn't have much to expel as she had begun feeling unwell before lunch and hadn't eaten. Diamond's shaking hand reached out to brush her fallen hair back from her hot check.

"Diamond?" Knox's voice could be heard through the closed door.

"Don't call me that." She might be down, but she wasn't out. She hated that name.

"Are you all right?" Diamond didn't want to hear the concern in his voice.

"I'm fine. You can go. It's a stomach virus I caught off my secretary. I hope you don't catch it."

"I don't get sick," Knox answered. "Can I get you anything?"

"No. Just lock the door on your way out." Diamond sat on her butt by the toilet, still afraid to move.

Just as Diamond heard him move away from the door then her outside door closing, her stomach began heaving again. She clung to the basin, thankful she was OCD about keeping a clean bathroom as she lost what little was left in her stomach. As sweat broke out across her body, Diamond tried to pull off her jacket, however she couldn't stop heaving long enough to do so.

When the bathroom door opened and she felt a wet cloth brush her forehead, Diamond whimpered in relief.

Her jacket was pulled off one side and she quickly grabbed the wet rag as he maneuvered her jacket completely off.

"You're burning up," Knox said, hanging her jacket on a hook on the wall.

Diamond began shaking harder.

"You're sure this is a virus and not food poisoning?" Knox asked, squatting down beside her.

Diamond nodded her head. "My secretary has been out two days with it." Brushing her hair back again, Diamond didn't want to imagine what she looked like with her fallen hair hanging over a toilet.

"You have anything for nausea in your cabinets?"

"No."

"I'll be back in ten minutes."

"Knox, I'll be fine. Just go home."

He ignored her, leaving the bathroom, then Diamond heard her front door open and close. Relieved that he had finally left, Diamond managed to rewet the washcloth in the sink and wash her face, however she found out that brushing her teeth was a huge mistake when she was once again over the toilet when Knox returned.

Diamond looked up at him in frustration. "I told you, I'll be all right."

"Shut the fuck up." Knox handed her the familiar pink medicine with a spoon. Diamond didn't resist taking a dose of the medicine as well as the cool liquid to swallow after it.

Her stomach finally empty, she tried to rise to her feet as Knox helped her up. Grasping the sink basin for support, she again washed her face and brushed her teeth, this time with better results.

Diamond turned from the sink to see Knox leaning against the doorframe. "Better?"

Diamond nodded her head, walking forward. Knox moved from the doorway, watching as she moved into her living room and then sunk down onto her couch where she laid her spinning head back.

Knox sat down in a chair, surveying the room. Diamond ignored the man who refused to leave.

"You got something against color?"

Diamond lifted her head weakly. "I like a calm environment."

"Any more calm and you'd be dead."

"Very funny. Maybe I should get mismatched furniture and put a bar in the corner, would that suit you better?" She refused to feel like a bitch about putting down the furniture at The Last Rider clubhouse when he was being so rude about her own decor.

"At least it would look like someone actually lived here."

"You can go anytime." Diamond lay back again weakly. "I'm over the worst of it." She watched as Knox stood to his feet.

"You sure?" he asked, hesitating. Diamond could tell he was anxious to leave.

"Yes." Diamond rebuffed the idea of being weak enough to need any help. "I'm sure."

At that, he left her sitting on the couch.

She began to feel sorry for herself as soon as he'd left and then promptly became angry at herself for wishing he had stayed. Diamond couldn't understand herself where he was concerned any more. He attracted her, and refusing to admit it was making the situation worse; that much was certain. It made her say ugly things that she didn't mean and act like those who had treated her the same when she had been a child. Diamond had learned long ago that ignoring something made it blow up in your face. It was smarter to realize you had a problem and put up defenses to stop it. She just wasn't sure how to get in front of this particular problem.

Ever since she had realized her father was a two-timing bastard, she had not let anyone close enough to rock the tame world she had built around herself. She didn't like an environment in turmoil and tension, which is what she'd lived in constantly with Sex Piston as a sister and with her father as the President of the Destructors. She wanted a quiet environment that she could enjoy, yet was reluctant to admit that it was also boring.

She got up from the couch and made herself a cup of hot tea at the same time that her childish instincts were kicking in, making her want to call her mom, but she didn't. Instead, she drank her tea and then went back to lay on the couch.

She must have dozed off, only waking groggily when she felt herself being lifted from the couch against a hard chest. Oddly, her panic instinct didn't click in, she just lay there as she was carried into her bedroom.

Sickly, she mumbled that she had to go to the restroom. She was carried into the bathroom to lose the tea she had drunk after another round of nausea. When she was finished, Knox washed her face off, removing the glistening sweat that showed her fever had risen.

"Do you need to use the restroom?" Diamond heard Knox's voice rousing her to her senses.

"Yes," her dry voice croaked.

"Go ahead." He left her, closing the door behind him. Diamond didn't take long. As soon as she had flushed the toilet, Knox was back, lifting her into his arms once more and then carrying her into her bedroom. Standing her on her feet by her bed, he began unbuttoning her blouse.

"Stop. What are you doing?"

"Getting you out of these clothes. You have vomit on your blouse."

Diamond flushed, losing her composure for a second. "I can do it."

Knox removed his hands, however when Diamond's shaking fingers only managed to fumble with the tiny buttons, Knox brushed her fingers away. His fingers had the shirt unbuttoned within seconds, sliding the blouse off before unsnapping her bra. Diamond reached out to cover her large breasts, but Knox ignored her efforts, stepping closer to her to reach his arms around her to unzip her skirt. When the skirt fell to her feet, leaving her standing in nothing other than her panties, Diamond's face blushed under her already heated skin.

"I can get myself undressed," Diamond snapped.

Knox ignored her and went to her chest against the wall. "Where are your nightgowns?" Diamond pointed to her dresser. "Top drawer."

Knox moved to the dresser, opening the drawer. He looked down for several seconds before pulling out a thin blue gown that had lace on the edges. Coming back to her, he slid the gown over her head. The nightgown came to her mid thighs.

"I see you do like color after all."

Diamond threw him a dirty look as she climbed into her bed. Her bright purple panties that were now covered by the bright blue gown didn't give her much room to argue. Knox pulled the covers over her before going back into the bathroom and returning with the nausea medicine. Taking it and the cold water he had gotten from the kitchen, she drank them then lay down on her bed.

Knox sat down on the bed next to her. "I'm going to crash on your sofa." Diamond opened her mouth to protest. "Call me if you need anything." With that, he left her lying there, not knowing what to do. Her cramping stomach finally made the choice for her and she relaxed into the soft bed, letting the medicine ease her back into a light doze.

Throughout the night, he helped her back and forth to the bathroom. Towards dawn, the cramping in her stomach eased and she was able to fall asleep. She kept kicking the covers off then would get cold again, pulling the covers back around her.

Finally managing to go into a deep sleep, she relaxed into the hard warmth at her back as her stomach was massaged by a warm hand, easing the tight muscles. Diamond lost all awareness and caring, only feeling the relief.

Sometime later, she tried to get up to go to the restroom only to find a hard arm pinning her to the bed. Stiffening, she realized that Knox was curved up against her back. Trying to slide out from underneath him, she felt his hard cock against her back. With a squeak, she tried harder to get out of the bed.

His hand slid to her hip over the silky material of her gown. "You going to be sick again?"

"No, I need to go to the bathroom."

When the hand at her hip released her, Diamond slid out of the bed.

Taking her time, she brushed her teeth and hair then put on her robe before returning to her bedroom where Knox was sitting on the side of the bed. His stubble was in direct contrast to his cleanly shaven head. His eyes surveyed her covered in her white robe as she came out of the bathroom.

"Better?"

"Yes, I think I'm over the worst of it."

Knox nodded his head before reaching down to grab his boots. Diamond watched as he put on his shoes.

"Why did you come back last night?"

"I knew you would be too stubborn to call anyone for help. I wouldn't want Sex Piston around me when I was sick, either."

"What have you got against my sister?" Diamond asked, thinking about defending her sister.

Knox looked up from putting on his shoes. "Other than she's as looney as that crowd she hangs with, not a damn thing."

Diamond changed the topic from her sister, knowing she didn't have a leg to stand on. They really were all crazy as hell. "Why did you get in the bed?"

Knox's face split into a sardonic grin. "You were crying because of your stomach. A couple of women at the club get bad cramps during their periods. Massage helps; I thought it would work on you. It did." Knox shrugged.

Diamond squashed the jealous feeling of another woman receiving his caring attention. She hadn't been the first woman he had rubbed away their pain, and she was damn sure she wouldn't be the last one.

"Well, aren't you just the master of knowledge where women are concerned?" Diamond said snidely.

Knox shrugged. "There's not much I don't know."

Diamond stared at him angrily. "You don't know shit about women, you know sluts."

"Now that wasn't nice."

Diamond agreed, furious at herself for being so petty minded. "I'm sorry. Your personal life is no concern of mine. I just don't like it when men assume all women are alike."

"I would never compare you to The Last Rider women, Diamond. They are flesh and blood and can admit when their pussy is wet."

Diamond stiffened, glaring at the arrogant ass who was now leaning back on his arms on her bed with his boot clad legs stretched out before him.

"I think it's time you left, Knox. Thanks for your help." Diamond dismissed him with an arrogant air of her own.

"I stayed the night, watching you puke your guts out and the only thanks I get is you shoving my ass out the door because you can't admit you're wet for me?" Knox leaned forward, anger filling his hard face.

"I'm not wet for you. I couldn't get wet for you. You're a man-whore; I saw that for myself. So, no, I'm not fucking wet."

"You're a bigger bitch than your sister, and I can prove you wrong," Knox said grimly.

"There is no proof, you moron!" Diamond yelled.

"We'll just see about that."

One second Diamond was standing there yelling, the next she was flying through the air, landing with a bounce on her bed. Before she had stopped bouncing, her robe and nightgown were jerked up to her waist.

"What the hell?" Diamond sputtered, trying to clench her thighs together, but Knox's hands pulled them apart as he stood by the bed before his fingers slid under her purple panties, finding the hot warmth of her pussy.

"Oh, yeah, you're wet," Knox answered smugly.

Diamond was stunned at the speed his fingers had found the evidence of her lie.

"You fucking bastard." Her foot tried to strike out at his gloating face, yet Knox caught her ankle in a hard hand, jerking it up into the air. Diamond found herself flat on her back as she heard her panties ripped from her.

"Let's see how much wetter you can get."

"Get your hands off me." Diamonds other foot struck out and was grasped by his other hand.

"My pleasure." Knox raised her legs up separating them as his face buried itself in her pussy and his tongue grazed across her clit then slid into the wetness she had denied existed. A whimper of denial escaped her lips at the unbelievable pleasure of him going down on her. Diamond's mind struggled for half a second before the pleasure of his tongue drove all plans of resistance away from her willing body.

Feeling her response against his tongue, he placed her legs over his shoulders as his mouth began to torture her into a need that had her shaking. With his hand holding her hips, he lifted her higher against him as his tongue with the barbell played with her clit, rubbing it insidiously, bringing her close to coming. He stopped, sliding his tongue inside her tight pussy to use the barbell to rub the sensitive flesh. Diamond writhed against his experienced tongue as he had her hips thrusting against him. Knox pulled his face away.

"You're so tight your squeezing my tongue." One of his hands went to her pussy, his fingers rubbing in her wetness before sliding one finger deeply into her warmth. Diamond moaned, helpless underneath him. "How long has it been since you've been fucked? As fucking tight and wound up as you are, I bet it's been a while."

"Go to hell!"

"Be careful, Diamond, or I won't give you my tongue back." Diamond opened her mouth to blast him before closing it with a snap.

"Smart woman." Knox removed his finger, bringing his mouth back to her pussy as he gave her what she needed.

The damn tongue ring was putting pressure against her clit, and with a hard push of the metal ball against the bundle of nerves, Diamond stiffened into an orgasm that had her hands smothering the scream she couldn't prevent.

Knox lowered her legs until they hung off the side of the bed. Diamond looked up to see Knox standing smugly over her satisfied body.

"You know where to find me if you want more." She then watched as he left her bedroom.

Rolling to her side when she heard the front door open and close, her hand that she had used to smother the sound of her climax curled into a ball as she bit her hand in a storm of regret.

He had just shoved her insults down her throat. She had never felt fear that he wouldn't stop, although she had been unable to make herself utter the words. The bastard had proved, without a doubt, that she had wanted him.

Diamond learned a hard lesson about challenging Knox. The next time she had a point to prove, she wouldn't do it in a bedroom.

CHAPTER TEN

Knox sat on his bike in the parking lot, trying to get his cock back under control. He was tempted to go back up the steps to her apartment and finish what he'd started. The only thing stopping him was the certainty that she would fight her desire tooth and nail.

Knox started his bike, going for a ride to clear his thoughts before heading back to the clubhouse. It didn't take a brilliant mind to know that Diamond was fighting her attraction to him. Knox was aware that the buttoned up lawyer was convinced she knew what kind of man he was. Besides that, both times she had come to the clubhouse hadn't helped in her low opinion of him.

Knox gunned his motor, taking the bike wide fucking open as he flew down the back county roads. His mind went back to the first time he had seen the luscious redhead at the clubhouse, interviewing Winter on her case against the school board. He'd had Natasha and Jewell at the bar, coming down from the upstairs. He was sure the activities they had participated in had been obvious.

Yesterday morning hadn't been any better. She had looked through the doorway to spy him with only a sheet around his hips and two women along with Rider in his bed. It had been disgusting to her and she had made no effort to hide it.

Knox smiled to himself. Two members of The Last Riders had just left his room. She would have really gotten an eyeful if they had all arrived just ten minutes earlier. He had nights like that often and didn't intend to apologize for his lifestyle.

"Fuck her," Knox said, the wind throwing his words back at him.

He could tell just from a distance that Diamond had issues going on with her family, and from the look of her biker father, he was going to get tarnished with whatever bullshit she had going on with him.

Slowing down, Knox turned around before he could reach the county line, bringing his bike back up to a speed he was comfortable with on the winding road. His thoughts went back to the woman lying on her bed with her spread legs and warm pussy. The desire burning his body had him actually considering making a play for the bitchy woman. Knox knew the woman would need careful handling to get her in his bed, although he wondered if it would be worth the effort.

"Dammit." Going through town, he slowed his speed and headed towards the clubhouse.

He needed a shower and to get caught up on some work, both would take his mind off the redhead that didn't know she had aroused a part of him he'd long since thought had disappeared. If he did decide to pursue the woman, he had to keep it in mind that she was only a fuck. He wasn't about to distract her from proving his innocence nor was he going to become too involved with a woman who obviously thought he was beneath her.

Knox bet the woman was angry; her body wanted him while she despised everything else about him.

* * *

It took Diamond two days to feel better. Thankfully, her secretary called to say that her case in court was delayed; Judge Creech having the same virus that she and everyone in town seemed to be suffering from. *I hope I gave it to Knox*, she thought vindictively. She hadn't seen him since he had left her apartment. Diamond, contrarily, didn't want to think of the number of women available at the clubhouse to tend to the sick man or to provide for his other needs if he wasn't.

With time on her hands, she decided to clean her apartment and wash clothes. She was folding the last few items when her doorbell rang.

She almost didn't open her door when she looked through the peephole and saw who was outside. Only the drama that would unfold in front of her neighbors had her unlocking her door.

"What do you want, Sex Piston?" Her sister and crew looked pityingly at her jeans and old t-shirt.

"Girl, you look like shit," her sister responded to her unwelcome response at seeing her.

"Thanks," Diamond responded casually, eyeing her sister's black booty shorts and thigh high boots, wondering how she wore the clothing with the cold weather outside. She had completed her outfit with a dark red t-shirt and leather fringe jacket. Her red hair should have clashed with her red top, but instead it made her look sexy and sassy, both of which Diamond was not.

Sex Piston brushed by her sister with her crew of bitches following her lead.

"Beth said you weren't feeling well, so I thought I'd swing by and check on you." Diamond looked outside to see her sister's green car that they drove themselves in when they weren't on the back of someone's bike.

"I'm fine," Diamond said, standing by the door while hoping Sex Piston would get her message.

"Damn girl, this apartment is white," Crazy Bitch remarked, sinking down on Diamond's sofa.

Diamond sighed. Closing the door, she came back into the living room and sat down to finish folding her clothes, knowing that the women would soon grow bored with her ignoring them and leave.

Sex Piston leaned forward, digging through her freshly washed, clothes and pulled out a bright pink pair of thong underwear and matching pink bra. "Can I borrow these?"

"No," snapped Diamond, taking them from her and placing them back in the laundry basket.

"Get out of the kitchen, Louise." Diamond refused to call her fat; the woman didn't weigh a hundred freaking pounds. The only thing big about her was her ass, which she was determined to put on display in the tightest pants imaginable.

"Why don't you have anything to fucking snack on?" Louise said, coming out of the kitchen.

"I'm on a diet."

"What for?" Sex Piston asked. "It's not like you care what anyone thinks."

"I don't." Diamond wasn't really, however she was well aware that she was much larger than her voluptuous sister, who was small with curves in all the right places, not the flabby ass and tummy Diamond had to deal with constantly.

"Ma wants you to come to dinner on Friday."

"I'm busy."

"Then get un-busy and get your ass there. She's cooking." Damn, her mom never cooked, and it showed with how terrible she was at it, but she always did it when she had bad news to impart. The last time she had cooked, she had told them her annual mammogram had shown a spot. Thankfully after a biopsy, it had proven to be nothing to worry about, yet Diamond's body tautened, knowing she wouldn't be able to miss the dinner.

"I'll be there."

Sex Piston nodded. "Heard you got a new case defending that fucker Knox. He kill the bitch?"

"No," Diamond replied irritably at the same time she took her red thong away from Crazy Bitch. Jerking her laundry basket away from the women, she carried it into her bedroom.

She knew it had been a mistake leaving the women alone when she returned to find them in her kitchen fixing themselves lunch. Giving in, she helped them to save her clean kitchen from being destroyed. Fixing sandwiches, they sat at her table, drinking the last of her wine she kept in the fridge.

"So why you so sure he didn't kill that bitch?" Sex Piston asked.

"Because I am." She refused to discuss Knox's case with her sister, instead she took her dirty plate to the sink.

Sex Piston narrowed her eyes at her sister. "Don't get attached to that fuckwad, Diamond. Beth told me what went on in that clubhouse before she married Razer. Now she doesn't tell me shit except that those parties and sex swapping are still going strong."

"I don't know or care what goes on in that clubhouse," Diamond answered, clearing the dishes from the table.

"Good. Because, if you can't handle what goes down with the Destructors, you sure as shit can't handle The Last Riders. And from what Beth said, Knox is the worst one. Says he goes at the women for hours."

"No shit?" Crazy Bitch asked, setting down her glass of wine.

"No shit," Sex Piston answered.

"Damn, the Destructors need to get some of that shit going on. Too bad that they don't look like The Last Riders," Crazy Bitch said wishfully.

"You're telling me; Ace and the rest of them all need to lose that spare their carrying around their middle."

"What's it matter? You've never let it bug you before?" Diamond said, picking up her empty wine glass. If Diamond hadn't been looking at her sister, she would have missed the hurt look before her sister managed to cover it with her usual blasé attitude.

"They broke up for good this time," Killyama answered

for her friend, throwing Sex Piston one of her pissed off glares.

"They never break up for good. They'll be back together by Friday. He'll have his ass sitting at Mom's table before I get there."

"Not unless that bitch he knocked up lets him loose."

"He got someone pregnant while he was seeing Sex Piston?"

"Nope, they were on one of their breaks. I guess it's more permanent than they thought it was going to be," Crazy Bitch said, looking at Sex Piston.

"I was done with his sorry ass anyway. He knocked up some eighteen-year-old. She can snuggle up to his hairy ass." Her chair scrapped back from the table.

"Sex Piston—" Her sister cut her off.

"Let's move," she said to her bitches. Her crew all stood to their feet, following behind her to the door. "See you Friday."

Diamond watched them leave, piling into their puke green car. Sex Piston's face was still set in her I'll-kick-your-ass visage she'd used since she was a little girl. Diamond had no doubt that Ace would rue the day he had cheated on Sex Piston.

* * *

Diamond had just put a pizza in the oven when her doorbell rang. Going to the door, she saw Rider and Knox.

When she opened the door, Rider handed her the keys to her car.

"All fixed."

"Thanks. How much do I owe you?" Diamond asked, stepping away from the door to get her purse. When she turned back around both men were inside her apartment. Still embarrassed from the way that she had behaved the last time Knox was in her apartment, she kept her eyes on Rider.

"Viper took care of it. He said he'd take it out of your payment for representing Knox." Diamond started to argue, but Rider held up his hand. "You got a problem with it, take it up with Viper. Don't shoot the messenger." Reluctantly, Diamond put down her purse.

"I won't. I'll settle up with him the next time I see him."

"Cool. That pizza I smell?" Rider asked, lifting his nose in the air.

"Yes," Diamond admitted reluctantly.

Neither man made a move to leave. Having dealt once today with her sister and her hungry crew, Diamond knew where this was headed.

"We didn't get lunch today, trying to get your car fixed and brought back to you. We figured you'd be recovered enough to get back to work tomorrow," Knox said. Diamond caved in at the reminders of his helping her when she was sick then fixing her car.

"Would you like to stay for dinner?"

"Yes," they both answered at once.

"Have a seat."

They sat at the kitchen table as Diamond took the pizza out of the oven.

"Got any beer?" Rider asked with hope in his voice.

"No, and I don't have any wine. Sex Piston and her friends finished it off earlier today."

"Thank God we missed them." Rider shuddered.

"That's her sister, dumbass."

"Sorry," Rider apologized as he pulled a slice of pizza free from the tray.

"It's okay. My sister and her friends are an acquired taste." Sitting down at the table, she put a pitcher of sweetened tea and glasses on the table before taking a slice of pizza onto her own plate.

As they ate, wiping out the pizza, Diamond barely managed to grab the last slice away from Rider, who gave her sad puppy dog eyes. When she was about to take a bite, his eyes dropped to her mouth as she opened it. Diamond closed her mouth and handed him the pizza.

"That wasn't fair," she chastised him. Rider took a large bite of the cheesy pizza, shrugging his shoulders.

"I don't remember the last time I had homemade pizza. Usually we get frozen from the freezer. I was willing to fight dirty," Rider explained.

Diamond found herself laughing at the friendly man. Her eyes went to Knox, surprised he had let his friend have the last slice. Her eyes met the heat in his, bringing the desire back into her body that had been missing since he left the other day.

Diamond broke eye contact and then stood to her feet and gathered the dirty dishes. As she turned around to get the glasses, she almost bumped into Knox as he carried the glasses to the sink.

"Let me do the dishes since we invited ourselves to dinner."

"No, that's okay."

Knox ignored her and began doing the dishes as she stood helplessly watching, not wanting to make an ass of herself by throwing out the two men who had temporally taken over her apartment.

Rider went into the living room and turned on her television set, making himself comfortable as he started flipping through her channels.

"Thanks for the pizza," Knox said.

"You're welcome." Diamond moved away to wipe the table down.

"Sex Piston stop by often?"

"Not really. We're not very close." Diamond shrugged, folding the dishcloth.

"She have any particular reason for stopping by today?" Knox asked. Diamond watched as he did a decent job at doing the dishes. For some reason she had assumed he would be clumsy because of his size, but his hands were expertly washing and rinsing them.

"We're having a family dinner on Friday."

Finishing the dishes, he turned to look at her. "From

your expression, you're not looking forward to it."

"Not really. I'm not very close to my family."

"Why?"

"No reason really; we're just different. We don't have much in common." Diamond turned away, determined to change the subject from her family. It merely reminded her that she was stupid even to be talking to Knox. It was not only unprofessional, but it would lead to a road she had no intention of taking.

Pasting her usual plastic expression onto her face, she decided to bring the impromptu evening to an end. Going into the living room, she stood by the couch. "Thanks again for bringing my car—"

"Do you mind if I finish this program? If I leave now, I'll miss the end." Rider glanced up from his show, hitting her with another puppy dog look. Diamond tried to stand strong, however Knox took a seat on the couch and then stretched out his long legs in front of him.

"No, I don't mind," Diamond found herself saying. She was about to sit down in the chair when she found herself gripped by the waist and hauled to sit between the men on the couch.

"You can see the television better from here," Knox explained, not taking his eyes off the television.

At first, Diamond sat between the men uncomfortably, remembering that both had been in Knox's bedroom the day the warrant was issued. When neither man made a move, she gradually relaxed to watch the show. After it ended, both men rose to their feet without any prompting from her.

"Thanks for dinner and the movie," Rider said with a grin. Diamond smiled back at the friendly biker. He was definitely the flirt of the group and had learned to use his good looks to his advantage.

"You're welcome, Rider. Thanks again for my car."

"Anytime." Rider went to the door, leaving with Knox following, but Knox paused as she came to the door.

Expecting him to go out the door like Rider, she looked at him curiously.

As he shut the door and pulled her to him, Diamond immediately stiffened, trying to pull away, yet Knox put his hand on her ass and pulled her against his hard body.

"I've had my mouth on your pussy, but I haven't had your mouth yet." Knox then lowered his head before Diamond could object, covering her mouth with his. She tried to tear her lips away, but Knox's hand buried in her hair, tilting her head to the side as he used the tip of his tongue to part her mouth. As he began thrusting into the warm recesses, gently exploring her mouth, her hands flattened on his chest as she stopped resisting.

His body turned, pressing her body against the door as his tongue raked against her own; the ball a reminder of how it felt against her clit. With that thought, Diamond tore her mouth away from his demanding lips.

"Knox, I'm not going to do this—"

He stepped back from her, staring down at her with a hardened face. "Why not? I know you want to fuck me just as much as I want to fuck you." Diamond winced at his blunt words.

"Because I could lose my license for one, and for another, I'm not going to become another woman in your big bed."

"Diamond I'm not going to affect your career because I didn't kill Sam. My bed will have you in it, whether anyone else is in it is up to you." Taking her by the arms, he set her away from the door before opening it.

"You jerk, I just told you we aren't going to happen. I have no intention of getting involved with you."

"Oh, you're going to be plenty involved when I put my dick up that tight pussy and you're begging for more.," Knox answered as he went out the door.

"Jackass." Diamond slammed the door behind him, furious at herself for letting down her guard enough to even let them in her apartment in the first place.

Knox was the type that, if you gave him an inch, he would take a mile. Because she had been temporally insane letting him give her an orgasm, he felt he was going to take anything else he wanted.

He was going to be disillusioned. She had dealt with arrogant bikers her whole life. She was going to put a stop to his plans before he cost her the career she had worked hard to achieve as well as, most importantly, the heart she had kept protected.

CHAPTER ELEVEN

Diamond came out of the courthouse, exhausted from having been in court since morning. Playing catch up after missing the last two days was going to have to wait. She was starving, having given away most of her dinner the night before and missing breakfast. She was more than ready for lunch. Crossing the street, she went to the diner, seeing she wasn't the only one wanting lunch in the packed restaurant.

Her attention was caught by a hand waving. Winter was sitting at a large table with two other women. Not wanting to encourage a friendship, she looked around the restaurant, but they had the only empty seat available. Her grumbling stomach made the choice for her as her reluctant feet carried her to their table.

"Hi Diamond; want to join us?" Diamond winced at the use of her hated name, although she accepted her invitation. As she sat down at the table, Winter made the introductions.

"This is my friend, Beth Moore, and her sister, Lily."

Diamond smiled at the pretty blond before turning to catch her first glimpse of her sister. As she had approached the table, she had only seen the black hair, which she had admired for its gleaming length, but she found her breath catching at the young woman smiling at her in welcome. She was beautiful. Diamond had never looked at another woman with such stunning looks, trying to think for a minute if she was a model or actress.

"Hello," Her gentle voice broke through Diamond's professional barricade with one word. No one could look at the gentle eyes and give her a set down.

"Hello." Diamond found herself returning her smile.

"Diamond is the lawyer representing Knox," Beth explained to her sister.

"I hope you can help him out," Lily said.

"I do, too. I'm working on it," Diamond said as the waitress came to take her order.

"So what are you ladies doing in town today?" Diamond questioned the women.

"I needed to pick up a few things that we need for the wedding tomorrow," Winter said.

Diamond's face flamed. Winter had invited her to the wedding, however she had declined.

"Are you coming?" Lily asked shyly.

"I—" Diamond felt awful as she was now faced with the three women staring at her. "I have a lot of work to get done on Knox's case." Winter stared at her in amusement as Diamond tried to extradite herself from the embarrassing conversation; she had declined the invitation before she'd taken Knox's case.

"Please come, you can keep me company. I've been around a few of The Last Riders since Beth married Razer, but I don't know them very well. It's in the backyard of the clubhouse so not many people will be attending because Winter didn't want a big wedding. It's going to be informal, so you don't have to dress up."

Diamond was going to refuse, but the pleading look on Lily's face prevented her from outright saying no.

"Lily, I'm sure that Winter doesn't want an unexpected guest," Diamond said, trying to get out of it one more time.

"I would like for you to come. There's plenty of room for another guest. Neither Viper nor I wanted to have a big wedding, just family and friends. I hope you come, Diamond," Winter said graciously.

Left with no choice, she accepted, not missing the relieved look which crossed Lily's face. Curiously, Diamond studied the young woman. She was dressed in a pretty blue dress that highlighted her dark hair. She didn't have on much make-up and she wore no jewelry. Diamond's eyes were caught by a red rubber band she wore around her wrist. Lily caught Diamond staring at it and self-consciously covered it with her other hand.

Diamond gave her a gentle smile before turning her attention to Winter who was discussing her wedding with Beth. Beth dragged her into their conversation and Diamond was surprised that, once she let her guard down, she had quite a bit in common with the three women.

They were unlike the other women Diamond had known who had been involved with bikers. Both Winter and Beth had careers and had no intention of making the biker lifestyle their whole world as her mother and Sex Piston had.

They were eating their lunch when Beth told Winter that Mrs. Langley wouldn't be coming to her wedding. It clicked with Diamond she had a resource she hadn't thought of yet.

"Beth and Winter, you've both lived in Treepoint your whole life, so you have an in where I don't." Beth and Winter stopped talking, listening to Diamond. "You," she motioned to Winter, "worked at a high school. Who did Samantha Langley see in Treepoint?"

"There isn't anyone she didn't sleep with. Even before The Last Riders, she would go with a boy for a week then move on."

"Can you make me a list? Go back as far as you can remember? Even if it's a one night stand that you know of.

I have to figure out who wanted her dead."

"Lily and she were in school together. We'll come up with a list of names for you and give it to you at the wedding tomorrow." Winter seemed excited about helping. Diamond smiled at the infectious warmth of the pretty woman. She could understand why Viper would have found her hard to resist.

Curiosity got the better of her. Beth had explained that she ran a business in town, caring for older individuals who needed help with their daily activities.

"Do you work with your sister?" Diamond asked Lily.

"No, I help out every now and then, but I'm a junior at Breckenridge College. I want to be a social worker."

Diamond stared at the beauty in front of her, the gentleness in her eyes. The world was going to take her in and spit her out. Her sister and she were something Diamond had never met; true humanitarians. Beth's gentleness was there to see while Lily held back more; her eyes holding secrets that Diamond didn't want to explore. She almost reached across the table to touch her hand. Bringing her mind back to the topic, Diamond couldn't believe how the woman affected her.

"That's very admirable," Diamond said tactfully. "But it's going to be hard seeing people need your help and only being able to do what your job tells you can be done."

"I'm stronger than I look. I can handle it," Lily said with determination.

Diamond had no doubts that the woman would be swallowed alive by the job she felt she had a vocation for. She cast Winter and Beth a concerned glance.

"She'll be fine. Lily will have both Winter and myself looking out for her," Beth answered her unspoken question.

"And The Last Riders," Winter spoke, not raising her head from her plate of food.

"I can take care of myself," Lily said firmly.

Diamond dealt with the same people that Lily would

inevitably be working with. No, the woman wasn't going to be able to handle it. Diamond barely could, and that was when they were behind bars and she had police in the vicinity. Not wanting to crush the woman's dreams, she changed the topic of conversation.

Diamond was on her second cup of coffee as they chatted when the door to the diner opened and The Last Riders entered. Beth smiled as a good-looking biker came up behind her and leaned down to kiss her. Beth blushed as her eyes caught Diamond's when she was released.

"Diamond, this is my husband, Razer. Razer, this is Diamond, she's representing Knox." The man smiled at her before taking a seat next to his wife, placing an arm over her shoulder while the empty seats on her side of the table were taken by Rider and Knox and Viper took a seat on Winter's side of the table. The final two men to have a seat were both not people that Diamond recognized; one was covered in tattoos and had a purely menacing appearance.

"Diamond, I think you know everyone here except Shade and Train." Shade was the one covered in tats and Train was the epitome of bad boy biker. Diamond could understand how The Last Riders managed to keep so many women interested in their club. The Destructors had maybe one or two good-looking men, yet most were older with beer bellies. There wasn't one of The Last Riders she had seen who had a beer paunch. They were in extremely good physical condition.

"What have you women been doing?" Viper asked Winter.

"Nothing, I finished what I needed for tomorrow. Sure you're not going to change your mind and leave me at the alter?" Winter teased.

"I'm sure," he replied, putting his arm around Winter's shoulders. The men, Diamond noticed, were possessive of the two women. Diamond found it amusing from what Sex Piston had said about how they believed in sharing.

Diamond's mind shied away from wondering if the two women participated in the club's activities; she honestly didn't want to know.

The men ordered their lunches and her lips twisted in amusement at Knox and Rider's big orders.

"What's so funny?" Knox asked.

"I think that you guys are as hungry as I was. I bet you could have eaten two more pizzas last night."

"Make it three and you'll be more on target," Knox said, sliding her a sideways grin.

When the women at the table began looking at her curiously, Diamond avoided their eyes as she gathered her things.

"I need to get back to my office." Diamond stood abruptly to her feet, feeling ridiculous when the conversation at the table stopped and everyone looked at her.

She left everyone sitting at the diner. It seemed the more she tried to distance herself from The Last Riders, the more she became enmeshed into their life.

She mentally chastised herself on her walk, however when she went into her office, she abruptly came to a complete stop. Holly was standing in the middle of an enormous mess, picking up papers from the floor.

"What in the hell happened?" Diamond was stunned at the mess her office was in. Furniture had been torn and the filing had been thrown everywhere. Her cabinets had been overturned and papers scattered all over the place.

"Someone broke into the office. I tried to call, but you were in court and didn't return my message. The sheriff has already been here; he took pictures and made a report," Holly said with a handful of papers in her hands.

"This is going to take days to clean up. Who would have done this?" Diamond asked, going into her private office and seeing it was in even worse shape. "How did they manage doing this?" Her desk had been overturned with the drawers and confidential papers scattered and torn apart.

"Do you think it has something to do with a client?" Holly asked.

"I don't know, although whoever wanted me distracted, succeeded."

"No they didn't," Knox said, entering her office.

Diamond and Holly both turned as the office filled with The Last Riders being followed by Winter, Lily and Beth, staring in shock at the vandalized office.

"I'll help," Lily offered as she went down on her hands and knees to pick up the papers.

"We all will," Winter said, taking out her cell phone. "Evie, could you and a couple of the women come down to Diamond Richard's office. Someone broke into it and she needs help cleaning up. Thanks."

"That's unnecessary; both Holly and I can handle this."

"Really. I think I'd be interested to see you try to lift those filing cabinets and desk," Knox said, moving forward with Rider to lift the heavy cabinets back into place while Shade, Train and Viper went into her office to lift the heavy desk.

"It took a couple of people to create this damage. The sheriff came into the diner after you left. He told us that your office had been vandalized. He thinks more than one person was responsible for the damage also," Knox said, righting the end tables while the others restored order to the rest of the furniture. Winter, Beth and Holly joined Lily on the floor.

"When the others get here we can get them back in order," Beth said.

"Please stop, Winter. You're getting married tomorrow; I'm sure you have things you need to take care of. I can handle—"

A sharp gasp from Lily, who was on the floor by the window, had everyone's attention going to her. She raised her hand with blood dripping from a wound.

"Beth…" Lily whispered, turning toward her sister and

giving another gasp of pain, reaching for her knees. Blood seeped onto the papers she was kneeling on.

Winter and Beth immediately moved towards the young woman, but before either could reach her, Shade was lifting Lily from the floor into his arms. The girl tried to struggle free with her eyes on her bloody hand.

"Where's the bathroom?" Shade snapped at Diamond. She pointed to the door outside her office. Shade strode from the room with a struggling Lily while Beth tried to follow.

"Beth…" Lily's whimper tore at Diamond's hardened heart. The sweet woman had jumped to help her and now she was hurt. When Diamond and Beth moved towards the bathroom, Knox caught her arm in a firm grip while Razer's arm went around Beth's waist.

"Let Shade handle it, Beth. He was a medic in the service before he became a Seal," Razer explained to his concerned wife.

"I'm a nurse, Razer. She wants me," she snapped at her husband.

"Give Shade time to get the glass out, Beth. It's going to hurt. Do you really think that you can do it?" Beth paled. "I'll go to your car and get your first aid kit."

Beth nodded. "Thanks, Razer." Razer left, going to Beth's car as everyone else stood tensely outside the bathroom door as they waited. Diamond wrung her hands, feeling terrible.

"Let's get this glass up before anyone else gets hurt," Knox suggested.

Diamond went to the hall closet, getting the broom and dust pan before going back into the office. Knox had already separated the glass from the paperwork. Diamond tried not to look at the bloody paperwork, wondering how the tough navy seal was going to be gentle enough to deal with the sweet woman who had generously sought to help.

* * *

"Stop it, Lily," Shade said, sitting Lily down on the

closed toilet seat.

Her eyes remained on her bloody hand as her eyes started to roll back into her head. A sudden shake had her eyes traveling back to Shade.

"Eyes to me, Lily," he snapped. "Don't look at your hand again."

"It hurts." Shade's lips tightened. He had almost protested when Lily had gone to her knees to pick up the messed up office, yet he hadn't wanted to interfere. He was angry at himself for not following his instincts. He was getting fucking tired of the fine line he was walking to keep everybody happy, especially since Lily was invariably the one getting hurt because he was unable to protect the accident prone woman.

"I'll get the glass out and get it cleaned up then the sting will stop."

"Beth is a nurse; she can do it, Shade. I want Beth," Lily replied stubbornly. Shade knew she was reacting to being in the close confinement of the room with him.

"I'm sure you do. Do you think Beth can pull out that glass with you crying and acting like a baby?" he said, hoping her anger would arouse her fighting instincts.

Lily stiffened. Shade could see her trying to gather her composure as her eyes tried to sneak a peek at her still oozing injury.

"Eyes on me," Shade snapped again, wetting paper towels and gently picking out the fine shards of glass.

He could feel her gaze on his face. She hadn't argued against his commands, even though he had been a bit harsh; the same nearness of the restroom that was unnerving her, was straining his control. As he finished her hand, he heard a knock on the door and Razer telling him he had a first aid kit. When he opened the door, a silent message passed between the two men before the door closed once more.

Shade opened the box, finding sterile gauze for cleaning her knees. One particular shard had become imbedded there, so he took great care in removing it. Lily's dress had ridden up her silky thighs, rattling his concentration. Shade's hands shook as he finished cleaning her knees, wiping it with an antiseptic and starting to wrap them with bandages. He felt her tremble as his hands touched the soft skin behind her knees, trying to clench her thighs together.

"Open your legs. I need to wrap your other knee."

He felt her legs open a scant amount and then he wrapped it softly, stroking the sensitive flesh behind her knee. When she would have pulled away, Shade rose to his feet, letting his hand slide across the top of her thighs with a delicate touch that the innocent girl would think was accidental.

Taking her hand, he applied the antiseptic to it and then wrapped it, taking his time once more, enjoying her eyes watching his every move. Unable to prolong the inevitable any longer, he took a step away.

"You're done." Her eyes immediately broke from him and she practically ran from the restroom.

Shade picked up the first aid kit, meticulously replacing the items he had taken out. Going to the sink basin, he washed his hands and sprayed cold water on his face, wondering how much longer he could resist from reaching out and taking what he was determined would be his.

CHAPTER TWELVE

The glass had been swept up by the time Lily reentered the room with wild eyes. Lily reminded Diamond of a frightened doe when she immediately went to Beth. Diamond envied the two sisters their close relationship as she watched Beth soothe her until Lily sat down on the chair and began organizing the papers The Last Riders were picking up.

Shade's eyes went to Lily when he came back into the room before he started gathering the papers while taking in Lily ignoring him. His grim visage was one of tension. Diamond watched the other Last Riders circle him. Diamond now believed Winter when she said The Last Riders would protect Lily as she did the job she wanted. After all, they were keeping her protected from the wolf in their own territory.

When the women from The Last Riders arrived minutes later, Diamond was introduced to Evie, Dawn, Jewell and Raci. All of them brushed aside her protests and began organizing her paperwork. Holly put them back in the cabinets when each folder was completed.

What would have taken a week to reorganize, took just one afternoon with everyone's help. When it was down to a final sheath of papers, Diamond stood, looking around the room, which looked bare now that the men had taken out the couch; it had been torn to such an extent that it had to be thrown way.

"Damn, any idea who did this?" Evie asked, handing her the last sheath of papers.

"No, but I think it involved Knox's case. It's too much of a coincidence with the search warrant for the jewelry, now this. Someone wants me to stop."

"I agree; they're escalating. This is becoming more dangerous than I anticipated. I don't want you going anywhere without back-up, Diamond," Viper ordered.

"I'll be careful, Viper," Diamond said.

"You better be," Knox stated sternly.

Evie and the other women paused at Knox's words, looking stunned, while Diamond turned away and busied herself by putting the rest of the folders back in the cabinet.

"We're done here. Holly can replace the sofa for me Monday. Thanks everyone. It would have taken several days for us straighten this mess out," Diamond said, truly grateful for their help.

"No problem. We're glad we could help," Winter said with a smile.

Winter, Lily and Beth stood. "I'm sorry about the cuts, Lily." Diamond continued to be stricken by the sight of the bandages on Lily.

"I shouldn't have over-reacted; it was just a few scratches. We'll see you tomorrow." The women left with Razer and Shade.

"We have to go to, but Knox will stay with you until you get home," Viper said, looking at the reorganized office. Diamond started to argue with him, but she had started to notice that it was a lost cause to bother once Viper's mind was made up.

"Okay, we're almost done here anyway," Diamond relented. Besides, she could tell by the way that Knox was leaning against the wall with his arms crossed over his chest he wasn't going anywhere.

"I called the locksmith, he's on his way to put on another lock," Holly said, hanging up the phone.

"Thanks, Holly." Diamond glanced at her watch and realized it was almost five. "You go ahead. I'll stay here until the door is fixed."

"Okay. If you're sure. I'll go by the furniture store before work Monday and pick out a new sofa." Holly left, leaving Diamond alone with Knox.

"Your friends really helped me out today."

Knox shrugged. "It's only fair since it probably was my case that brought the bastard out who did this." His hand rubbed over his bald head. "This is fucking messed up. If I had just kept my dick in my pants, none of this would be happening."

Diamond didn't say anything because he was probably right, someone had used Knox's interlude with Samantha to set him up. The question was, how had they known?

"Did you see anyone that day? Someone had to have seen you so they could turn the cops in your direction."

"I didn't see anyone. No one saw me wreck or Sam pick me up."

"How about when you left the hotel?"

"No, it was empty."

Diamond saw something flash across his face. "What?"

"I thought I heard something, but when I looked around, it turned out to be nothing. I didn't see anyone."

"Where did you think the noise came from?" Diamond felt a brief flare of excitement.

"There's a big oak tree on the edge of the parking lot. I thought it was just the wind, but someone could have been hiding there. I'll send Cash to have a look around."

"I could go by on my way home," she said, anxious to have a look around.

"No, it's better if Cash goes. He's a tracker; he might pick up something we would miss." The locksmith knocked on the door as Knox made his call. Diamond purchased the strongest lock possible, yet she didn't have high hopes that it would prevent another break-in.

The door repair didn't take long. When it was finished, Diamond and Knox were finally able to leave. She glanced down at her watch as she headed to her car.

"What's the hurry?" Knox asked, his long strides easily keeping up with her fast steps.

"I'm going to be late to dinner at my mother's," she answered, opening her car door.

"You're driving to Jamestown?"

"Yes."

Knox stopped her from entering her car by taking her arm. She started to jerk away until she noticed that he was pointing to her tire.

"Damn it. What is going on? This day is one disaster after another." Diamond started to pull her phone out of her pocket to cancel dinner.

"I can drive you on my bike. I would just have followed anyway or Viper would have had my ass."

"I'm not riding on your bike to my mother's house."

"It doesn't look like you have much choice. It'll take at least thirty minutes for someone to bring you a new tire."

"You could change my tire for me. I have a spare," Diamond suggested.

"Your spare is for shit. I noticed it the other day when we worked on your alternator. Your whole car is one big accident waiting to happen," Knox said, shaking his head.

"I was going to get another one as soon as I get a few more clients. I needed Holly more than a car."

Knox looked at her skeptically. "Maybe if you're driving around town within walking distance of everything, but if you're driving to your mom's, then no, it's not safe."

Diamond knew he was right, therefore she bit back the sharp retort she had been going to make. At the same time, Knox went to his bike, getting on and handing her the helmet.

"You going home or to your mother's?"

Diamond almost went home. Only the importance her mother had placed on her dinner made Diamond climb on the back of Knox's bike.

Putting on Knox's helmet, Diamond grabbed him around the waist as he rode out of the parking lot. Diamond had forgotten how much she loved riding on the back of a motorcycle. She hadn't done it in years, since she had quit going for rides with her father. The first time she had ridden with Knox, she had been too sick to appreciate the short ride.

Sex Piston had bought her own motorcycle and took it out often after her father taught her how to ride, but Diamond had never been tempted to own her own. She knew she didn't have her sister's skill for the feel of the machine. As they went around the tight curves, she let her body go loose, holding on to Knox and following the moves of the bike.

It didn't take long before they were pulling up in front of her mother's house. Diamond climbed off, handing the helmet to Knox.

"Thanks for the ride. I'll get Sex Piston to bring me home." Diamond started to walk up the path to her mother's house, stopping at his next words.

"I'll wait." Knox turned off his motor.

"Don't be crazy. You can't sit out here while we eat. The neighbors and my parents will wonder who you are."

"So tell them." Knox shrugged, making no effort to start his motor.

Diamond stared at the stubborn man, realizing he wasn't going to give in. "For Heaven's sake, just come in. You can have dinner with us, but remember when Sex Piston is driving you crazy that you brought it on yourself." Diamond stomped to her parents' house with Knox following behind.

She ignored Knox's raised brow at her knocking and not going on inside the house.

When her mother answered the door at her knock, her eye's widened as she took in the man standing beside her daughter. "Diamond, I was beginning to get worried."

"Mom, this is Knox. My car had a flat and he was nice enough to give me a ride. I invited him to dinner, if that's okay?" Diamond explained in one breath.

"Of course, dear, you know when I cook I always make enough for leftovers."

Diamond was afraid of that. . She hadn't had time to warn Knox about the lack of cooking skills her mother had or that she only felt the need to subject the family to said cooking in order to impart a piece of news that she felt was important to them all. Diamond studied her mother, looking for any signs of illness she might be hiding and was relieved when her mother looked healthier than she had in years.

"What in the fuck is he doing here?" Sex Piston asked as she set the beer on the table when they entered the dining room.

"Sex Piston, watch your mouth," Diamond's mother snapped at her daughter.

"You don't care you have a murderer sitting at your table?" Her mother cast Knox a sharp glance.

"He's innocent, Mom." Knox stood there quietly, not trying to defend himself.

"I'm sure he is." Her mother tried to stop the argument brewing between her two daughters.

"He sure as fuck isn't," Sex Piston retorted, her hand going to her hips.

"Shut up. My car had a flat and he gave me a ride here," Diamond explained, hoping that it would calm her sister.

"Well, you're here now. I'll give you a ride home. See ya," Sex Piston smarted off to Knox.

"Sex Piston, stop it," her mother scolded. "Everyone, sit down. I'll get your father." Diamond and Sex Piston shot dirty looks each other's way as they sat down at the table. Knox sat down next to her at the table across from Sex Piston.

"I should have warned you sooner. My mom's not the greatest cook, so make sure you take small portions," Diamond warned.

"I bet it tastes better than prison food," Sex Piston snapped.

"Sex Piston, if you don't quit bugging your sister, the police are going to be charging me with another crime," Knox threatened.

"Bring it on, asshole," Sex Piston taunted, picking up the carving knife and laying it beside her on the table.

"Cut it out." A sharp voice from the doorway had all eyes going to her father. Sex Piston's mouth snapped closed. Diamond was relieved when her sister called a halt to her antics and picked up her beer. Her father came into the room, holding his hand out to Knox.

"I'm Skulls."

"Knox."

Diamond watched the two bikers introduce themselves.

"Have you met Sizzle?" he asked, pulling out her mother's chair.

Diamond wanted to crawl under the table when her father told Knox her mother's nickname.

"It's nice to meet you both." Knox barely managed to keep from laughing. Diamond threw him a dirty look.

Her father took his seat at the table. "Sex Piston told us Diamond is representing you for killing a woman in Treepoint."

"Yes." Knox looked her father in the eyes.

"You do it?"

"No. I couldn't stand the bitch, but I didn't kill her."

"Good, let's eat. Sizzle, bring on the food." Her father barely managed to hide his grimace.

Her mother brought out a roast on a platter with potatoes, carrots and rolls. The whole table stared at the food as her mother took a seat. Serving everyone took several minutes as the roast was almost impossible to cut. It had practically been burnt to a crisp. Passing the rolls, she shook her head when her mother offered them. She could tell by looking at them that they were raw.

Not even for her mother would she gag down raw bread dough. Her father and everyone else at the table hadn't been so smart. She couldn't hide her vengeful smile when Sex Piston wasn't able to prevent the retching noise as she took a bite of one.

To Knox's credit, he managed to clean his plate, which was a big mistake as her mother forced seconds on him. Her father manned up and took seconds for himself, not wanting Knox to outdo him. Washing the dried meat down with several swallows of beer, she managed to eat half her plate. Throwing Sex Piston a who's-a-pussy look when she couldn't eat as much.

"Anyone want dessert?" her mother asked happily.

"No," the whole table chorused together.

The crestfallen expression on her mother's face had everyone retracting their answer except Diamond. Been there, done that.

"I'm on a diet, Mom," she responded to Sex Piston's threatening glare accompanied with the finger behind her mother's back.

Her mother returned to the table with a cake that looked remarkably good, but Diamond had learnt that looks were deceiving where her mother's cooking was concerned. She always waited for the consensus before jumping for a slice of chocolate cake. The look of horror on their faces confirmed her fears.

"Sizzle, we need some milk. Beer and chocolate don't go together." Her mother went back into the kitchen and everyone sprang into action. Sex Piston dumped her cake onto her father's napkin and he dumped his there also then left the room just as her mother returned with the milk and paper cups.

Diamond wanted to go through the floor, wondering if

the night could get any more embarrassing as she watched Knox when her father returned to the room, explaining to her mother he'd had to go to the restroom. Knox managed to take a couple of bites before even he couldn't gag any more down.

"I'm not a big sweet eater," Knox explained to her mother when she cast him a questioning glance.

"I'm not, either, but I know they enjoy it when I make something sweet to finish off dinner."

"It was a delicious meal as always, Sizzle," her father lied.

Diamond had, with that, had enough. She wanted to escape before she had to have any more time in her father's company.

"Mom, what did you want to tell us? Knox can leave, go in the other room while we talk—"

"There's no need, Diamond; it's not bad news. I just wanted to ask you two girls if you'd be my bridesmaids. Your father and I have finally decided to tie the knot." Sex Piston whooped, getting up to hug both parents. Her mother's smiling face turned toward her as Diamond rose carefully from the table.

"I'll talk to you later, Mom. I need to leave. I don't want to hold Knox up any longer than necessary. I was worried you may be sick again. I'm glad it's good news." Diamond put her chair back under the table. Not waiting for Knox, she practically ran for the door.

"Diamond, what on earth? Wait a minute. The wedding is going to be at the Destructors' clubhouse. We're going to have a caterer and everything." Diamond could hear the tears in her mother's voice, but didn't stop.

"I can't, Mom. I just can't," Diamond answered, pulling open the door and going for Knox's bike.

"Damn it, stop, Diamond," her father yelled.

Diamond stopped; her back to her family, sensing Knox stopping by her side.

"What's your fucking problem?" Sex Piston yelled.

"Why are you being a bitch to Mom? They've been together for years. You should be happy."

Diamond swung around facing her family.

"Why should I be happy to see her marry a man who has fucked around on her for years? Now that he's an old man and not president of a motorcycle club the pussy probably doesn't come as easy as it used to, does it, Pops?" Years of hurt along with feelings of betrayal welled and found their target. The stunned look on her father's face had her wanting to inflict more hurt. "You haven't deserved Mom for years, so no, I'm not going to watch you get married to my mom when you damn sure don't deserve her now."

"You bitch!" Sex Piston yelled at her sister.

"You're calling me a bitch? You're the bitch; always in heat for some man. You're just like him, chasing anything with a dick—you and Ace both. The only difference is you didn't get knocked up like that woman he's got now."

Diamond saw the look of pain on her mother's face, and with a sob, went to Knox's bike, getting on and putting on his helmet. He paused, but then hopped on to the bike, starting it and pulling out. Diamond cried all the way back to Treepoint. Angry at her parents for springing the news on her and even angrier at her mother for putting up with her father's shit for all the years they had been together.

She was also embarrassed that she had let loose in front of Knox. She should just have left, but she had lost control when she had faced her father. All the admiration she'd had for him as a little girl when she would have at one time been overjoyed for her parents to get married were washed away by the memory of him with that other woman at the Destructors' clubhouse.

The hardest thing to admit was that she could finally understand her mother after all these years; the attraction of wanting someone you knew was incapable of being faithful and being the man you wanted him to be. The torture of a body in need versus a mind that said it was a heartache in waiting. Knox was like the wind rushing passed them, uncontrollable and free. He would never be the man she needed to make her happy.

CHAPTER THIRTEEN

As Knox pulled up in front of Diamond's apartment, she barely managed to wait for him to stop to jump off.

"Thanks for the ride." Handing him the helmet, she took off for her door. When she was there, she realized too late she had left her purse in Knox's saddlebag. As she turned to go back, she bumped into Knox.

"Diamond, what's wrong with you? Don't fucking jump off my bike like that again," Knox growled, handing her purse to her.

Diamond ran her hand through her flattened hair. "I made a fool of myself. I didn't mean to drag that crap out in front of you. I'm sorry." Digging in her purse, she found her keys and then opened the door. She started to tell Knox goodnight, only to find herself propelled forward into her apartment.

"What are you doing?" Diamond said, startled.

"I'm going to check your apartment out before I leave," Knox answered, brushing past her to walk through her apartment, checking each room.

"I believe I would notice if someone broke in," Diamond said sarcastically.

"Your neighbors aren't home next door. Who's going

to hear if you yell for help?" Knox said, unfazed by her attitude, which only irritated Diamond further.

"I have a cell phone," she snapped.

"Yeah, you tell the man who breaks in and is waiting to take you out that you need to make a call. I'm sure he'll listen," Knox said sarcastically. "Until we find out who broke into your office, you need to play it safe, Diamond."

In the turmoil of the last few hours she had forgotten about her office.

"I wasn't thinking. Next time, I'll be more careful," Diamond admitted.

"Good. Now do you have anything to eat, I'm fucking starving."

"I think I can manage something." She laughed, setting her purse down on the table.

"Good, because I hate to tell you this, but your mama isn't a good cook," Knox said with a grimace.

Diamond had to agree. "How was the cake?" she asked, going to the refrigerator and pulling out lunchmeat, lettuce and tomatoes.

"I think she mixed up the salt with the sugar, and the chocolate was God awful," Knox said, picking out an apple from the fruit bowl on the counter.

"She always manages to mix up the different types of chocolate. Sorry my dad didn't help you out."

"Hell, I understand; in that situation it was every man for himself." Diamond laughed harder.

"Thank God, she doesn't cook often. Usually it's about something pretty bad, and I guess, tonight was no exception," Diamond said, her laughter dying.

"You don't want your parents to get married?" Knox went to her fridge, pulling out a grape soda. "How long have they been together?" he asked, taking a bite of the apple.

"Thirty-five years. Twenty years longer than they should have been."

Knox paused, unscrewing the bottled grape drink. "Is

that the reason you yelled at them out in their front yard?"

Diamond made the sandwiches, cutting and slicing them, even removing the crust. Then, setting them on a couple of plates, she carried them to the table.

"Yes." When they sat down to eat, regret began to bloom in her chest, making it hard to swallow.

"I bet they hate me." Diamond got up, throwing the rest of her food away and putting her plate in the sink.

"No, they don't. They aren't real happy with you right now, but they don't hate you," Knox said. "I have to say, though, if a man can eat that kind of cooking from a woman, there has to be a lot of love there." Diamond had to partially agree; her mom was a terrible cook, although she had never seen him complain, acting like each meal she served had been prepared by a five star chef.

"Sex Piston hates me."

"That's probably true," Knox said, finishing his sandwich, then rose to put his own plate in the sink. Diamond leaned against the counter, trying not to laugh.

"Gee, thanks."

"I don't believe in bullshit. What you said tonight, nothing was wrong with saying it. You simply should have done it sooner. That shit's been festering awhile for you, hasn't it?"

"Ever since I was fourteen and saw my dad fucking one of the sluts that had been hanging around the clubhouse." Diamond turned away, walking into the living room. "She was always so friendly with Mom and me when we went to the clubhouse; both before and after I saw her with my dad. It didn't bother her at all she was doing him behind my mom's back."

Knox followed her into the living room, sitting on the sofa. "You sure your mom didn't know? They've been together a long time for her not to know he's fucking around on her."

"We never talked about it. I couldn't tell her, and I'm damn sure my dad didn't." Diamond sat down at the end of the couch.

"It wouldn't be something your mom would talk to you about," Knox said in a matter-of-fact tone.

"Are you saying my mom knew he was fucking around on her and she stayed with him anyway?" Diamond asked angrily.

"I'm saying that what went on between your parents is their business. Maybe she did know and it didn't bother her; she accepted it," Knox reasoned.

"Are you crazy? What woman is going to stay with a man who is constantly fucking around on her?"

"Some couples don't mind sharing," Knox said, turning on the television with the remote.

"Yeah, The Last Riders for one. Don't tarnish my parents with the same sick kinks your club shares." Diamond grabbed the remote from his hand. Knox reacted by taking her hand and jerking her down on his lap.

"What do we do that's sick?" he asked, easily keeping her on his lap as she tried to wiggle off.

"You, Rider, Evie and Bliss in one bed. That's sick."

"No, that was fucking great," Knox said, dipping his head and taking her mouth in a demanding kiss she was determined to resist.

Diamond jerked her head back, tearing her mouth away from his. Undeterred, Knox's lips traveled to her throat, seeking the sensitive flesh as his hand traveled up her thigh under her dress.

"Have you ever had dick up your ass and pussy at the same time, Diamond?" Knox murmured against her throat. Diamond shivered as the image played across her mind. "You can have a lot of fun sharing that beautiful body of yours, Diamond, if you just let yourself relax and enjoy the pleasure." His fingers slid under the band of her panties, finding the wet warmth of her pussy waiting for his attention. His rough finger sought and found her clit, stroking it until the tiny bud quivered, sending flares of need screaming through Diamond's body. "That's it, baby, give me all that cream, you're going to need it."

Diamond's head tilted to the side and Knox seized the advantage by taking her mouth with his again. This time the pleasure prevented Diamond from retreating, instead she returned his kiss, stroking his tongue with hers and searching his mouth in a duel of dominance. His tongue ring caressed her tongue as his finger plunged into her warm passage, creating a rhythm her hips rose to meet. Escalating her passion, he added another finger, only withdrawing when her arms clasped his shoulders, pulling him close while her legs thrashed as she tried to move to the couch.

Knox rose in one movement, carrying her into the bedroom and laying her down on the bed. His hands went to her hips, pulling down her stockings and panties. He then removed his shirt, exposing his chest. Diamond's mouth watered at the bare expanse of the muscular chest, her fingers wanted to explore the tats on his arm and her mouth wanted to trace the tats on his chest. She watched breathlessly as he took off his boots, standing again to take off his jeans, exposing his huge, pierced cock.

Diamond's eyes widened at the sheer size of his cock and the piercings that had several balls on the flesh around the head. She, even with her limited experience, knew that this would be no gentle round of love-making from the tensed look on Knox's face. The size and piercings were enough to scare the desire from her body, add the fierce expression and Diamond knew he would be too much to handle.

Diamond rose to her knees on the bed as he pulled on a condom, her flight or fight instinct kicking in when faced with the frightening proposition of being fucked by a cock that she was afraid would rip her to shreds in more ways than one.

She tried to scramble off the other side of the bed, however she found her hips grasped in his hands and her ass dragged backwards to him.

"If you didn't want to fuck, you would have said so before I pulled my dick out." He pulled her dress up to her waist, baring her ass and pussy to his gaze. Stepping up between her thighs, he fit his cock against her opening.

"Knox..."

Knox inserted the head of his penis into her wet opening, pumping in and out in small increments. Diamond felt the balls of his piercings rub against her tender flesh as he moved against her, attempting to fit inside. His hands moved her thighs wider apart as he slid another inch inside her at the same time that Diamond's fingers grasped her comforter as her knees tried to brace herself while he continued to shove his length inside her. His thumb found her clit again, stroking her. The rush of wetness allowed him to continue to slide within as she felt him stretching her. Diamond tried to buck him off and move forward, but Knox held her still, bending over and pinning her shoulders to the bed with his chest.

"You can take me, just relax."

"That's easy for you to say," she said, trying to ignore the small bite of pain as he began a steady pumping that was driving him deeper within her. The piercings on his cock rubbed the walls of her pussy and it was eliciting a response that had her involuntary moving backwards against her better judgment.

"That's it, fuck me back." His mouth found the back of her neck, sucking a piece of flesh into his mouth and biting down.

The slight flare of pain arched her back, driving him further into her. Diamond whimpered as he began to move harder and faster inside her. The stretching fullness of his cock breached her tight opening, arousing her to feelings of lust she had never felt before. Losing control, she began to move back against him in demands of her own as she felt him fill her completely.

Knox controlled her wild movements with his

experienced hands, moving her hips in the direction that maximized the feel of those piercing against her g-spot. The pain of the tightness of her cunt only added to the excitement of his cock driving forcefully within her. His mouth sucking against her neck merely stimulated her further as she moaned, trying to find her release.

"You want to come?" Knox's hand on her clit pressed against her harder, lifting her off the bed as he used his hand against her body to lift her while he continued to fuck strongly within her.

"Yes!"

"I'm not ready to come yet; you going to suck me off if I let you come?"

"Yes!"

Knox lowered her knees back to the bed. Removing the palm of his hand, he started rubbing her clit as he pumped inside of her. Within two hard thrusts of his cock, Diamond felt her climax strike her in waves of sensations that had her incapable of doing anything except letting her orgasm run its course.

Knox pulled out of her, and with an arm around her waist, he lifted her from the bed. Turning, he sat down on the side of her bed, setting her down between his thighs on the floor.

Still shuddering with her climax, she heard his command. "Take the condom off." With shaking fingers, Diamond reached out and removed the slick condom, dropping it into the small trashcan she kept by her bed.

"Get on your knees." Diamond dropped to her knees between his splayed thighs. Knox's hand went to her now messed up hair, pulling her down to his cock.

"Suck me off." Diamond took his cock into her mouth, giving him what he wanted, although she had only ever given head a few times and she knew she wasn't very good at it.

Knox's hand in her hair took into account her inexperience, showing her what he wanted. Knox was not a lover that took it easy on you; he demanded, going past her defenses to get her to take more of his cock than she thought she would be able to. When he felt her begin to gag, he pulled back, but only gave her a moment's respite before surging back within her mouth.

His fingers unbuttoned the front of her dress, pulling a breast out of the cup of her bra. Finding her nipple, he pinched until the nub hardened, turning a light red. Diamond groaned around the head of his cock.

"Use your tongue." Again Diamond followed his instructions, using her tongue to explore the hard flesh and teasing the piercings that had driven her crazy when he had been buried in her pussy.

"Do you know how sexy you look with my cock in your mouth, wearing those uptight business clothes with your tits begging me to pinch them? You look fucking hot." His praise had Diamond trying harder to please him, endeavoring to take more of him while going up and down his long length.

"That's it; show me you want it." His hand in her hair grasped her tighter and his hips began to thrust. Her tongue found the piercings again, playing with them while her fingers went to his balls, feeling them tighten. His length hardened even further as he finally achieved the orgasm he'd wanted.

When she removed her mouth, he picked her up by the waist, laying her on the bed and curving against her. His mouth went to her neck, placing kisses on her. Diamond felt warm and tired. Her eyes closed from the disaster of a day, which hadn't ended badly.

"Get some sleep. I'm going to fuck you again in an hour," Knox said, reaching out to turn the light off.

Diamond dozed off, thinking that he was overestimating his stamina, but it was Diamond who spent the night amazed at the amount of times he kept waking her. She found herself continuously submitting to the demands he placed on her body. It was only towards dawn that she felt him climb from the bed, pulling on his clothes. Diamond watched, barely able to move her sore body.

"I'll see you this afternoon at Viper's wedding. You better get some sleep; you're going to need it." He left her without another word.

Diamond heard the door open and close behind him, wondering what in the hell she had started.

* * *

Diamond soaked her stiff body in hot water until she felt her flesh begin to wrinkle. Her mind was in turmoil at what she had allowed to happen with Knox. The sexual attraction she held for him was nothing she had ever encountered before. Of the few men she'd had sex with, she'd had an emotional attachment to all of them before they had explored the sexual side of their relationship. With Knox, she didn't know how she felt about him, yet her body wanted his until it almost consumed her with lust.

She admired the things he had done with his life, but she hated that he belonged to The Last Riders and the lifestyle he made no bones about enjoying. Diamond had no illusions; if he wanted to fuck one of the women at the club, their one night together wouldn't stop him. Feeling a knife of jealousy plunge into her stomach, Diamond rose from the tub, drying off.

She went to her closet and picked out a purple dress that buttoned up the back. It was pretty and sexy. Diamond had picked it out in the department store in town and hadn't worn it yet because the deep v in the front wasn't appropriate for the office or court.

Dressed, she put on heels and brushed her red hair until it fell down her back in curls. When she went to get her car keys, she realized she had forgotten her car was still at the office. Not to mention, her keys were now missing. A knock at the door sounded just as she was going to pick up her phone to call and have it fixed.

. With a sense of déjà vu she opened her door to the grinning Rider and an impassive Knox.

"We brought your car back, all fixed with a new tire," Rider said, handing her the keys.

"Thanks, Rider."

"And before you can mention money...—" he continued.

"I know, Viper took care of it." Diamond finished for him. "The way it's going I'm going to owe him money."

"Cheaper to get a new car than fix everything wrong with that piece of junk," Knox said.

"I told you that I can't afford to get a new car yet."

"Then I suggest you get busy getting me off the hook for Sam's murder so that you can buy one."

"Why don't you make it easy on me and just confess," she snapped.

Rider burst out laughing. "As much as I'm enjoying this bickering, we're going to be late for Viper's wedding. Knowing Winter, she'll make me take a punishment."

"Take a punishment?" Diamond questioned Rider, but was ignored as Knox took her hand and pulled her out into the hall. Rider locked and closed her door, following behind.

"Slow down Knox; we're not that late," Diamond said, trying to keep up. Knox slowed his steps and Diamond walked between the two men.

A truck was parked by her car. Diamond started to go to her car, however Knox opened the truck door. "Get in."

"But I was going to take my car."

"Leave it. I'll bring you back tonight." Diamond gave in, sliding into the passenger side of the truck then scooting over as Knox got in beside her. Rider climbed in behind the wheel, expertly backing the truck out and onto the road.

"Did Winter invite anymore unexpected guests?" Diamond asked curiously.

"No, just The Last Riders, you and Lily. Mrs. Langley was invited, but under the circumstances, she declined."

"I know; Winter told me. I feel horrible that she doesn't have any family left," Diamond said, knowing the sweet woman had to be lonely.

"She has a great-grandchild if Sam hadn't decided to keep it a secret with what she had done with it," Knox said, staring out the window.

"Vincent Bedford refuses to tell?" Diamond asked.

"Yes. The sheriff is looking into the situation," Rider answered.

Knox placed his arm against the back of the car seat. Diamond was unsure how to act around him. She didn't want to act like a girlfriend, but she didn't want to be the cliché one-night stand, either. She was confused as to what exactly she did want.

Rider pulled the truck into the parking lot of the clubhouse. The huge house sat on top of a hill facing the mountain. Diamond noticed a path being dug alongside the long flight of steps leading to the door.

"You're putting in more steps?" Diamond asked.

"No, we're trying to level it off so that a winding path will take you to the back door of the house to make it easier on Winter's back. Viper worries that she will fall."

Diamond had come to respect the way Viper treated Winter. During her school board case, he had let her take the lead, supporting her in the decisions she made and had backed her up with the wealth he had at his disposal. He saw her through the violent attack that had cost her several months of physical recovery and even now was making sure her safety was taken seriously.

They climbed the steps, and when they reached the front door, Knox opened it, letting her go first into the huge room. Diamond came to a stop, seeing the inside had been redecorated. The furniture had been changed since she had been to see Winter. The mismatched furniture had been replaced with expensive leather couches and recliners in several groupings. Two long sectionals were also along opposite sides of the walls. The bar where she had seen Knox with the two women stood empty with the overhead lights off; the liquor bottles and glasses gone. It looked like the bed and breakfast it was intended to be, not the motorcycle club that had been evident a few months before.

"What happened?" Diamond asked, amazed at the transformation it had gone from a haphazard assortment of furniture into a casually elegant welcoming environment.

"We redecorated," Rider said in amusement.

"It looks wonderful," Diamond said, looking at the shiny wooden floors and plants scattered throughout the room.

"Winter and Beth spent the week getting it ready," Rider said, taking off his jacket and placing it in the closet. The door opened behind them and Beth, Lily and Razer came in behind them.

"Hi," Beth and Lily spoke in unison.

"Hello," Diamond returned their greeting. Beth looked gorgeous in a pretty blue dress and Lily was wearing a pink dress that highlighted the darkness of her long black hair, making her look feminine and graceful. Beth hung up their coats as Lily looked around.

"It's very nice in here, Beth," Lily told her sister. The look of relief on Beth's face brought understanding to Diamond. The redecorating had been for Lily's benefit.

"You haven't been in here before?" Diamond asked Lily. Everyone surrounding her tensed. Even Knox stiffened, his hand grasped her upper arm, giving a squeeze. Diamond didn't understand the secrecy about the change, but decided to ask Knox about it later, instead of making an issue of it.

"No. The clubhouse is off limits to me." Lily lowered her eyes. Sensing her hurt, Diamond took a step toward her. Knox's hand dropped away from her as she wound her arm through Lily's.

"I'd make it off limits to you, too, if you were my sister. Too much testosterone." Diamond gave a mock shudder, making Lily laugh. Turning back to the men, she asked, "So where's the wedding?" Diamond twined her arm through Lily's, and Beth gave her a grateful smile.

Diamond and Lily only managed a brief glimpse of the house as they went through into the backyard. The day was sunny with above-average temperatures for the late fall. The backyard was huge with two picnic tables set up with white tablecloths and flowers. A gazebo had flowers decorating it, which a minister was standing in front of, talking to Viper. Diamond had never met the Pastor who was extremely handsome with a sex appeal that made the ministers from her youth seem old-fashioned.

"Grab a seat; it's about to start." Knox ushered the women to a grouping of empty chairs toward the front. Beth had already gone to join Winter as her matron of honor.

"Winter didn't want bridesmaids. She picked Beth to be her matron of honor and Viper picked Cash as his best man," Lily whispered at her side.

Knox and Rider sat down next on the opposite side of Diamond. Diamond gazed at the guests already seated. All of them, The Last Riders and the female members, were waiting expectantly. Diamond felt terrible she had initially refused Winter's invitation now that she saw that she had invited no outsiders other than Lily and her. Diamond didn't understand why she had invited her, though. She hadn't been friendly to the woman when she had represented her and had made no effort to get to know her since her case had been resolved.

They weren't waiting long when someone started some light music and the door opened as Winter and an older man walked out. Winter was wearing a white dress that had long sleeves made of lace which wasn't long, stopping at her calves, fitting her slight body to perfection. She looked beautiful with the smile and love on her face when she caught sight of Viper waiting with the Pastor.

"She looks beautiful," Lily said beside her, speaking her own thoughts.

"Yes, she does."

The man handed Winter over to Viper and took a seat in the row in front of Diamond. The ceremony was brief and eloquent with both Winter and Viper speaking their own vows. When the minister pronounced them man and wife, Viper scooped Winter up into his arms, twirling her around. The loud cheer from the crowd had Diamond and Lily smiling at each other.

"Thank God, that's over," Knox said, rising to his feet.

Diamond sent him a reproving glance as they went to Winter and Viper to congratulate them. The happy couple greeted her with warmth, making Diamond feel welcome among so many strangers. Viper introduced Diamond to his father, Ton; the older man who had walked Winter down the aisle and now stood grimly at the couple's side.

"You look beautiful," Diamond complimented her.

"Thanks." Winter smiled.

"I was afraid for a few minutes that Ton was going to run off with her," Viper joked.

"Let's get the pictures over with, so I can get some food. You already took all the fun out of it by hiding the booze." Everyone sent the man a quelling look while Lily looked stricken with a faint blush rising to her cheeks.

"Diamond let's get some food. You can come with us, Lily. Beth will be a few minutes taking pictures." Knox took both women by the arms, leading them into a huge kitchen where a large amount of food was sitting in warming trays. Evie and Bliss were ahead of them in line, filling their plate. Diamond avoided their eyes after the women greeted her with smiles.

Lily and Diamond filled their plates, watching as Knox and Rider overloaded their own. They took a seat at the large table in the dining room where Lily sat across from her while Knox and Rider sat down next to her, one on each side. When Evie and Bliss joined them at the same table, their friendly demeanor put Diamond at ease despite their history with Knox.

Lily kept her entertained by asking questions about her job and where she had gone to college. She was familiar with Lexington and the University of Kentucky, and they talked for several minutes before a breathless Beth took the seat next to Lily.

"Razer is getting my plate. I didn't want to fight the line." As Knox and Rider had gone back for seconds, Diamond could understand. When they returned and they resumed their seats, Beth stared at them for several seconds before giving Razer a concerned look as he handed her a plate of food.

His carefully bland face gave Diamond no clue as to what was upsetting Beth. Knox drew her attention with a hard look at Beth as he asked Diamond if she had heard anything else about his case.

"No, it goes to trial in January, giving me a couple of months to prepare, but I'm basically at a standstill until we get the final results from Frankfort."

"I'll be glad when this bullshit is over," Knox said, picking up his glass of Champaign punch.

"I need all the time I can get. If something new doesn't turn up, it's not going to go well for you," Diamond warned.

"I made the biggest mistake of my life that day," Knox said, the anger evident on his face.

Diamond squeezed his hand in sympathy as Evie and Bliss got up from the table, excusing themselves to wash dishes. Diamond and Lily started to rise to go help.

"Let them take care of it; it's their punishment." Knox stopped her with a hand on her arm.

"Punishment?" Diamond questioned, seeing Lily's eyes widen.

"They screwed up an order that went out last week. The kitchen is the punishment they drew."

"You punish them when they make a simple mistake?" Lily questioned.

"It wasn't a simple mistake; a customer was kept waiting for the supplies they needed. They gave us a bad review and took their order somewhere else," Shade said, pausing by their table.

"Then write them up," Lily snapped back. "But punishing them like children is ridiculous."

"Is it?" Shade said. "Do you think a written paper telling them they made a mistake is as effective as making them wash all the dishes and clean the kitchen for a week?"

"For a week?" Lily asked. "They should report you to OSHA."

Shades lips twisted into what Diamond thought was his version of a smile. "It was handled as a club punishment, which is different than what we would have done if they had been one of the hired employees."

"What would you have done to a hired employee? Make them mop the floors for a month?" Lily asked with fight in her eyes.

"No, we would have fired their asses," Shade answered.

A thought occurred to Lily, who turned to Beth. Diamond would have bet her law degree on the question that was coming next. "Do you have to take punishments like that?"

When Beth didn't answer immediately, Lily drew taut beside her sister. Diamond almost found herself smiling at the young woman who was like a spitting kitten trying to protect her sister.

"Then you don't need to belong to the club anymore," Lily declared.

"She's Razer's; she belongs to him and the club," Shade said bluntly. Lily stared at her sister, wanting her to deny their ownership.

"We'll talk about this later, Lily," Beth said, taking Lily's hand. "But I love Razer and you do, too, and you know it. The Last Riders are a big part of his life; he considers them family. I did know that he was in a motorcycle club when I fell in love with him, and it's not like it's an overly harsh punishment. The worst thing that could happen is dish pan hands."

Lily gave her sister a rueful smile. "I'm sorry I overreacted, I just couldn't stand the thought of you taking any punishment for any reason." The women shared a private moment. "Besides, it's your life and I know for a fact you're very happy."

"Yes, I am." Beth smiled.

Shade once again started to walk on until Lily's next words stopped him dead in his tracks. "We need to go to Arizona; they have cowboys, Diamond," Lily said to her mischievously.

"Cowboys?" Diamond asked, not understanding the abrupt subject change.

"I'm going to marry a cowboy. Their gentlemen, kind and protect their women," Lily said with authority.

"They do?"

Lily nodded her head. From the look on Shades face, the only cowboy in Lily's future would be wearing leather instead of chaps and a motorcycle instead of a horse.

Beth laughed at her sister's idea of a perfect husband. "Our father wouldn't let us watch television. The only shows he would take us to every now and then were cowboy movies. Lily has been infatuated with them ever since," Beth explained.

A chill ran down Diamond's back at the expression on Shades face. His hands clenched and unclenched as he stood still.

"Shade, Razer is waiting on you." Winter's voice broke the tension-filled moment as she came up behind him, her eyes flashing a warning. Shade leaned over Lily, reaching for Diamond's empty plate.

"You think cowboys don't know how to punish their women, Lily? They have whips and spurs they use on their horses." A terrified look came over Lily's face and her hand went to the wrist with a rubber band. Shade's hand covered the wrist before Lily could touch it. "I'll take that to the kitchen for you, Diamond. At least when I punish someone, I don't leave a mark," he said suggestively, rising with Diamond's plate in his hand, leaving the quiet group behind.

Rider started laughing, breaking the tension. "I think I'll get another plate."

Diamond stared at him in surprise. "Rider, you've been back twice."

"I have to have plenty of energy for the dancing," he said with a meaningful look at Beth, laughing at her red face while she gave her husband a threatening glare.

Rising to her feet, Beth took Lily's hand and went upstairs to help Winter get out of her wedding dress.

Diamond looked at Knox. "I don't want to know what that was all about, do I?"

"Nope, just do what I do."

"What's that?"

"Stay out of it," Knox said.

"That's good advice." Diamond didn't want to invade Lily's privacy and she wasn't about to piss off Shade. That man took the term intimidating to a whole new level.

"Let's go outside and sit." They went outside, finding a couple of chairs.

"I didn't realize this backyard was so big."

"The property extends for several miles. Razer and Beth are building a home over there." Knox pointed to a clearing that had several piles of lumber stacked and a frame already well under way. It was close to the house, but not too close; giving the impression of privacy while still having the feeling of being close to the main house.

"They wanted to have it finished by next year when Lily graduates. There was another clearing farther away with its back to the mountain. That's where Shade plans to build his house when Razer's is finished."

"It's a beautiful spot."

Music began playing. "Dance with me."

"I shouldn't, Knox. I shouldn't be doing any of this. I could get censured." Diamond attempted to half-heartedly resist.

"No one is going to open their mouth about you even being here today." The thought suddenly occurred to her that he had driven her, not letting her take her own car, ensuring that no one would see her car parked outside for any length of time.

They went to where several of The Last Riders were dancing in a spot that obviously had been used to dance several times. Diamond was amazed at how tame everyone was; no liquor, the women were all dressed modestly and on very circumspect behavior. Her dad's former club would have torn the place apart by now, celebrating an occasion of their president getting married. Diamond knew of two instances where fires had been inadvertently set.

Everyone in the club was dancing, so Diamond and Knox danced several times before Lily, Beth and Winter came outside; Winter having changed into a cream dress that suited her and wasn't as formal. While Viper and Razer grabbed their women for a dance, Lily saw Diamond and came over to them to sit down by her and Knox.

They sat, talking until Diamond began to feel uncomfortable. It was obvious Lily wanted to dance, yet no one had asked her. Diamond tried to give the hint to Knox with a shake of her head when Lily wasn't looking, however she received a firm "No" in response that made Lily jump and Diamond want to kick him. She thought Razer would ask, yet when he approached with Beth, they only joined them to sit and relax. Beth also tried to unobtrusively get Razer to dance with Lily, which was ignored.

Diamond noticed that all the men in the group gave

Lily a wide berth, which led Diamond to draw two conclusions; one was that because of Razer they were showing respect by leaving his sister-in-law alone, the second that they were afraid of someone. Diamond had grown up with bikers; when they wanted a woman, no harm no foul, anything was game on.

So that left the only conclusion; they were afraid, and she had a feeling she knew who they were afraid of. The man in question was dancing with Bliss who had been in Knox's bedroom the day they had served the warrant. She was also the woman her sister and crew wanted to beat the shit out of because she had been the woman Razer had two-timed Beth with.

As Lily sat talking with Beth and Razer, she never once looked at Shade and Bliss. The oblivious woman had no clue of the wolf stalking her.

Knox caught her staring with a raised brow. Diamond said nothing at first then became slightly mischievous and decided to dance again.

"Let's dance." Agreeing easily, Knox stood up, going ahead to where the group was dancing while Diamond turned back to Lily. "Want to dance with us?" The enthusiasm on her face made Diamond's breath catch. "Lord have mercy," she mumbled under her breath, taking Lily's hand. Knox threw her a look when she approached with Lily. She thought he would walk off the dance floor, but Lily's joyful face stopped him as did the threatening glare from Diamond.

Resigned, he danced with the two women, although he did dance close to Diamond's side, staying as far away from Lily as the crowded floor would allow. Lily stayed on Diamond's other side, dancing with youthful enthusiasm. She was good. Her lithe body moving to the music had her smiling at the two people she danced with as a rosy glow crept onto her cheeks. She twirled when the music ended, laughing at Diamond's astonishment at her skill.

"You're very good," Diamond complimented her.

"Beth and I used to dance in our bedrooms when we were little. We were terrible, but it was just us, so we didn't care," Lily confessed.

"You're not terrible now, you're really good."

"My roommate has been teaching me. She likes to go to some of the college parties and she makes me go with her." Her voice was a little loud so she could be heard over the music. She twirled again, and this time when she twirled, a hard body was waiting. Lily immediately shied away from Shade.

Diamond was about to take a step forward to intervene when Knox put his hand around her waist, holding her back, although he did stay close enough to keep a watchful eye on the situation. "You started this, now leave it alone."

"You dance with guys at these parties?" Diamond heard Shade ask Lily.

"No," Lily said, trying to break away. Shade loosened his grip, letting Lily put some space between them.

"Dance with me," he said persuasively, loosening his hold.

Razer and Beth came to dance next to them with Beth sending her an encouraging smile. Lily slowly began to dance to the music, yet she didn't regain the fluidity of before. Her hand went to her wrist, but Shade sent her a warning glance and she removed it. Diamond was as relieved when the music ended as Lily was, leaving the dance floor with a sense of reprieve.

"It's time I leave. I'm going back to school tonight. My roommate is picking me up at my house. She's visiting a family friend. Beth didn't want me to drive back in the dark." Lily accepted her sister's over-protectiveness without complaint herself before they could reach their chairs. She hugged Beth and Razer goodbye. "See you in a couple of weeks."

"Bye, little sis," Razer said with his arm around Beth's shoulder.

Lily turned to Diamond, giving her a quick hug. "It was

nice seeing you again, Diamond."

"You too, Lily. Drive careful."

"I will," Lily murmured, stepping towards the door, avoiding Shade's sharp gaze. The tension seemed to evaporate with Lily's departure.

Knox led her back to the dance floor. This time the music seemed more erotic, his hands going for her hips, brushing her against his own hips and thighs. Diamond stared around her, noticing the change in the others also; the movements more erotic and sensuous.

When the dance was over she thought they would go back to their chairs, yet Knox seemed to have other ideas. "Let's get a beer." They went into the kitchen where beer coolers were now sitting on the counters and several members were already drinking. Grabbing them two ice-cold beers, Knox took her into the living room, finding a spot for them on one of the couches.

"Why didn't you have beer earlier?" Diamond questioned Knox.

"Lily has a few issues with alcohol. We thought it would be better to wait until she left." Diamond felt the difference in the vibe around the club. The alcohol wasn't all they had been hiding from the young woman.

No sooner had she begun to notice the changes than Rider took a seat across from them on a chair, pulling a woman down on his lap. Diamond watched as Viper's best man, Cash, went up to Evie who was sitting on one of the bar stools. His mouth dropped to hers as his hand slid up her thighs, widening them and stepping between them.

"Knox, I think it's time I went home." She watched as Cash's hand disappeared under Evie's skirt, obviously playing with the woman's pussy. When Evie then grabbed onto the bar, Diamond was sure it was time to leave. She turned to Knox who was watching her in amusement.

"We'll leave in a little while, just relax. They're simply having some fun," Knox told her as his hand slid behind her hair and he turned towards her. His mouth found hers and his tongue went inside of her mouth.

Diamond tensed as he kissed her in front of the woman and Rider. She had never kissed someone in public before and was not enjoying it now, feeling as if everyone's eyes were on her and Knox. Moving her lips away from his didn't stop him, his lips simply went to her throat.

"Watch; he'll have her coming in a few minutes." Diamond tried to tear her gaze away, but ended up watching in helpless fascination as the woman sat there, letting Cash bring her to a climax in front of the whole room.

Razer and Beth entered the room, followed by Viper and Winter. Both women stared at Diamond in concern, but Viper led Winter upstairs while a grinning Razer pushed Beth behind the bar. Razer talked to Cash as he continued to stroke a shuddering Evie while Beth no longer met her gaze, standing behind the bar, drinking a beer.

When Knox's lips traveled lower to the tops of her breasts, she reached up to push his head away when his head lifted and his gaze met hers. "Kiss me. Forget there's anyone in the room," Knox suggested.

"Knox…" Her mouth opened to protest, finding his mouth on her again. This time he was determined to find a response. Diamond couldn't resist the stroke of his tongue; unexpectedly aroused by watching the couple across the room.

"That's it, relax," Knox murmured against her mouth.

Diamond let her body relax against him, allowing herself to enjoy him kissing her. Her guard lowered and Knox took advantage by caressing his hand across the back of her knee before sliding underneath her dress, rubbing her thigh. When he didn't try to go any further, Diamond didn't resist. As his mouth went to her throat again, sucking the flesh under her ear, Diamond shivered in need, becoming aroused. Her eyes lifted self-consciously, looking toward Rider and seeing that he was sucking on the woman's breast.

"Damn, Jewell, you taste good," he said, his lips tugging on the woman's nipple. Jewell pulled away, pulling off her top then lifting her skirt to her hips, showing a tiny black thong. Straddling Riders hips, she pulled his cock out of his jeans. Diamond watched in shock as the woman then took a condom from Rider and slid it on his cock before moving her thong to the side and plunging herself down onto him.

That did it. Diamond started to jump up from the couch, but Knox used the opportunity to slide his hand further up her thigh, reaching her own pussy. Sliding underneath her panties, his finger found her clit, rubbing the moisture he found.

Diamond fell back against him, squeezing her thighs closed.

"Open," Knox ordered. Diamond stared. "Open your legs."

Diamond slowly opened her thighs as she watched the woman across from her slide up and down the cock inside of her. Rider leaned back in the chair, squeezing the woman's breasts, but his eyes were on Diamond as Knox's hand rubbed her pussy, building her to a climax she couldn't believe was dangerously close.

"You want me to fuck you here or upstairs?"

Diamond couldn't believe she was even going to answer. She should be getting to her feet and getting the hell out, instead she found herself answering, "Upstairs."

Knox stood to his feet, picking her up and carrying her up the steps. He opened his door with one hand, turning on the light and then shutting the door before crossing the bedroom to lay her on the bed.

"Get your clothes off," Knox said, already pulling his off. Diamond didn't hesitate, pulling her dress off then removing her bra. She sat on her knees, watching as Knox pulled off his boots, but left his jeans on, unzipping them to pull out his cock.

"Come here." When Diamond crawled across the bed toward him, Knox reached down to lift her up as he sucked her breast into his mouth before turning and doing the same to the other and then setting her back down on the bed.

"Get back on your knees, facing me." Diamond did as he told her. His hands went to her breasts, pushing them together. "You know what I wanted to do the first time I saw you?"

"What?" Diamond asked seductively.

Knox covered his cock with a condom then pushed it between her clenched breasts. His hips began pumping as he fucked her breasts. His teeth clenched and he held her breasts tighter together.

"When I get enough of this, I'm going to fuck you harder than you've ever thought you could take. You still want to go home?" Knox said with a clenched jaw.

"No," Diamond answered honestly.

His cock was sliding faster between her breasts. Knox took a shuddering breath then pulled back. He wrapped his hand around her waist, turning her until she was again on her knees, facing the mirror of his dresser this time. She watched as he plunged into her wet pussy without stopping; stroking himself in until Diamond groaned at the tight fit.

"You're so tight; it's going to take a couple of months of me giving it to you for you to get accustomed to it. After that, it'll get easier or you'll get used to it. Either way, you're going to be getting my dick all the time. You won't remember what it was like not to have me in you all the time. I'll be fucking this pussy anytime I want it and you're going to give it to me anytime I want it, aren't you?"

"Yes," Diamond whimpered.

"Anytime?" Knox asked

"Yes," Diamond whimpered again.

"Any place?" Diamond wasn't that far gone that she gave him that answer. Knox laughed. "You will."

His cock pumped into her hard, driving her forward on the bed. Knox reached forward, taking her breasts in his hands to use them as he dragged her back onto his hard cock. Diamond began moaning; as her climax built, she tried to stifle the scream.

"Don't worry about the noise; you'll be hearing it from the other rooms the rest of the night. No one here gives a fuck about the noise."

Diamond couldn't hold back her release any longer, letting the climax take her as Knox gave a deep thrust. She felt him climax through the thin barrier of the condom then she lay passively on her stomach as he removed his jeans. Shifting her further up in the bed, Knox lay down next to her.

"Aren't you glad I didn't take you home now?" Knox asked.

"Yes," Diamond replied, almost asleep, tired from her lack of sleep last night and exhausted from his sexual demands.

"Get some sleep. I'll wake you up when I want some more."

Diamond opened her mouth to let him have a piece of her mind, yet then shut it before she said anything. She wanted him to wake her; the lust he aroused in her body had her wanting him again. Diamond didn't know how to get herself back under control. She had thought earlier that Lily was oblivious, however it was herself that didn't know what was going on. She'd lost touch with reality. Diamond mocked herself for living in never, never land. The scary part was, she didn't want to find her way back.

CHAPTER FOURTEEN

Diamond showered in Knox's bathroom, determined to go home as soon as she was dressed. The night had been spent exactly as it had been the night before, both of them seeking each other during the night to have sex. Each time was more exciting and challenging than the time before.

Diamond grinned. She had discovered a side to herself she hadn't known existed. Knox made sure he kept control at all times, restraining his strength with her while at the same time making sure she had no control of her own responses.

She had found herself doing things with him she would have never considered with another man due to Knox's blasé attitude about sex, which made her comfortable trying new positions and ways of having sex she had never contemplated before. Her body was now reaping the consequences. She was sore and she was even sure that, if she looked, he had left several marks on her neck and breasts.

Determined not to think about her behavior until she was back in her own home, she dried off then dressed in clean sweats and a t-shirt Knox had borrowed from Beth.

When she finished, she went out into the bedroom to see Knox waiting for her.

"Hungry?"

"I'm starved," she answered.

"Lunch should be ready; let's go downstairs." Knox held the door for her. Diamond seriously wished she had made up an excuse to leave, hoping not many Last Riders would be downstairs.

As she entered the kitchen, she was embarrassed to find the large room filled with the members in line for food and several already eating. She looked around the room, seeing neither Beth nor Winter. Knox handed her a plate and she got in line behind him, going down the line of a vast array of food. They had hamburgers and hotdogs with salad and several vegetables.

They found a seat at one of the occupied tables. Knox left then returned with a beer for each of them. Evie and Jewell both smiled at her when she sat down. She picked up her fork when Bliss and Rider also joined them at the table. At first the conversation was stilted, but then they began talking about the factory that they ran next door.

"What do you make?" Diamond questioned.

"Medical kits, solar batteries and generators. Basically anything a prepper or disaster victim would need to survive without help from outside resources," Evie answered her question. The woman was friendly, giving no evidence of jealousy of her spending the night with Knox. She didn't seem to mind that Knox had another woman sitting next to him. "We also have a large variety of seeds and want to expand our horticulture to include more."

"How are the new employees Viper hired working out?" Diamond asked, the promised jobs had been one of the main reason's the school board had given Winter a job as principal at the alternative school.

"Makes life a lot easier on us. We don't have to pull as many shifts, or work long hours. We actually have time for more relaxation," Bliss added happily.

"Like you let that stop you before," Knox joked. Bliss stuck out her tongue at Knox. "Be careful or I'll make you put that tongue to good use," he said, leaning back in his chair.

Diamond turned to him, throwing him a look for giving the woman a suggestive comment in front of her.

"Hell, no; I'm not going through this shit again." Diamond jumped when she heard Jewell's voice.

"Excuse me?" Diamond said to the woman staring at her.

"We lost Razer because Beth couldn't share. Then we lost Viper because Winter damn sure wasn't going to share. Let me tell you, those men could fuck for hours, so losing them was a big fucking deal. Knox has skill no one else has and we're not giving him up." She put her hands on the table, leaning toward Diamond. "Take Train he's pretty good, or better yet, take Cash; he never shares his bed. I'm even willing to sacrifice Rider, and let me tell you that will be taking a big hit, if you know what I mean, but you can't have Knox. He's a fucking sex machine. There's no way you can satisfy him by yourself. Actually, we'll be doing you a favor." Jewell nodded her head. "You can have him during the days and we'll take care of him during the nights. Plus, you can have Sundays."

Bliss and Evie didn't say anything, although Diamond could see the agreement in their eyes. Rider looked pissed and the men that she thought might be Train and Cash had stopped eating and were just as livid.

"I work days." Diamond tried to control her temper.

"We do, too," Jewell snapped back.

"Well, that's too fucking bad, and you having him nights and practically the whole weekend doesn't work for me, either." Diamond couldn't believe she was negotiating over Knox's cock.

"Deal with it, because you're not having him to yourself," Jewell snapped.

"Aren't you going to say something?" Diamond turned

to Knox.

"We let the women handle this on their own," he answered in amusement.

"Asshole." As Diamond started to stand up, everyone at the table started laughing. She sat back down. "Very funny," she muttered.

"You deserve it, getting all uptight about him making a comment to Bliss. You can't pretend he hasn't fucked everyone here at this table, or ask him to treat them different because your ass is sitting here. If he hadn't said something, then he would be trying to hide shit."

"You're right," Diamond admitted to the woman.

"Good, glad we got that shit straight. Can I eat my lunch now?" Jewell asked, picking up her fork.

"Yes." Diamond laughed, finishing her own food.

It was easy to see how Beth and Winter had adjusted to The Last Rider's lifestyle. The women were nice and didn't try to stake their claim, instead they were friendly and yet let you have your own space and privacy. Evie was obviously the leader and confident. Bliss was shy with the women, but more outgoing with the men. Jewell was an in-your-face, tell-it-like-it-is type of personality, which Diamond could admire. She felt a friendship developing between them as they sat there, drinking another beer.

Rider stood up, taking his plate. "Since no one cares about me, I'm going to go work on my bike."

"I didn't say I wasn't interested," Jewell said, looking at him, leaving no doubt what was on her mind.

"Later. My manhood has taken a blow. It's going to take time to recover."

"More likely you used it up last night with Dawn and don't have anything left."

"Later, Jewell." Rider didn't deny Jewell's theory.

"I'll be waiting," she answered.

Everyone gradually wandered off, leaving Knox and her sitting alone. "I like your friends."

"They can be a pain in the ass sometimes, but they

have become a family to me," Knox said.

"What about your parents?"

"My dad is in prison for drug trafficking and my mom disappeared when I was a kid; don't know or care where she is."

"I'm sorry."

"Don't be. I haven't given a damn about it since I joined The Last Riders. They have my back and I have theirs." He shrugged.

"I'm glad you found that, Knox," Diamond said and meant it. Knox obviously meant a lot to The Last Riders.

"I met Evie when I was in the service and she introduced me to them. After a few months, they asked me to join the club when Gavin and Viper were first starting it. I got along with them all so I joined in and took a stake in the company. It was the best and smartest decision I've ever made."

"Were you and Evie…?" Diamond questioned carefully.

"At first I thought Evie was in love with me, but she knew I didn't return her feelings. She was the first woman I was with, Diamond." Diamond was shocked by his admission. "Picture me as a kid in high school."

"Oh." His size alone would have set him apart, and his harsh features wouldn't have been attractive to a high school girl.

"No one after high school?"

Knox ignored her question. Diamond had already learned that when Knox didn't want to talk, he didn't. She thought that he probably had become involved with someone then she must have dumped him. Diamond didn't blame him for not wanting to discuss a broken relationship.

"It must have been hard when you joined The Last Riders and saw her with the other men," Diamond probed.

"The first time I saw her with another man I dreaded it because I thought it would bother me, but it didn't. I just thought about how hot it was. I knew I wasn't in love with her, but I didn't know how I would feel about sharing someone I was in a sexual relationship with, then I discovered that I enjoyed it. Then the other women became available to me and I went pussy crazy.

"The feelings Evie had for me died somewhere along the way or they weren't there to begin with. Now we're good friends and neither of us want it any other way. For some reason, whenever someone new joins, they picture us as a couple, but we aren't. We never really were."

Diamond knew why, but didn't tell Knox. That was Evie's secret. The only reason she knew was, God help her, she was beginning to feel the same way for the big man.

"Want to go for a ride?" Knox asked, standing up.

Diamond was aware that she should refuse, go home and put this weekend behind her, but she couldn't resist a few more hours with him. "Yes."

They grabbed their jackets and went to his bike. Knox drove them down the mountain roads that were no longer used by the coal trucks. Diamond enjoyed every bit of the ride. It was breathtaking when she looked down and realized exactly how high they were. Diamond enjoyed the scenery and the closeness to Knox. When they returned to the clubhouse she wished they could have stayed out longer.

The clubhouse was quiet when they returned to his room and lay on his bed where they watched television as they explored each other's bodies until Knox stopped. Diamond whimpered, wanting him to finish what he'd started.

He grinned at her. "Stay here." He left to go downstairs, returning with a pizza box and beers. "Sundays are always pizza night." They sat cross-legged on his bed, eating the pizza and drinking the beer.

Knox had every zombie movie ever made, so they ended up watching two of them back to back before

Diamond couldn't take the blood and guts anymore.

"Enough. Put in a comedy," she demanded.

"How about we just forget the movie." Knox moved the pizza box and pulled her to him, his hand slid under her sweat pants to find her soft and wet. His finger traced the opening of her pussy and Diamond couldn't help the small jerk of her hips.

"Sore?"

"A little," Diamond admitted.

"I have a remedy for that." Knox got up from the bed and reached down to take her hand, dragging her from the bed. Her mouth watered as she looked at him. He had removed his shirt and his tats made him look like the bad ass biker he was. He was only wearing jeans and was barefoot.

"Where are we going?"

"It's a surprise." They left the room and went down the stairs. Diamond began to wonder exactly what remedy he could have. He went to the kitchen where he opened a door at the side, showing steps that led to a basement. "Go ahead." Diamond went down the steps and found a large room that had a gym set up with different machines. There were even workout mats leaning against the wall.

"Wow." Diamond admired the workout area.

"We had a pretty good set up before Winter came here after her attack, but when she came here to do her rehab, Viper bought top of the line," Knox explained.

"I've never seen this much equipment outside of a gym."

There was also a big screen television and entertainment center with a large sectional couch. A huge pole in the middle separated the two parts of the room.

"We just added that. The upstairs can get crowded sometimes when Winter and Beth are here," Knox said cryptically.

"You guys have a sweet set-up here."

"We enjoy it. Treepoint doesn't have much to offer for

amusement."

"No it doesn't." It was extremely small. Even Jamestown, just a twenty minute drive away, had more to offer than Treepoint. "You want me to exercise?" Diamond questioned why he had brought her downstairs.

"No, I have something that's going to help that soreness." He led her out of the gym through another door that had a hallway. A door to the left stood open. "That's the bathroom. It also has a shower. That door at the end is Shade's room. It's off limits unless invited," Knox warned.

Diamond and Knox went through the open door on the right and she gasped at the hot tub bubbling inside. "That looks like a dream come true." Diamond laughed. "But I don't have a suit."

"No problem. We have extras." Knox opened a cabinet, showing several swimsuits. Picking out a white one, he handed it to her. "Go get changed."

Diamond took the swimsuit from him, looking at the tiny pieces before going to the cabinet and pulling out a blue one that looked like it would fit much better. Shutting the cabinet, she gave Knox a gloating smile before going to the bathroom.

She quickly lost her gloating smile when she realized the bottoms were bigger than the thong, but the bra was much smaller. Scowling she wrapped a towel around herself before going back to the hot tub room.

Knox was already in the large tub that would easily sit eight people. Leaning back, his dark eyes watched her drop the towel on a bench before carefully climbing inside the hot tub. Sinking down onto a seat next to Knox, she enjoyed the hot water relaxing her muscles. The jets shooting out the water eased the soreness in her thighs.

"Better?" Knox grinned.

"Oh yes," Diamond groaned.

Knox leaned over, his hands rubbing her thighs, which helped even more. "I should have taken it easier on you."

"I'm fine." Diamond remembered a couple of times had been of her own initiating.

Knox's mouth found hers, his tongue laving her lips until they parted, letting it slide into her mouth. The metal ball in his mouth never failed to arouse her. Knox lifted her until she was on his lap her back to his. She discovered he wasn't wearing anything when his cock brushed up against her.

"You're not wearing trunks?"

"You've seen my dick; everyone in the club has seen my dick."

"Winter and Beth, too?" Diamond asked, surprised.

"Seen, not touched. They only do their men, but they get off watching," Knox said, surprising Diamond. Diamond was learning more than she wanted to know about the sexual aspect of the motorcycle club Knox belonged to.

Knox's hand slid into the front of her swimsuit as he began to rub her pussy. "Still sore?" Knox asked his mouth going to her neck.

"No," Diamond moaned.

Knox undid the swimsuit top that was too small and was cutting into her flesh.

"Knox give me my top back," Diamond protested, feeling decadent as she sat half naked in the hot tub.

Knox threw it over the side of the hot tub. "It's too small. I could see your nipples anyway." His hands continued to play with her while his lips teased with tiny kisses.

The opening door was lost on Diamond as his finger began plunging inside of her. She lifted dazed eyes when she heard a noise at the side of the tub. Rider was removing the towel he had wrapped around his hips and his hair was wet, so he must have taken a shower.

"Mind if I join you?" Rider asked, staring at Diamond's naked breasts.

"No," Knox said.

"Yes," Diamond groaned as Knox thrust another finger deep within her while sucking on her neck. His free hand took a breast in his hand, lifting it out of the water. Rider slid into the tub, moving towards them.

"Knox?"

"Relax, lean back against me," Knox coaxed.

Helplessly, Diamond leaned back against Knox's chest, exposing even more of her breasts to Rider's gaze. Diamond's hips twisted on Knox's fingers, trying to bring herself to a climax at the same time that small whimpers escaped her.

"Shh... baby, we're going to take care of you." Knox's fingers searched deeper, but still didn't fill that aching void that wanted his cock.

When Rider's lips dropped to her breast, sucking a nipple deep into his mouth, Diamond almost jumped off Knox's lap, but his hand on her pussy held her still. Rider's teeth bit at her nipple, turning it into a hardened nub. When he removed his lips, his fingers squeezed tightly as his mouth went to her other breast.

"Feels good, doesn't it?" Knox asked.

Diamond didn't answer and Rider took his mouth away, each hand now torturing her nipples until she reluctantly admitted, "Yes."

"Good girl," Knox murmured against her throat. Rider removed his hands, going to sit on the side of the hot tub. His cock wasn't as large as Knox's, but was wider. Diamond watched as his hand began sliding up and down the length while he watched Knox bring her to the brink of an orgasm.

Knox stood up and Diamond shivered as the cool air hit her hot skin. With a hand on her back, he pushed her down until her hands rested on the side of the tub by Rider.

"Hand me a condom." Rider reached over, grasping inside a drawer at the side of the tub and then handing Knox the requested condom.

"Knox, let's go upstairs." Diamond tried to regain what little sanity she had left as she heard him tear open the condom and put it on.

"Diamond, this isn't going to wait until we get upstairs," Knox said as he notched his cock against her opening.

Knox's cock slid deep with a hard shove of his hips. Diamond tried to arch up, but Rider's hand on her back held her still as Knox's hands grasped her hips for leverage to pump his hard length inside her. Diamond groaned as she felt the metal balls of his piercings rub against the sensitive flesh of her pussy.

Grabbing the side of the tub to prevent herself from falling, Diamond stood as Knox fucked her while Rider's hand slid up and down on his cock. Diamond couldn't help watching as a pearl of liquid escaped the head of his cock.

"You want his cock?" Diamond didn't answer Knox, her desire was rising to the extent where she was losing control, driving her to do what before would have been unthinkable.

Then she felt Rider's hand in her hair, tilting her head until his cock was within reach of her mouth. He stopped moving her towards, playing with her hair as he left the decision up to her.

Diamond opened her mouth, sliding his cock in. A hiss escaped Rider as she began to suckle his cock.

"Fuck," Knox said as he surged against her. "Suck him hard. He likes it when you use your tongue." Diamond followed his instructions, liking the taste of Rider and his gentle hand in her hair. Having him in her mouth made her feel naughty with Knox pounding into her from behind. Every fantasy that Diamond had played through her mind as both men moved within her. Rider's legs splayed wider and Knox lifted her, making it easier to reach his cock without straining her neck, enabling her to take him deeper.

Her fingers went to his balls, stroking them while her tongue played with the head of his cock until she felt Rider take her hair in his hands and push her down further. Diamond began sliding her mouth up and down on him while her tongue teased the silky flesh. She felt his cock tighten just before he groaned his release into her mouth, gripping her hair tightly. When he finished she raised her head as Rider slid back down into the water, his mouth going to her nipple.

"Did you enjoy making Rider come?" Knox asked, thrusting high within her.

Diamond hesitated, but eventually admitted the truth to herself and them, "Yes."

"You going to make me come now?" Knox grunted.

"Yes," Diamond moaned.

"Then push that pussy back on my cock." Diamond began moving back on him as hard as he was fucking her.

"God, it's making me hard again watching you two fuck," Rider moaned against her swollen nipple

"Once is all you're getting tonight. You want pussy, go find one of the other women," Knox said through gritted teeth.

"Damn. If you change your mind, let me know." Rider pressed her nipple against his teeth, using his tongue. The tiny nip of pain rose her passion to an orgasm that had her moaning. Rider, feeling her shudders from climax, slid out of the tub and wrapped the towel around his hips before hurriedly leaving.

"I've got to find Jewell," he said as he left.

Diamond groaned as she felt Knox thrust inside her, jerking as he came, driving her into another orgasm that she was afraid would make her pass out. She leaned her head on her hands that gripped the side of the hot tub, shaking.

Minutes later, reality returned with a rush of shame and recriminations. Diamond scrambled over the side of the tub, picking up the towel and wrapping it around her body.

Her hands went to her hair, pushing the tangled mess from her face.

"Oh God, oh God. I did not just do that. I did not just do that!" Her voice was getting louder each time.

"Fuck." Knox took off his condom, stepping out of the hot tub. "Calm down, Diamond."

"That's easy for you to say; this is normal for you. I don't do shit like this. I am going to lose my license, and I just had sex with two men at the same time." Diamond had never had an anxiety attack, yet she knew that was exactly where she was headed because of letting her attraction to Knox undermine everything she had worked for years to accomplish.

"You're not going to lose your license." Knox tried to reason with her, but it was a lost cause as she started to run to the bathroom for her clothes.

Knox grabbed her around the waist, picking her up and putting her wiggling body over his shoulder. Leaving the room, he went through the gym and up the stairs.

"Have you lost your mind; you're naked and I am, too," Diamond screeched.

Knox didn't stop, just continued through the kitchen where Evie, Raci and Bliss stood with their mouths hanging open. As he carried her through the living room Winter, Beth, Razer and Viper turned from the bar to watch as he continued through the room and up the steps. Diamond buried her face in his back.

"I'm going to kill you for this, Knox. So help me, when you let me down I'm going to kick your ass," Diamond threatened.

Knox stopped in the hallway, opening his door and carrying her into his bedroom. He stood her wiggling body on the floor by the bed.

"You going to calm down?" Knox asked.

"Fuck you!" Diamond screamed.

"That's it." Knox sat down on the side of the bed, pulling Diamond across his lap.

"What do you think you're doing?" Her bottom was smacked with a large hand.

"Ouch." Diamond said, hitting his leg with her fists.

"Are you going to calm down so that we can talk?"

"Go to hell!" Diamond tried to bite the side of his leg.

"Woman, you're going to regret that." His hand smacked her ass twice more. The swat on her bare bottom stung.

"You bastard." Swat.

"I'm going to make you eat your nuts!" Swat.

"I'm going to be the one that pulls the switch when they fry your ass." Swat. Swat. Swat.

"Got any more smart-ass remarks?" Knox's clenched jaw showed his temper was under control, but he wasn't going to put up with her hysterics.

"No."

Knox lifted her up, sitting her on his lap facing him with her knees on the bed beside his hip. His hand buried in her hair, lifting her head so that he could hold her eyes with his own. "You ready to talk?"

"Am I going to get spanked again if I say no?" Diamond asked mutinously.

"Diamond..."

She drew in a deep breath, managing to get her riotous emotions back under control.

"Better?" he asked, a glint of amusement appearing in his eyes. "That's some temper you have."

"Yes," Diamond answered both questions with one word.

"So I take it you were freaked out about Rider?"

Diamond threw him a look that doubted his intelligence.

"Careful, Diamond. How did I know that it would freak you out? You could have said no at any time. Do you think I wanted that from you?" Knox asked, obviously worried that she might have felt pressured.

"I didn't think at all," Diamond admitted.

"That's the point; you enjoyed it. Don't start that crap about feeling guilty for something that was what you wanted. We all enjoyed it; it was fucking great. I've never seen Rider get hard so fast." Knox's fingers went to her breasts, playing with her still red nipples.

"I shouldn't have done it. It was crazy! I don't act like that, Knox. I don't fuck around with a lot of men. For me to have sex with you while blowing Rider is scaring me."

"Diamond, you're just letting go. Your body has demands that you've been pushing down, afraid to let loose. I've never seen a more uptight woman than you. Don't feel bad about letting your sensuality loose; explore and find out what you want out of sex, experiment a little. You did admit you enjoyed taking Rider and me at the same time." Diamond turned her face away, but Knox had her turning back to face him. "Don't be ashamed of finding pleasure doing new things."

"I'll try." She didn't know how successful she would be, but it had happened and Knox was right, it had been great.

"Cool, then if you want him to join us again, he will. If you don't, he won't. It's up to you."

"Okay. But I already know I don't want to do that again," Diamond said, looking him firmly in the eyes.

"Whatever you decide to do, Diamond. I aim to please." As Knox's head dropped to the nipple he had been teasing with his fingertips, Diamond's arms circled his thick neck, her hand turning so that her palms could lay flat against his bald head. The ball of his tongue's piercing pressed against her sensitive nipple, sending a renewed sense of desire through her clenching pussy that was aching to be filled as if they hadn't just fucked less than fifteen minutes ago.

Diamond felt Knox reach for a condom from his nightstand then he turned with her still on his lap until she lay on the bed with him between her thighs. He took less than a minute to expertly slide the condom over the piercings on his cock.

"I'm on the pill." Diamond arched as he slid his covered cock into her warm pussy.

"I never fuck without a condom. I've already broken one of my rules for you," Knox said, surging within her. His head went to the spot he preferred on her neck, right under her ear. She didn't understand what he was talking about, however she lost track of their conversation as he began to fuck her.

She had wanted to feel his naked length inside her, but liked that he kept himself protected. Diamond gasped as she lost herself to his passion, returning to the place that only Knox could take her. She let her recriminations and doubts leave her, determined to spend the rest of the night in Neverland.

Tomorrow, reality would arrive soon enough.

CHAPTER FIFTEEN

Knox dropped her off at her apartment before the sun rose the next morning. She climbed off his bike, pausing before going to her apartment.

"Come here." His arm went around her waist. "I'll watch until you're inside."

"Okay."

"Later."

Diamond nodded her head, stepping away from his warm body.

She went up the short flight of steps to her apartment. Putting the key in the lock, she unlocked the door and turned on her lights then turned and waved to Knox, who waved back before leaving. Diamond went inside her apartment, locking the door behind her and then stared around the white, emotionless room.

She realized then that there was no going back to the vacuum she had turned her life into. Knox had awoken the emotions of desire she had buried deep within her that day she had caught her father cheating on her mother.

Going into her bedroom, she took off her clothes and went into the shower. She let the water get warm as she turned around and caught sight of her body in the full length mirror she kept on the back of the bathroom door. Her breasts and neck had faint marks Knox had left behind. He hadn't been rough and had never caused her any pain, but the marks seemed to reinforce the possession he had taken over her body.

Turning away from the mirror, she got into the shower, hoping it would wake her up. She hadn't slept much this weekend and she had a feeling it was going to be a long day.

* * *

The motorcycle drove steadily up the mountain road, taking the curves at maximum speed. He passed Rosie's bar on his way back to the clubhouse and the patrol car beginning to pull out of the parking lot. Seconds later, he saw the flashing blue lights in his rear view mirror. Slowing down, he pulled carefully off the road.

He turned off his motor as he watched the sheriff get out of his car. The thought struck him that he was walking slower and his face had become more lined since the last time he had seen him just last week.

"What are you doing out so late?" The sheriff greeted him with the gruff question.

"Couldn't sleep."

"Knox just passed ahead of you; something going on that I need to know about?" The sheriff always tried to stay alert to possible trouble involving The Last Riders.

"No."

The sheriff stared at him silently, patiently waiting for more information.

"Nothing's going on. Knox took his woman home and was going back to the clubhouse," he explained, knowing he would worry.

"Anyone I know?" he asked curiously.

"Diamond Richards."

The sheriff whistled. "Never would have guessed that one."

"You're looking tired."

"I am. I'm a deputy short." The sheriff sighed, raising his hand to rub his eyes. "When Cash asked me to come up here and check on Beth and Lily, I never expected to stay this long."

"I know."

"Rach wants to travel. Lost one wife not listening to what she wanted, don't plan on getting another divorce in this stage of my life."

"She won't divorce you, maybe stop cooking for you, but she wouldn't leave you."

"I asked Lucky, if I retired, if he would take over," The sheriff said, looking up the dark road ahead.

"What was his answer?"

"He told me to shove it." The sheriff didn't try to hide his disappointment at wanting to turn the reigns of the sheriff's office over to someone he could trust.

The sheriff turned the conversation back to the reason he had made the stop. "Penni stopped by to see us; she was pretty upset about you calling her to jump on her ass."

"She doesn't need to be going to parties, and she damn sure doesn't need to take Lily with her."

"Go home and go to bed, Shade. You're looking tired yourself. You're not going to find what you're looking for on this mountain road." The Sheriff turned to walk away, but then turned back "And slow your ass down."

"I will. Night, Dad." Shade started his motor, pulling out onto the road.

"Night, son."

* * *

Diamond stayed busy the next two weeks, going over the list of names that Beth, Lily and Winter had given her at the wedding. They had told the truth; the list was overwhelming in the number of men Samantha had intimate contact with. They had even made a separate category for those names she had a brief relationship with.

Several of the men had moved out of town, became married or could care less that Samantha had been murdered. The woman had no friends that she could find and Diamond was becoming increasingly worried that she wouldn't be able to come up with a viable alternative suspect to switch the focus off Knox.

She stared out her window that faced the back of the church and provided a view of the parking lot. The sight of the church never failed to bring feelings of guilt about her relationship with Knox.

She had spent every night of the last two weeks either in his bed or hers. He would wait until dark and pick her up on his bike to take her to the clubhouse or he would knock on her door and they would stay at her apartment for the night. She refused to allow herself to think about the time he was at the clubhouse without her.

She got up from her chair and went to her window, lowering the shade so the image of the church wouldn't be staring at her accusingly.

As she returned to her desk, her cell phone rang so she looked at the caller ID. Sex Piston was calling her. Diamond didn't answer, dodging her sister yet again. She hadn't been able to bring herself to talk to them since that disaster of a dinner.

She sighed, making her mind up to go over tomorrow night and face them. She would apologize and paste one of her fake smiles on and then stand by them with gritted teeth as they married.

Her cell phone rang again. Picking it up, thinking this time it might be her mother, she saw that it was the Commonwealth's Attorney calling.

"Hello?"

"Di, this is David.

"What can I do for you this morning?" Diamond was dreading further bad news on Knox's case.

"We're dropping charges on Knox. The official autopsy and toxicology reports finally got back from Frankfort. Apparently, Treepoint needs a new coroner because he missed the mark on this case."

"What did the autopsy show?" Hope had Diamond clenching the phone tighter in her hand.

"Samantha Bedford had a genetic kidney disease. The coroner said it was unbelievable that she had lived as long as she had with the shape they were in. I talked to the grandmother; none of the family or Samantha had any idea that she was sick.

"Besides that, the doctor said the hit on her head wasn't hard enough to kill her, that her kidneys shut down. Even if we can prove the assault on her, which led to the trauma to her head, a good lawyer would get him off because of her condition. You're an excellent lawyer, so I'm not going to waste the state's money until we can prove without a doubt it was Knox she had the altercation with. Our office is going to drop the charges."

"Thanks for calling me. I'll give Knox the good news." Diamond couldn't hide her excitement.

"Don't get to complacent, Di. If I can find some way to prove he was the one that caused that head injury, I'll prosecute him for involuntary manslaughter."

"Understood." Disconnecting the call, Diamond was elated that Knox wouldn't be facing a trial in the near future, but she continued to be worried he would have the specter of Samantha Bedford hanging over his head until they did find out who she'd had a fight with after Knox left her that day.

She pushed in Knox's phone number.

"Yeah?" Knox answered with his grumpy voice.

"Where are you at?" Diamond tried to tone down her excitement, wanting to surprise him.

"Having lunch at the diner with Razer and Viper."

"Can you come to my office when you get done, I have some good news."

"Be there in five; we're done here."

"Okay. Bye." Diamond could hardly wait to see his reaction.

She walked into her front office, smiling at Holly. "You

can go to lunch."

Her secretary returned her smile. "I take it you're having a good day."

"The best." Diamond couldn't restrain herself, she hugged her startled secretary.

"Want me to bring you something back?" Holly offered.

"No thanks. I might not be here when you get back. I'll lock the door if I leave," Diamond told her.

"Okay. See you tomorrow then." Diamond nodded happily, going back into her office. A few minutes later, Knox came in. Diamond ran across her office, throwing herself into his arms.

"The Commonwealth's Attorney's office dropped the charges against you. Samantha had a genetic kidney disease that was the cause of death."

Knox's arms squeezed her. "What?"

Diamond nodded her head. "It's true. Even if they find evidence of an argument between you, which they won't," Diamond added hastily, "they would have to do involuntary manslaughter and that would be hard to prove unless someone actually saw you inflict the injury on Samantha."

"It's over?" Knox asked, relief filling his face.

"Yes, I'm still going to try to find who attacked her because I don't want that hanging over your head, but you're free now." Diamond didn't try to hide how happy she was for him.

Knox twirled her around in a circle before putting her back on her feet.

"Want to go back to my apartment and celebrate? I don't have any cases this afternoon." Her arms circled his neck, leaning her body against his while her hand went to the belt at his waist. Knox's hand grabbed her ass, pulling her against his hard body.

"Have you lost your fucking mind, Diamond?" Sex Piston's voice from the office door had Diamond stepping away from Knox and turning to face her sister.

"What are you doing here?" Sex Piston never came to her office.

"I came to see why in the hell you haven't returned any of Ma's and Pop's calls. Now I see why. You're giving them shit while you're screwing that fuckwad."

"Don't talk about him like that, Sex Piston," Diamond snapped angrily at her sister.

Sex Piston's eyes narrowed dangerously. "You're taking up for him? You've been fucking him after throwing up your high and mighty morals to me for years. I don't think so, bitch. You're letting someone fuck you that I wouldn't let touch me."

"Shut up."

"Why? You don't want to hear what I got to say? Too fucking bad, I've put up with your shit for years." She nodded to Knox. "If you've been fucking him, then you've done Rider, too."

Diamond turned white, taking a step away from Knox. "What are you talking about?"

"They're the welcoming committee to The Last Riders. They double team the women that are joining the club. He tell you how the women become members?"

"Like pop's club; you become a member's old lady or fuck buddy."

"Don't tell me you're that fucking stupid. None of those women belong to any of the members, they are members."

"How do they become members?" Diamond looked towards Knox. His face was impassive as he listened to Sex Piston talk about The Last Riders.

"There are eight original members. The women that want to join fuck six out of the eight. When they've accomplished that milestone, they go get themselves tatted with the date they got their final vote. Now isn't that too sweet?" Sex Piston said harshly.

Diamond was deathly afraid she was going to pass out.

"You been to one of their Friday night parties?" Sex Piston asked.

"What?"

"It's their weekly fuck-fest where they swap sex partners and decide if any new women are going to become members." She nodded her head. "I heard that he has a regular smorgasbord every week."

For the last three weeks they had spent Friday nights at her apartment while they had spent the weeknights at his room at the clubhouse. Diamond felt sick.

"If you didn't make it to one of their Fridays, then he has no interest in you joining. You're less than those women; you're just a temporary fuck."

"Get out." Diamond had heard enough from her sister. Sex Piston's mouth closed with a snap. Throwing both of them dirty looks, she stormed from the office, slamming both doors as she left.

"Is it true?" Diamond asked.

"Yes." He made no attempt to deny any of Sex Piston's accusations.

"All of it?"

"Yes." As he stared her straight in the eyes, the true depths of her humiliation hit home.

"Even the part about me being a temporary fuck?" Diamond braced herself for his answer.

This time his answer was slower, but Knox was always bluntly honest. "Yes."

"I see." Diamond walked to the door, opening it. "Please leave."

"Diamond." She held up her hand, halting any words he may have spoken.

"Leave." Knox hesitated a minute longer before leaving without looking back at the devastation he had caused. Diamond went to the front door, locking it then went back into her private office. She picked up her cell phone and called Holly.

"Hello?" Holly answered.

"Take the rest of the day off," Diamond said, trying to keep her voice steady.

"Are you sure?"

"Yes, I'll see you tomorrow."

"All right. Thanks." Diamond disconnected the call then threw her phone against the wall before going to sit behind her desk on shaking legs.

Tears blinded her eyes as she stared at the empty doorway, hoping he would come back and make it all right between them. She began praying that it wasn't really the way Sex Piston had described. That he had cared for her, at least in a small amount. That his big body would come back and explain everything away, or say that none of it mattered, that he had come to care for her. Anything... she would take any explanation from him...

Her tears flowed faster as the doorway remained empty.

CHAPTER SIXTEEN

Knox walked to his motorcycle and got on, putting the key in the ignition. Instead of starting it, his hands went to his head. His mind told him to start the motor and get as far away from Diamond as he could. Another part of himself that he had thought long dead was telling him to get the fuck off his bike and go back inside. He had never meant the good time they were having to get out of control. He should have known the first time he had kissed her to walk away, but again, he had proven how stupid he could be.

Starting the motor, he drove out of the parking lot and out of her life. He had always intended to walk away from the beginning, each time together the last, but each night he had found himself on his bike heading to her apartment.

He had started it angry that every time she saw him she looked at him as though he was beneath her contempt. The first time he had seen her she had curled her lip at him in disgust which had brought back his high school and college days, and the looks the girls had given him; how they had treated him.

When they had begun fucking, he had discovered she

was nothing like those women, and despite his best efforts, had felt himself falling for her. *Just like...* Knox's mind closed down, refusing to go there. He drove away from Diamond and the resurgence of emotions; that was the only thing that he would back down from, knowing he wasn't strong enough to win that particular battle.

For the first time, he pulled into the clubhouse parking lot without wanting to go inside. Getting off the bike, he went inside, going to his room. He lay down on the bed and stared at the ceiling. He hadn't been there long when he heard a soft knock at his door.

Bliss had seen him come in; he had no doubt it was her knocking on his door. Rolling to his side, he ignored the sound until eventually she gave up, leaving him alone.

* * *

Thanksgiving and Christmas passed in a blur for Diamond. She kept herself busy with court cases. For the first few weeks, she had been an emotional mess, eating anything she could get her hands on, unable to sleep because of the memories of Knox's skills. Her body had shown the effects.

Diamond went to her closet to get the dress she was wearing to her parents' wedding. Her mother had picked out the dresses for her and Sex Piston, and they'd shown that her mother had no concept of her daughter's tastes.

Both dresses were a pale yellow that looked amazing with their red-gold hair, but she had picked out two different dresses of the same color for her daughter. Hers was low cut with spaghetti straps and it clung to her body, showing each curve. Thankfully, she had begun to regain control of the weight she had packed on; the dress was still tight, though it was wearable.

In direct contrast, Sex Piston's dress was more demur yet seductive. The neckline was high in the front while leaving a plunging back that showcased Sex Piston's best asset. The dress flowed loosely against her body, hinting at the curves that Sex Piston loved to flaunt. Diamond had even asked her mother twice to make sure she had intended those particular dresses for them and hadn't mixed them up. Her mother had merely given her a sad look, refusing to change her choice of dress.

She had spent the least amount of time as possible with her parents, not even going for Christmas or Thanksgiving, using her caseload as an excuse. Everyone knew she was lying, however they didn't say anything. She had thankfully also avoided Sex Piston since that day at the office.

Diamond dressed, going to the table to get her car keys and purse. Going out the door to her car, she thought again of going to purchase a new one, yet was unable to bring herself to do so.

Viper had brought the money for Knox's case, but she had refused all of it except the actual hours she had worked on the case, explaining that she hadn't been the one to prove his innocence. The State of Kentucky had done the job they were supposed to do.

Viper had argued, but had eventually given up, leaving her with enough to buy a new car. However she couldn't bring herself to do so, remembering Knox had promised to help her pick one out.

She pulled out of the parking lot, not noticing the lone biker sitting where she couldn't see him.

* * *

The wedding was being held at her father's motorcycle club where he used to be president. Diamond pulled into the parking lot, surprised at the number of bikes in front of the small building, wondering who they belonged to. The Destructors' members would never be able to afford the bikes she was staring at and they sure as hell had never had more than twenty members. She was looking at more than sixty bikes.

Curious, Diamond parked her car and climbed out. She once again studied the bikes as she went inside the club where she came to a stop when recognizing a few of the jackets of the men inside the club. The Blue Horsemen were inside, mingling with the Destructors.

Diamond tried not to let her mouth drop open, but was unable to prevent the surprised expression on her face.

Startled, she managed to squeeze through the crowd, searching for her mother. She finally located her in one of the rooms at the back of the club. She was dressed in a cream dress that made her look pretty and carefree, which exemplified her mother. Her sister looked gorgeous as well. The pale yellow dress really went well with her hair and gave her a maturity and sophistication that Diamond had never noticed before.

"You look beautiful," Diamond said, going to stand by her mother's side.

Her mother and Sex Piston both turned at her voice.

"You look beautiful, Diamond." Her mother grabbed her and hugged her tightly.

Sex Piston didn't say anything, studying her sister's face with tight lips.

"What's with all the Blue Horsemen?" Diamond asked.

"The Destructors have merged with them. We're a big family now."

"What?" Diamond asked, confused.

"If you ever happened to answer your phone, you would know shit," Sex Piston said snidely.

Diamond avoided her sister's eyes, going to her mother for an explanation as she started to pull her hair up off her neck.

"I was doing that," Sex Piston snapped. Diamond's hands dropped away and she went to sit on a chair as Sex Piston resumed fixing their mother's hair.

Silence filled the room as Sex Piston worked her mother's hair until it was on the top of her head and fell in curls against the back of her neck.

"Why did they merge?" Diamond asked.

"Because Joker and Ace can't handle the club. They

had a couple of fights three months ago and several of the members were seriously hurt. They can't handle the club without your father and your father doesn't want the responsibility of the club every day anymore. His heart isn't as strong as it used to be; the doctors said, if he doesn't take better care of himself, he's headed for a heart attack." Her mother's voice wobbled on her last words.

"Stud and your pops have been friends for years, and he asked him if they were interested in merging. He said no, but he took the Destructors on as a charter of the Blue Horsemen."

"So basically the Destructors are no more?" Diamond couldn't believe it. She had thought they would be like cockroaches who could survive a nuclear blast.

Her mother looked close to tears. "It's for everyone's safety. If Joker and Ace can't protect the club, then someone could get killed with their attitude. They can't back up their brothers."

Diamond had known all along that the younger members weren't up to the standard her father had expected, although she had, of course, kept that knowledge to herself.

"How do the Destructors feel about the change?"

"Oh, I think the men are all happy with the change. Most of them are followers, not leaders," her mom said, her smile returning as she put on lipstick.

"The women?" Diamond questioned, but she didn't need to really. Sex Piston's face said it all. She was the leader of the women. If she wasn't happy then her crew sure as shit wasn't.

"They'll adjust." Her optimistic mom said, picking up her bouquet from the dresser. Diamond couldn't help the smile curving her lips at her sister's mutinous face. "The Blue Horsemen don't let their women become involved in club business and usually, uh..." Her mother's face turned red. "They don't talk back to the men with disrespect." Her mother cast Sex Piston a censorious look.

Diamond could just bet the hostilities between the women of the Destructors and the Blue Horsemen was quickly becoming legendary. With their father the President of the Destructors since their birth, Sex Piston had pretty much been allowed to do anything she wanted and her crew were just as bad.

Having met the Blue Horsemen when she was investigating Knox's case, she didn't think the arrogant bikers were going to tolerate the attitude of the women. It was going to be interesting to see who would win the forthcoming battle. As much as she hated to admit it, from firsthand experience, the Blue Horsemen wouldn't be able to deal with Sex Piston, Crazy Bitch and they sure as hell wouldn't be able to deal with Killyama.

A knock sounded at the door.

"Don't take all fucking day, I got shit to do." Killyama's voice on the other side of the door only reinforced her thoughts.

"I'm ready." Her mother smiled, taking each daughter by the arm. Diamond opened the door, walking slowly down the hallway into the crowded room where one of her father's friends was going to marry them. Diamond couldn't help wondering exactly how legal the ceremony they were participating in was; she hoped the man had done the necessary paperwork. Pushing those thoughts away, her eyes drifted to her father as he turned around and Diamond's breath caught at the expression on his face. All the love he felt for her mother was there for everyone to see.

When they drew near, her mother moved forward to stand beside her father. He turned, hugging Sex Piston as Diamond drew away to go sit down. Her father grabbed her hand, stopping her as Sex Piston stepped away. He pulled her close and Diamond stood stiffly in his embrace before he released her.

"I love you, Diamond." Her father's voice sounded strained with emotion. Tears filled her eyes as memories from her childhood surged through her mind, reminding her of the special bond they had once shared.

Diamond didn't say anything as she stepped back to watch the ceremony.

It was short and sweet, and when it was over, they kissed like they had never kissed before with cheers and raucous comments from the audience. Her parents broke apart with a raucous comment themselves.

Diamond winced, going to get a beer from the coolers set up on tables against the wall. Pulling one from the ice, she noticed Crazy Bitch already had one as she stared back at her.

"You look all choked up with emotion, Diamond," she said sarcastically.

"Kiss my ass," Diamond snapped.

"Looks like there's more of it, that's for fucking sure." Crazy Bitch stared pointedly at her ass.

Diamond blushed, she had become best friends with Chunky Monkey ice cream the last several weeks and her dress had become tight across her butt. She hadn't been raised in the Destructors without being able to handle herself, though. "How's it going with the Blue Horsemen?"

Crazy Bitch's mouth snapped closed as several of them came to take beer from the cooler. Diamond threw her a satisfied smile before moving away from the table because she was also not stupid; she knew that Crazy Bitch would beat the shit out of her if she pressed too hard. Diamond wasn't afraid of her, but she didn't want to ruin the wedding day her mother had waited years for, either.

She found a couple of older members that she knew and stood talking with them about their children now grown when the President of the Blue Horsemen walked by.

"Diamond, have you met Stud?"

Diamond stared at the biker. "We've met," she said with a quirk of her lips.

Stud paused, looking her over. "You look different without your suit."

Diamond shrugged. "The Destructors don't mind my suits when I'm bailing them out of jail."

Stud's mouth twisted. "Good to know that we have a lawyer in the family, could come in handy."

"I don't belong to my parent's club," Diamond said hastily.

"Don't matter if you are or not. If you're Skulls's kid, we'll watch out for you."

"You'll do well if you can keep Sex Piston out of trouble without worrying about me."

At the mention of Sex Piston's name, his facial expression changed. "Your sister isn't going to get in trouble anymore."

Diamond laughed in his face. "Good luck with that."

His face darkened, not appreciating her humor. "You doubt that we can control her?"

"I know so. Sex Piston and her crew are going to drive you and your men nuts. But don't worry, maybe I'm wrong." Diamond doubted it, though hey, miracles could happen.

"What did you just call me?" A loud roar sounded from across the room where the biker that had offered Diamond his lap was arguing with Killyama.

Diamond started laughing when a fuming looking Stud moved toward the table where the argument was going on between the two. Diamond saw her mother and father standing together and walked toward them.

"I'm going to go. Congratulations." Diamond brushed a kiss across her mother's face and then turned to say goodbye to her father. He was looking younger than his years; obviously having the weight of the club off his shoulders was beneficial to his health.

"Can't you stay a little longer?" he asked.

"I have some work that I need to do. I've been busy."

"So I've heard," he said, searching her eyes.

Diamond should have known that Sex Piston wouldn't keep her mouth shut.

"I heard that the charges were dropped against him."

Diamond nodded.

"You still seeing him?" her mother asked with her discerning eyes on Diamond's face.

"No. Look, I've gotta go. I'll give you a call." Diamond managed to escape, avoiding Sex Piston who she saw had joined Killyama in the argument with the bikers. Their eyes met briefly before Diamond went out the door. Sex Piston's eyes searched hers, easily seeing the pain that Diamond was trying unsuccessfully to keep hidden.

Diamond drove home, passing the diner as she went through town where The Last Riders on their motorcycles ended up in front of her. Knox was easy to spot amongst the group. Bliss was on the back with her arms wrapped around his waist.

One of the bikers must have said something because Evie and Raci turned their heads around, waving at Diamond. Diamond forced herself to wave nonchalantly back. Giving her blinker, she turned off the main road several streets before hers, taking the longer way home, but it was worth it not to have to watch Bliss riding with Knox.

Diamond parked her car and then went inside her lonely apartment. Taking off her dress, she slid on the sweats and top she had worn home from Knox's that first weekend she had spent with him.

Then, grabbing her Chunky Monkey ice cream, she went to her couch, dropping down on it. Bored, she shoved the papers she had been working on to the side, knocking off one of the folders. She watched the contents spill over the floor before picking them up.

She stared at the list of men's names that Sam had been intimate with in high school. Diamond could tell from the addresses beside each name that they were from the better part of town. Samantha hadn't become involved with the less savory men in Treepoint until after she had turned eighteen. Diamond's spoon paused with the ice cream still on there, halfway to her mouth. A sudden thought occurred to her.

Picking up her phone, she called Beth. "Hello?"

"Hi, Beth this is Diamond I was wondering if I could have Lily's number. I have a quick question for her."

"Yes." Beth gave her the number without questioning why Diamond wanted it.

"Thanks, Beth." Diamond cut off the conversation before Beth could say anything. Feeling guilty, Diamond regretted being rude, but she had heard the laughter and music in the background and her stomach couldn't take the images of Knox being there.

Her call to Lily was answered on the first ring.

"Lily, this is Diamond Richard. Do you remember me?"

"Of course. How are you?"

"I'm doing well. I have a quick question."

"Okay." Her sweet voice brought a true smile to Diamond's face for the first time in weeks.

"When you were in high school, who was considered the bad boy in your age group? Someone that would freak a parent out if their daughter got involved with them?"

Silence met her answer. "Most of the boys in my class were pretty nice; they were into clothes as much as the girls."

"How about a grade ahead of you then?"

"I can't think of anyone that... wait a minute, there was someone, but he didn't graduate with his class; he was a year ahead of Samantha and me and dropped out before graduation. I heard his grades were bad enough he would have to come back during summer school and he wasn't going to do that, so he just dropped out completely."

"Who?" The name Lily gave her convinced Diamond she was right in her assumptions.

"Thanks, Lily. That's all I needed to know. How's

school?"

"Good. I'm glad I only have a year left after this semester, I'm getting sick of being away from home." Diamond heard the homesickness in her voice.

"I understand. Just hang in there. It will be worth it when you graduate."

"I will." They talked for several minutes more before they hung up. Diamond got up from her couch and put the melting ice cream back into the freezer.

She went into the bedroom to put on her tennis shoes then grabbed her keys before she went outside. It was getting dark. Almost deciding to turn around and wait until tomorrow, Diamond got into her car, curiosity driving her to lose her commonsense about finding their home in the dark.

She had to know for sure if she was right because, if she was, she had just found out who was responsible for Samantha Bedford's death.

CHAPTER SEVENTEEN

"Who was that?" Razer asked.

Beth sat, staring at her phone with a hurt expression on her face.

"Diamond Richard," she said, glancing at Knox who was sitting across the table from her, eating his dinner.

"What did she want with Lily's number?" Shade and Knox both stopped eating at Razer's question.

"I don't know. She hung up before I could ask."

They continued eating until Razer couldn't avoid the glares from the men sitting at the table.

"Maybe you should call and find out," Razer suggested.

Beth picked up her phone and called her sister while the men waited impatiently for several minutes until Beth hung up.

"What did she want?" This time it was Knox who asked.

"She wanted to know if there was a boy in her and Sam's class that would freak a parent out if their daughter became involved with them."

"Was there?" Knox asked, getting a sick feeling in his gut.

"Yes."

"Who was it?"

"Dustin Porter."

* * *

Diamond pulled her car in front of the Porter's house. The older, wooden house's front porch was lit with a spotlight, showing not only the front porch, but a great expanse of the yard. When Diamond got out of her car, almost blinded by the light, the door opened and a man came outside to stand on the porch.

"Is that you, Ms. Richards?"

"Yes, Dustin." Diamond licked her lips. "Can I talk to you for a few minutes?"

He lowered the shotgun he was holding. "Sure, come on in."

Diamond walked up the short flight of steps to the front porch. Dustin's face was in the shadows as if he suspected why she was there, making her unable to read his feelings on her being there. Diamond walked into the old fashioned living room that had a braided rug on the floor and an old, flowered print couch.

"Where are your brothers and sister?" Diamond questioned, going into the living room, regretting her decision for coming out alone to his house. She should have gone to the sheriff, however she'd been too excited at the prospect of being right to think of what she was doing.

"They went into town to see a movie. Not much else to do on a Friday night," Dustin replied.

"I've been finding that out myself. I'm from Jamestown; it's not much bigger, but at least it has a little more entertainment than Treepoint does." She made an effort to keep the conversation casual until she could get out of the situation she had placed herself in.

"What brought you out here at this time of night?" Dustin asked, studying her tense face.

"I just wanted to check and see how everything was going since the hearing. I like to check in with my clients. I also thought I would invite Rachel to lunch. I haven't made many friends since coming to Treepoint." Dustin didn't say anything after her answer. "Since she's not here you can tell her to give me a call," Diamond continued on, casually walking towards the door.

"How'd you figure it out?" Dustin asked, making no move to stop her.

Diamond paused, looking at the man nervously. She thought about denying it, but something told her it would be useless. Selling pot for a living would give him the advantage of being used to determining when a person was lying.

"Sam flaunted everyone in front of her parents; it only made sense to wonder about the man she kept secret."

"I embarrassed her." Dustin made a wry face, his hand running through his curly hair. "We began seeing each other when she was a freshman in high school. She didn't tell anyone because she didn't want her rich daddy to know."

He took a step toward her and Diamond backed away towards the door. Dustin stopped then walked over to the table, putting the gun down.

"I'm not going to hurt you, Ms. Richards."

Diamond let a sigh of relief escape.

"We were in love," he continued. "She wasn't like she was until after we broke up. She was always a handful and a smartass, but she wasn't mean and a slut until after she broke up with me. When her mother died, we were going to sneak away and get married. She was just waiting until the end of the school year then we were going to leave town."

"What happened?" Diamond asked.

"I don't know, but I think her father found out and he threatened my family. I tried to talk to her, but she wouldn't listen to me. She didn't think I could protect her." Diamond saw the pain on the man's face; he looked much older than his years.

"She disappeared for about six months, and when she

came back, she wouldn't talk to me and then she began seeing every man in town who had a hard on for her."

Diamond felt terrible about every name she had called Samantha Bedford. The young girl had lost her mother then found out she was pregnant. She could only imagine the threats her father would have made to the young woman when he realized she was pregnant by a boy whose family was the biggest pot dealers in the county, if not the state.

"Did you know she was pregnant?"

Dustin gave a shake of his head. "I only found out the day she died."

"That was what the argument was about?" Diamond guessed.

"Yes. I went into the sheriff's office to see Greer when a phone call came in to the receptionist. I heard her talking to someone from Jamestown. They told her that no further information was available. No one knows what happened to my kid, do they?"

"I don't think they do, but the sheriff's office is trying. You know the sheriff better than me, you think he'll give up?"

"No, but I'm afraid to find out, too. I didn't know the Sam that opened that motel door. She thought I was Knox coming back for more." His face showed the pain in his soul that loving the woman had cost him. He was too young to go through this.

In that instant, Diamond hated Vincent Bedford more than she had ever thought it was possible to hate another human being. He was sitting in a jail cell while he was responsible for one man's death and had precipitated the actions that led to his daughter's death. If he hadn't interfered, Dustin and Samantha would probably have married and raised their child together. Vincent Bedford deserved more punishment than he was getting.

"What happened when she saw it was you?"

"She freaked out."

Diamond was sure she had. Samantha had probably been using men to forget Dustin for a long time. To see him walk in, she could only imagine how humiliated the woman had felt.

"She started screaming at me, throwing stuff. I tried to calm her down and ask about my kid. She told me to get out and started pushing me toward the door. I shoved her back and she fell and hit her head on the side of the table." Dustin buried his face in his hands. "I called the ambulance and left. I knew that, with my reputation, everyone would think I did it deliberately. I didn't even really shove her, I just jerked my arm away from her and she lost her balance. I don't know anymore. I keep going over it in my head and all I keep seeing is her lying there on the floor," Dustin confessed.

"Dustin, I wish you would have come to me. I would've helped." A sudden thought came to mind. "Are you the one who destroyed my office?"

"No, why would I do that?" he asked, confused.

"That's what I want to know," Diamond said. Now she was the one confused. If he hadn't trashed her office, who had?

"I didn't touch your office," Dustin said.

"We did." Diamond turned towards the door, seeing Greer, Tate and Rachel standing in the doorway.

"I did," Greer corrected his family, walking into the room and going to the table to pick up the shotgun. "I wanted to distract you from nosing around. I heard that you were asking about Sam's men."

Rachel and Tate closed the door. Rachel was pale as she came to stand next to Diamond at the same time that Tate went to stand next to Greer.

"I'm not going to press charges," Diamond said.

"I'll pay for the damages," Rachel burst out.

"That's not necessary," Diamond said. "The couch was the only thing I had to throw out and I like my new one."

"What are we going to do? She's going to go to the

sheriff," Greer asked his brothers.

"No, I'm not. We're going to the sheriff together." Diamond kept her voice firm. "Dustin will always be looking over his shoulder for the rest of his life if he doesn't. He's going to face it and get it over with then start over."

"My brother isn't going to jail," Greer said angrily.

"No, he's not. Samantha died because of her kidneys, not the blow to her head. I can get the charge dropped to involuntary manslaughter. I'll talk to Caleb and see if we can work out a deal."

"Listen to her, Greer," Rachel said, going to her brother, trying to take the gun from him.

"They're not going to offer him a deal! They've been trying to lock one of us away for years, and all because of that slut they are going to get one of us!"

"I told you not to call her that!" Dustin said.

"You were always blind where that bitch was concerned! I told you to stay away from that stuck up pussy, and did you listen to me? Hell no! Now look at the mess we're in all because you had to have that slut!"

Rachel attempted to take the shotgun away from Greer again before her brothers came to blows. Frightened of their altercation with the weapon, Diamond went forward to get the girl back when the gun went off.

Everyone froze in shock. Diamond took a breath of relief when she realized the shot went through the back of the ugly sofa.

"Thank God," Rachel said.

The door suddenly crashed open and The Last Riders came into the room. Diamond didn't have a chance to move before she was turned around and Knox's hands were going over her body.

"Are you okay?" he asked hoarsely.

Diamond batted his hands away. "I'm fine. Why are you here?"

"Beth called Lily to see what you wanted, knowing your

track record about going at things alone, I had a feeling that you would come here," Knox explained angrily.

"I didn't need anyone's help. The gun went off accidently," Diamond snapped back.

"Guns don't fucking go off by accident if you're not holding one," Knox said, looking at Greer who was staring guiltily at his sister.

"I'm sorry, Rachel," Greer apologized to his sister.

"I've told you that temper of yours is going to get someone killed," Rachel told her brother.

Diamond felt bad for Rachel; she had not one but three brothers that were a pain in the ass. The Last Riders were itching for a fight and were holding themselves back because Rachel and she were in the room.

"Diamond, take Rachel outside and wait for me," Knox ordered, staring at Greer with deadly intent.

"We're not going anywhere." Diamond refused to leave the men alone.

The Last Riders were spreading throughout the room. Rider and Razer were by Dustin. Cash and Viper were next to Tate, and Greer had Train and Crash standing by him. Rachel was shaking, still standing next to Greer while Shade simply stood by the door.

"I didn't ask." Knox lifted her off her feet, turning towards the door.

"Stop it, Knox. You don't even know what's going on. I'm Dustin's lawyer and I came out here to discuss his court case with him."

"Which one? The one where he sold pot to an undercover cop or for Sam's death?" Knox mocked her, letting her know they had already figured out why she had come to the Porter's house.

"Put me down!" Diamond knew there was no arguing with Knox when his mind was made up.

Cash took Rachel's arm, moving her away from Greer. "Don't fucking touch her!" Greer yelled, moving forward. Viper had him in a second; held immobile as Rachel struggled against Cash.

"Stop it, listen to me. He didn't mean for the gun to go off. Rachel tried to take the gun from him. You know he wouldn't hurt his sister. Knox, calm down and listen to me." Diamond quit trying to struggle against him, letting her body go pliant. Turning against him until she was plastered against his front, she took his face in her hands, drawing his furious gaze back to hers.

"They had no intention of hurting me," Diamond told the partial truth. Greer she wasn't sure about, but she chose to give him the benefit of the doubt to save his life even if he was a jackass.

Knox stared down at Diamond with a look she barely caught before it was smoothed out and once again his demeanor returned to the impassive one she was so familiar with. Knox released her, stepping away from the closeness of her body.

"Let her go, Cash," Viper ordered. Cash released a still struggling Rachel who, when he released her, turned around and planted her foot in his balls.

Cash went immediately to his knees.

"Don't fucking ever touch me again." She started for the downed man again, but a laughing Shade moved forward, blocking Cash who was bent over in agony.

"I think he got the message Rachel," Shade told her.

Rachel pulled her shirt down, which had ridden up her flat stomach. Planting her hands on her hips, she earned Diamond's admiration when she let the men have it with her vicious tongue.

"You're going to buy me a new door, Knox." She turned around and pointed her finger at Greer. "You're going to get your ass out of bed in the morning and buy me a new couch." Now, turning to Viper, she let him have it, too. "Next time you come to my house, fucking knock first." She looked around at a smirking Shade to see Cash trying to get to his feet. Shade offered him a hand, but was met with an angry scowl.

"You have a whole club of women to haul around, don't touch me again or the only thing you're going to be able to touch them with are your damn fingers."

Taking a deep breath, she turned to Diamond. "Now, can you help Dustin or not?"

"Yes," Diamond said softly, seeing the fear for her brother behind the bravado. "I'll go with him to the sheriff's office to make a statement. I'll talk to the Commonwealth's Attorney to try to work out a deal, but he knows he doesn't have much of a case. I sent for the coroner's report from Frankfort; Samantha Bedford was in bad shape. She needed a kidney transplant and wasn't even aware she had a problem. I talked to her grandmother; it could have possibly been what killed her mother. It was a genetic condition that the family was unaware of."

"Could my kid have it?" Dustin asked.

"Possibly. Dustin, right now we have to deal with Samantha's death. I'll do what I can to see how I can get more help for you to find your child, okay?" Diamond meant it, she would try. Dustin deserved to know what had happened to his child.

"All right. I don't have a choice, do I?" Dustin said unhappily.

"No. I'm sorry, you don't. Samantha made several bad decisions, but I do think she cared about you, Dustin, and if she did, she would have seen your child was taken care of. You have to hold on to that hope."

Dustin nodded his head.

"Let's get this over with."

"Wait a minute, who planted the jewelry in my bedroom?" Knox asked

The Porters stopped, looking at each other.

Greer faced Knox. "I paid Tara and Stacy to plant it for me. I gave them a month's supply of pot for doing it and then to tell me which room was yours. Then I called the state police."

"Who are Tara and Stacy?" Diamond asked, confused.

"They're twins that are hanger-ons. They come to the clubhouse every Friday," Viper explained, not able to look her in the eyes.

Diamond really wanted out of the house before she made a fool of herself. She walked toward the door, keeping her face averted from Knox and The Last Riders.

The Porters started to follow her until Knox took a step forward and punched Greer in the face. Tate managed to catch his brother before he fell to the floor then Tate started to move towards Knox, but Viper's words stopped him.

"If it wasn't for Diamond and Rachel, we would have had a different outcome tonight. Don't press your luck. Get your asses to the car before I change my mind and don't care if they see us get even."

The Porters didn't hesitate, going out to the front yard which was also full of The Last Riders.

Diamond went to her car, ignoring Knox who was watching her.

"I'll meet you at the sheriff's office," she told the Porters. She looked towards Viper who had come out of the house and was standing by Knox. They stared at each other, both knowing that despite her taking up for the Porters, it could have been a dangerous situation if they hadn't shown up.

Viper silently acknowledged her thanks with nod of his head.

Diamond got in her car, carefully turning it around and once again going down the treacherous driveway until she was on the road leading into town with The Last Riders following. Diamond had hoped she wouldn't see them again that night. She had wanted to avoid seeing Knox, however Diamond was not going to get another of her prayers answered that evening.

CHAPTER EIGHTEEN

She was at the sheriff's office for several hours. David Thurman made an appearance as Diamond sat by Dustin's side while he retold his story. Afterward, Diamond and Commonwealth's Attorney went out into the hallway.

"Well?" Diamond asked.

"I'm not going to press charges. No jury is going to convict him after he tells that story. I've been trying to get the Porters in jail for the last two years, but that man's being punished enough. He has no idea where his child is?"

"No. Samantha and her father covered their tracks," Diamond explained.

"I'll see what I can do in the morning," David offered. He started to leave, but paused. "That was good work, Di. You ever want a job in my office, let me know."

"Thanks, David." Diamond went back into the room to give Dustin the good news.

It was another hour before Diamond made it back to her apartment. Exhausted, she went to the refrigerator to get a drink when a knock on her door startled her. She went to the door, looking out the peephole to see Knox on the other side.

"Go away, Knox."

"Let me in, Diamond."

Diamond's head fell against the door. She knew what would happen if she let him in. It wouldn't matter that she hadn't seen or heard from him for the last two months. Where Knox was concerned, she knew her weakness.

"Diamond." Knox's cajoling voice almost had her weakening.

"Knox, if I let you in, we both know what will happen; that's why you're here."

Silence from the other side of the door.

"I want you, Knox, so bad. You know I do."

"Let me in then." His voice turned seductive.

"I care about you, Knox, but us in my bed wouldn't mean anything to you. The saddest part is, I don't even care that you'll leave here and be in someone else's bed. I want you that bad. I'll open the door if you can tell me you care about me. I have to know that much at least. That's all I'm asking, Knox, please."

Without even a pause to show he'd thought about it, Diamond heard the sound of his boots walking away then the loud sound of him riding out of the parking lot. She slid down the door until she sat on the floor, leaning against the door, crying.

She had taken a leap and had asked little in return. She hadn't asked for commitment, love or even fidelity. The only thing she had wanted was to know that, when they were having sex, he cared about her. He hadn't been able to give it to her. She didn't know why her heart was breaking over a man like Knox, yet something inside her told her she was losing a prize worth fighting for.

* * *

Diamond closed the folder, stacking it with the others she had just updated.

"Ms. Richards?" Holly said, sticking her head in the doorway of her office.

"Yes, Holly."

"There's someone here to see you; they don't have an appointment."

"Who is it?" Diamond was about to leave for the day, but she didn't have anyone to rush home to, so a few extra minutes at the office wasn't really going to make a difference.

"Pastor Dean. His church is the one across the street."

"Show him in, Holly." Holly disappeared for a minute before her door reopened. Pastor Dean walked in, giving Holly a smile that had her blushing and smiling back.

"Ms. Richards, my name is Pastor Dean. I wanted to introduce myself and see what it would take for you to give my church a visit."

Diamond smiled at his forthright approach. "I'm afraid you have an uphill battle there, Pastor. I'm not much for going to church." Diamond rose from her desk to greet the Pastor, extending her hand to shake his. Diamond was surprised how rough and calloused his hand was, expecting a smooth one. This man was used to doing labor.

"I'm sorry to hear that. If not church service, then on Wednesday we have a potluck dinner that everyone in the community is invited to. It would give you an opportunity to become more familiar with the townspeople and build your client base."

"Pastor Dean, you're not trying to bribe me with potential clients to get me inside your church, are you?"

"All roads lead to God, Ms. Richards," he said, not denying his attempt at coercion.

Diamond couldn't help laugher laughter at that. It didn't take him long before he'd turned the humor into finagling a clothing donation out of her, and changing her firm no at attending church services to a maybe.

"You're a very convincing man, Pastor Dean. I'm willing to bet you give an excellent sermon."

"I try." He tried to appear humble, though somehow Diamond had a feeling this man had plenty of confidence.

Diamond motioned for him to have a seat on the chair

by the window as she walked over to take the other one. Pastor Dean followed her to the seating area, pausing before he sat down to look out the window.

"You have quite a view of my church."

Diamond nodded. "It can be a pain sometimes when I'm thinking of billing my customers for an extra hour and look outside to see the church; keeps me from padding the bills," Diamond said wryly.

"I have a good view also. Perhaps we should learn a signal. I could signal you when I have a parishioner that wants to stay forever and you could signal me when you have a client you can't get rid of," he joked.

"Don't temp me; I've had several of those."

"I noticed Knox coming by several weeks ago, but he hasn't been around for a while, why is that?" Pastor Dean inquired.

Diamond was surprised that he'd bluntly let her know he had noticed Knox coming into her office as well as his question. "His case was dropped, so there wasn't any need for him to come around anymore."

Pastor Dean nodded his head. "I was glad to hear it. Knox and I were in the service together," he explained.

"You're friends?" Diamond asked in surprise.

"Yes, I consider myself one of the few honored with that position. We started out in the service together straight out of high school. Knox didn't have many friends then, still doesn't. The Last Riders are his friends and family, but I think that's it. He ended up in foster care when he was pretty young. He told me he had been in over fifteen foster homes before he graduated and joined the service."

"Fifteen?" Diamond was shocked.

"Yes, I imagine that was hard growing up; every time you became attached to a new family, being sent away."

Diamond felt the pain for Knox in her chest, aching for the man when he was a child who had been unable to control his own life. It would have been doubly hard on

Knox who had such a dominant personality.

"I knew his wife also," Pastor Dean said, watching her reaction.

"His wife?" Diamond whispered.

"They got married about a year after he joined the service. She was very pretty and shy. I can still see her in my mind on their wedding day. They were both nineteen and thought nothing could touch them. They didn't even have time for a honeymoon. They wanted to get married before Dena got shipped out. It was the first wedding I performed. She was shipped out thirty minutes later. They didn't even have time to consummate their marriage, yet they didn't care. Both of them simply laughed and held hands while they waited on the chopper to pick her up."

"What happened?" Diamond whispered, seeing that Pastor Dean's hands had clenched at his side.

"She was killed by a roadside bomb two days later. I was the one who had to tell him. I've had to deliver that news sixty-three times, but Knox was the worst. He was a friend and I saw something inside of him die that day." Diamond couldn't help the tears that fell from her eyes. "He met Evie and joined The Last Riders two years later, but he never let himself fall for another woman. It would be a leap of faith for him to do that and I think he gave up on God the day Dena died."

"Why are you telling me this?" Diamond asked, finally realizing that he'd had more than one purpose in coming to her office.

"As I said, my church has a perfect view of your building."

Diamond's face flamed, remembering the night she had worked late and Knox had showed up. He had lifted her onto her desk and taken her until she had begged for mercy, promising she wouldn't be late meeting him again. Pastor Dean must have gotten an eyeful.

"He had a look on his face I hadn't seen in years. Frankly, I was happy to see someone in his life that he cared about again."

"He doesn't care about me," Diamond said. "I asked him, he wouldn't tell me."

"Knox isn't much of a talker. That's for damn sure, but I'm not surprised he's running away, especially if he cares for you. He won't willingly put himself out there to be hurt again," Pastor Dean advised.

"He wouldn't. He's a marshmallow," she agreed with his assessment.

"A marshmallow?" Diamond nodded. "Yes, well, I don't know if I'd agree with that analogy, but if it keeps you from playing 'Rolling in the Deep' over and over again, I'm all for it."

"You can hear that?" Pastor Dean nodded. Diamond couldn't help but laugh. "You and my secretary won't be hearing it again," Diamond promised.

"Thank God," Pastor Dean declared, standing up.

"It was nice to meet you, Pastor Dean, and I think I will take you up on your invitation. I'll see you Sunday."

"It was nice to meet you, too, Diamond." Pastor Dean left her office, closing the door behind him.

As soon as he left, Diamond went to her desk phone, pushing in Knox's number. She wanted to talk to him. She didn't know what she would say, she just wanted to hear his voice. He didn't answer on her first call, he didn't answer the next six times she called, nor did he return any of her texts or messages. After an hour of failed attempts, Diamond left her office, going to her car.

She had somewhere to go now.

Driving carefully through the tears clouding her vision, she went in search of the one person who could make it better.

CHAPTER NINETEEN

No one was home as Diamond put her key into the door, going inside the quiet house. It was ironic that the last few weeks her parents had called and Diamond hadn't returned their calls, yet now that she wanted someone to talk to, no one was around. Diamond walked around the empty house, unsure of what to do. She went outside onto the back porch, sitting in the swing that faced the yard. Her foot gently sent the swing into motion.

She heard the back door open and close. "Diamond? Why are you sitting out here? It's freezing out."

Her father walked around to the front of the swing.

"What's wrong?" He sat down beside her.

"I love Knox. I love him so much." Diamond buried her face in her hands. "I don't even know why I love the big jerk." Her father put his arm around her shoulder. Diamond turned to him, crying on his shoulder.

"How does he feel?" Her father looked over his shoulder to his wife and Sex Piston standing silently behind the swing. He started to get up and let his wife handle the situation, but Sizzle shook her head.

"He doesn't love me back." Diamond cried harder.

"Are you sure?" Her father pulled her closer.

"Yes, now he won't even talk to me."

"Then make him," he said matter-of-factly.

"What?" Diamond looked up from his shoulder.

"Make him talk to you. It's what your mother did."

"When?" Diamond couldn't remember her parents ever even having an argument.

Her father took a deep breath. "When you girls were little, we broke up for a while. We argued over custody so we decided to live together until you girls were older. It was the worst six months of my life. I loved your mom, but she was sick of me putting the Destructors first. She didn't want me to leave the club, she just wanted equal time. I was stupid and put the club first and you guys second. When I missed Sex Piston's birthday party, she'd had it. Living with your mom and yet not being with her was terrible. I'm ashamed to say I did stupid shit that I regret, that I will always regret, Diamond."

"How did you get back together?" Diamond asked.

"It was because of you, Diamond."

Her eyes widened in surprise. "Me?"

"After you saw me at the club with that woman and didn't talk to me, your mom and I talked. She couldn't understand the change in you towards me. You went from being a daddy's girl to not wanting to sit at the dinner table with me, so yeah, she knew something was wrong."

"How did you know?"

"One of my men saw you running from the back of the club. When I got home I could tell from the way you treated me that you had seen. I didn't know what to say to you, and your mother finally made me tell her. It was the worst day of my life, confessing I had cheated on her and had been for a long time. The thing was, she had known all along and that was another reason she'd had a problem with the club. We talked all day and night, Diamond, and worked it all out, but I paid for that day for years. It destroyed my relationship with you and your mother wouldn't marry me for a long time. I had lost her trust; it took all these years to get it back, but I lost my little girl forever.

"Diamond, go after Knox, make him talk to you." Her father looked at her with watery eyes.

"But you loved mom, Knox doesn't even care about me."

"He ever give you a nickname? Even when you were messing around?" Her father turned red at his question.

"No."

"Not once?" he pressed.

"No, he always called me Diamond."

"Do you know why we called you Diamond?" her father asked, his voice gruff.

"No."

"Because the second we saw you, we knew you were going to be the most precious thing in the world to us. Our precious jewel, our little Diamond."

Diamond burst into tears, her arms going around her father, crying for how much time they had lost.

"If Knox hasn't called you anything else, then he knows what he's got, probably just too stubborn to admit it. Go talk to him, sweetheart."

"Maybe I'll go see him tomorrow," Diamond prevaricated.

"Fuck that. Get off your ass, I'll take you." Shocked at the sound of Sex Piston's voice, Diamond stood up, seeing her mother and sister behind the swing.

"Go ahead, Diamond. What have you got to lose?" her father urged.

"My dignity?"

"Dignity isn't going to keep your ass warm tonight, move it." Sex Piston took her hand, dragging her inside the house. They were almost out the door when Sex Piston changed her mind and turned towards her bedroom.

"You can't go on a manhunt wearing that shit you got on." She went to her closet and pulled out a pair of jeans and jerked a top off the hanger. "Get dressed."

Diamond looked down at herself. She was wearing the dark blue suit she'd been in all day, and for once, she agreed with her sister. Taking of the suit, she managed to squeeze herself into her sister's jeans and pulled on the top. Her breasts were larger than Sex Piston's and the top was low cut. The globes of her breasts were displayed to an extent that Diamond didn't think was decent.

"Do you have another top I could borrow? This one is too tight." Diamond looked at herself in her sister's mirror. The top was practically indecent.

Sex Piston closed the closet door with a pair of high-heeled boots in her hand. She handed them to Diamond. "Put them on, and no I don't have a bigger top. That's the largest one I have," she lied.

Diamond sat down on the side of the bed, putting the boots on. When she was done Sex Piston pushed her down at her dressing table and took down her hair, styling the thick mass until it was curled and fluffy.

"Now you're done. Let's go."

Diamond followed behind her sister, her resolve weakening. "Sex Piston, I think I'm going to wait until I've thought this over a little more."

"Think over what?" Crazy Bitch asked, coming out of the kitchen with Killyama and T.A..

"Damn, I forgot we were supposed to watch Stud's kids tonight while they had their meeting," Sex Piston said, coming to a halt.

"Stud has kids?" Diamond asked.

"Yeah, three kids from hell. Is Fat Louise here?" Sex Piston asked, thinking fast.

"She's in the kitchen," Crazy Bitch answered.

"Fat Louise!" Sex Piston yelled. Fat Louise came out of the kitchen, eating a Pop Tart.

"You go on to the club and watch Stud's kids, we have somewhere we got to go."

"I ain't watching those monsters by myself," Fat Louise argued back.

"If you do it, I'll take you out to dinner, anywhere you want to go."

"Anywhere?"

Sex Piston hesitated. "Yes."

"Even Popeye's?" Fat Louise's eyes lit up.

"Yes. We are going to The Last Riders' clubhouse to get Knox for Diamond."

"Why?" Fat Louise asked, confused. "We don't like that asshole."

"We don't, but Diamond's in love with the mother fucker, and what she wants, she's going to get," Sex Piston said resolutely. "Let's go; time's a-wastin'. It's Friday night at that club; things will be getting freaky there."

Diamond tried to interrupt Sex Piston, but found herself dragged outside by her and Crazy Bitch.

"My keys are in the house," Diamond said.

"They can stay there, we're taking my car." Killyama opened the back door and Diamond barely had enough time to lower her head before she was shoved into the back seat.

"Scoot your ass over," Killyama said, sliding in next to her.

Crazy Bitch got in the front seat with Sex Piston and T.A. grabbed the last seat, sliding in next to Diamond in the back seat.

Sex Piston put the car in gear, accelerating with a squeal of her tires. Driving like a bat out of hell, her sister drove towards Treepoint.

With each mile, the butterflies in Diamond's stomach made her more and more nervous. Completely sure this was a terrible mistake, she attempted to get Sex Piston to turn around.

"Fuck, no, we ain't turnin' around," Killyama said. "I've been dying to see one of their parties ever since Beth told us about them. Who knows, maybe we'll like them more than the Blue Horseman and we'll start hangin' with them instead."

Diamond stared at the grim-faced women in the car. The Last Riders had no idea what was headed their way. God help them.

CHAPTER TWENTY

The Last Riders' parking lot was filled with motorcycles and cars. It was the one day of the week that hanger-ons were allowed in the clubhouse. Diamond, Sex Piston and her crew got out of the car, staring up at the huge house. Music could be heard from where they were standing.

"Sex Piston, I've changed my mind." Her sister glanced at her before walking over and taking her hand.

"You can do this, Diamond. I'll be right there with you. I shouldn't have butted in when I saw him at your office. Now, get your ass up those steps," she said, giving Diamond a shove on her back.

"What if I see him with someone?"

"Beth caught Razer fucking Evie. She got over it." She shrugged.

Diamond wasn't so sure she would be able to get over seeing him with another woman.

When they walked up the steps, Diamond tried to hesitate at the door, but Killyama pushed her through. The sight that met Diamond's eyes were her worst fears confirmed. The Last Riders were as Diamond had never seen them before.

Cash had Jewell on his lap, sucking her bare breast,

196

while Crash had a woman pressed against the wall with her skirt up around her waist as he was fucking her. Razer and Beth were sitting on the couch, necking, and while they were the most circumspect of the group with their clothes still on, Diamond wasn't so sure what she would've found if they had come in a few minutes later.

"Do you see him?" Sex Piston asked.

"No, he's not here."

"He must be in his room. Where is it?" Sex Piston asked.

"Upstairs." Diamond felt a hand on her back, pushing her towards the steps.

"Stop pushing me T.A.," Diamond hissed, seeing Beth's eyes widen and jerk from Razer's arms before coming towards them.

"What are you doing here?" she asked as she drew close.

"Diamond is going to talk to Knox. He upstairs?" Sex Piston told Beth as if they stopped by for a visit regularly.

"I don't know. We just got here. Go outside and wait. I'll get Razer to go get him for you."

"We can get him ourselves." Sex Piston ignored her offer. Diamond felt herself move toward the steps and then up them. As Beth followed behind, she saw Razer get up, coming after them.

"Sex Piston, I really don't think this is a good idea." Beth tried again to stop them. The woman ignored her, reaching the top of the steps.

"Which one is it?" Sex Piston asked. Diamond almost didn't tell her, but she knew that she would go into each and every room until she found him.

Diamond took a step toward Knox's door. She was going to knock, but Sex Piston opened the door before she could. The light from the bathroom shined into the bedroom, highlighting the people on the bed. There were four people on the bed.

Diamond took one look and then turned around,

running into Sex Piston who knew the instant she saw Diamond's face that she had made a mistake in making her confront Knox in his room.

"Mother. Fucker," Sex Piston said angrily.

Diamond pushed through the group of women, her hand to her mouth. She got to the top of the steps before she stopped. Sex Piston, Killyama, Beth, Crazy Bitch and T.A. all came to a stop behind her as Razer stood at the top of the steps, watching the women. She saw the recognition in his eyes; he was aware of what she had encountered. Diamond turned around, unable to face the sympathy she saw in the hard ass biker.

Taking a deep breath, Diamond tried to breathe through the pain tearing her heart apart. She had seen the short blond hair on top of the man on the bed while Rider had Evie on the other side of the bed and was fucking the woman.

"Bliss is mine," Diamond said, pissed off like she had never been before. Sex Piston and her crew all gave a grin.

"Let's kick some ass." Sex Piston let Diamond take the lead.

"What?" Wait!" Beth yelled.

Diamond rushed back into the bedroom before Beth or Razer could react, burying her hand in Bliss's hair and jerking her off the cock she was riding. At the same time, Sex Piston went for Evie who was straddling Rider's lap, pulling her off backwards to land on the floor. Through all of this, Crazy Bitch held Beth and Razer back at the doorway, threatening them with a lamp she had quickly picked up from the dresser.

"What in the fuck?" A man growled, though Diamond didn't even pay attention to the male voice coming from the bed.

Bliss screamed, trying to get away, but Diamond had a good grip on her hair. Evie was doing better defending herself against Sex Piston, but not by much. As Rider tried to jerk Sex Piston off Evie, Razer finally managed to get by

Crazy Bitch.

Diamond glared at him as he approached her. "You get away or I'm going to smash your nuts."

No sooner had the words left her mouth than the doorway filled with Last Riders trying to get into the bedroom and someone hit the light switch.

"Diamond!" Knox yelled from the doorway. He stood there, dressed in jeans shirt and boots with his jacket on.

"What is going on in here?" Viper came to the doorway with no shoes or shirt on. The tribal tattoo he had on his arm and shoulder and the huge one he had on his chest had Sex Piston and her crew pausing to look at the biker despite the turmoil going on in the room. Knox gave Diamond a threatening glare when he saw her eyes linger on Viper's display of muscular perfection a little longer than he deemed necessary.

"I thought that Knox was in here." Diamond reluctantly tore her attention away from Viper, giving Bliss's hair a final tug before releasing it. Evie and Sex Piston were still fighting despite Rider trying to separate the women when Train got up from the bed, grabbing Sex Piston so that Rider could help Evie get to her feet. Sex Piston's hand reached behind her back and grabbed Train by his nuts. To Train's credit, he bellowed, but he didn't release the bitch.

"Sex Piston, stop!" Viper yelled.

She let Train go reluctantly, who fell back onto the bed holding himself. Sex Piston's top was torn and her hair was a mess from Evie using it to pull away when she had tried to strangle her.

"What are you doing here, Diamond?" Knox asked.

"I wanted to talk to you?" The statement came out as more of a question because Diamond felt self-conscious with everyone listening.

"Did you ever think of just calling me?" Knox asked, looking around at the pandemonium in the room.

Diamond looked confused. "I did, you never answered.

Besides that, I texted and left messages."

Knox searched his pockets for his phone. "I've been out riding my bike all day then I went for a walk at Cash's homestead. I must have lost it."

"You weren't ignoring my call?" Diamond asked with a wavering voice.

"No," Knox answered, staring deeply into her eyes.

"You would have answered?"

"Yeah," Knox said softly.

Diamond smiled, walking toward him, this time not worried about making a fool of herself. She walked up to him and circled his waist with her arms.

"I've missed you," Diamond confessed.

"I've missed you," Knox said.

"Well, isn't that sweet," Killyama said in a sickeningly sweet voice. "Does that mean we can stay for the party?"

"No," everyone answered at once. Diamond laughed into Knox's chest.

"We help you out and we can't even get a beer?" Crazy Bitch asked Diamond.

Diamond looked up pleadingly at Knox.

"One beer," he agreed reluctantly.

"Knox," Viper said in warning.

"One beer then they'll leave," Knox promised.

Sex Piston and her crew nodded their heads in agreement. As Knox and Diamond left the room with everyone following, she noticed Viper turning to go to a bedroom at the end of the hall where Winter stood in the doorway with a sheet covering her body. When she saw Diamond's eyes on her, she shut the door just as Viper was about to enter. Unable to stop his momentum, he ran into the door.

Before she could so much as laugh at the spectacle it had created, they reached the top of the steps and saw the front door open and Stud enter with several of the Blue Horseman coming in behind him.

Cash, who was at the bottom of the steps, turned

toward the door. "What in the fuck do you think you're doing?" he asked Stud.

"We want our women."

"What women?" Cash asked, blocking Stud from coming any further into the clubhouse.

"Sex Piston, Crazy Bitch and T.A., you can keep Killyama," Stud said, looking up the steps. Catching sight of the women at the top of the steps with Rider and Train half naked sparked a fury within him that Diamond hadn't expected the emotionless man capable of.

"What in the hell are you doing here, Stud?" Sex Piston yelled, leaning over the railing. Her hair messed up and her top torn, she looked down at the President of the Blue Horseman.

"Which one touched you?" Stud yelled back.

"What?" Sex Piston asked in confusion.

"Which mother fucking asshole touched you? Because they're going to regret touching something that's mine."

"I'm not yours!" she yelled, putting her hands on her hips and glaring back.

"You damn sure are. Get your ass down here now!"

"We're not going anywhere, we're staying for a beer." Smugly, Sex Piston continued to ignore his order.

"Yeah?"

"Yeah!"

Stud signaled his men at her response. Knox didn't waste time, he moved Diamond back as Stud charged up the stairway after Sex Piston at the same time that the Blue Horsemen came through the doorway in a mass.

Sex Piston tried to take off running down the hallway, but ran into Viper who had come back down the hallway when he heard the commotion.

"Just a minute," Viper said, preventing Sex Piston from getting away.

As Stud reached the top of the stairs, seeing Viper holding Sex Piston seemed to piss the biker off even more.

"Let her go, Viper."

"My pleasure." Viper let Sex Piston's arm go, and before Sex Piston could move, Stud had her.

"Let me go," she said, trying to twist free.

"Pike." Stud turned and one of the Blue Horseman came up the steps. "Take her to the truck." Sex Piston tried to struggle away, but found herself tossed over the big man's shoulder.

Stud turned back to the rest of Sex Piston's crew.

"Now, you can go with her or be carried away, which is it going to be?"

T.A. immediately went after Sex Piston, giving Stud a wide berth while Crazy Bitch and Killyama merely stood there with their arms crossed over their chests.

"Fuck off," Crazy Bitch said.

"Back off, bitch," Killyama snarled.

Stud didn't argue. "Rock, Blade."

Two men came up the steps slowly. One took a step forward and grappled with Crazy Bitch before he managed to get her in a tight hold, tossing her over his shoulder then went down the steps with the woman threatening to cut his dick off.

"Blade," Stud ordered.

"Do I have to?" Stud threw the man a look that had him taking a step forward taking on Killyama. The woman fought the man dirty, ramming his nose with her fist then jerking out the loop in his ear before he managed to get her, still struggling, out of the house to a cheering audience.

"Now which one touched Sex Piston?" Menace filled the hallway.

"None of them did. She came in here and started a fight with our women," Viper said sharply.

"That true?" Stud asked Diamond.

"Yes," she answered from behind Knox's back.

Stud looked at the women in the hallway. Bliss, who had pulled on a robe, had a black eye and Evie, who had put on Train's shirt, whose hair was a total mess from Sex

Piston's hands.

"I don't suppose we could switch Killyama with one of these women?" Stud quipped.

"No." Viper apparently wasn't in a joking mood, although Diamond wasn't so sure that Stud had been joking from the look of disappointment on his face.

"I didn't think so." Stud turned to go back down the steps. "Sorry about the interruption to your party. That's two markers we owe your club."

"Don't pull this shit again, Stud. Next time you come to our club like this, I'll take it as a sign of war." Viper made his position clear.

Stud stopped, turning back. "Next time I hit your club with our women here, war won't describe what I'll do," Stud said, making his own stance equally evident.

Viper nodded. Both Presidents coming to a mutual agreement.

After Stud and his men cleared the club within minutes, Knox moved to the side, letting Diamond free. Everyone stared at her accusingly.

"Sorry." Diamond felt terrible about the commotion she had caused.

"You two need to get your shit straight," Viper said, turning back to his bedroom.

Knox took Diamond's hand, leading her back to the hallway and going into the room across the hall from his.

CHAPTER TWENTY-ONE

"Why do you have a different bedroom?" Diamond asked. The room was half the size of his previous room. His blanket that had once lain on a huge, king-sized bed now lay across a full bed. She couldn't believe he even fit on the bed.

"I didn't need the big bed anymore."

"You didn't? Why?" Diamond asked, studying his face.

Knox didn't answer, instead he asked a question of his own. "Why all the hurry to see me? It would have been easier to open your door last night. Nothing's changed, Diamond."

Diamond stood there, wanting to be the woman that could let him have it while he stood arrogantly with his arms crossed over his chest as if he held all the cards. To be the type that had more respect for herself than to be humiliated in front of a man, however Diamond wanted Knox. If she took a chance, she might win him, and having him meant everything.

"I've decided it doesn't matter if you care about me or not."

"It doesn't?" Surprised, his arms dropped to his side.

"No, I was wrong. Just because I care about you,

doesn't mean that you have to return my feelings."

"What feelings?" Knox asked, going still.

"I'm in love with you," Diamond confessed, staring him straight in the eyes.

"No, you're not."

Diamond nodded her head. "I am. You know I am, that's why you left that day. I bet you were relieved that Sex Piston gave you an out."

"I didn't need Sex Piston to give me an out. I was done," Knox said emotionlessly.

Diamond's heart plunged, although there was something that was hiding in his eyes that gave her a spark of hope. It was a tiny spark, but Diamond was going to play the hand of her life and that didn't mean folding.

"What were you done with, Knox?" Diamond walked to stand beside the bed. Taking off her top, she managed to unsnap her bra, letting her breasts free. She then sat down on the side of the bed, pulling off the boots before she stood back up, unsnapping the tight jeans she had to wiggle out of. Kicking them away, she remained standing in nothing more than a tiny pair of black panties, which she slowly slipped her finger under the sides of before she slid them off, now naked before him.

Her eyes went to the front of his jeans where his erection was thrusting against the front of them. Feeling a rise in her confidence, she walked towards him, making sure she put an extra swing into her hips. Her hands went to the bottom of his t-shirt, raising it up his chest. She didn't try to take it off the man standing as still as a statue. Instead, she leaned toward his chest, taking one of his nipples between her teeth and biting gently before letting her tongue lave the tightening nipple.

"I'm surprised that, as much as you like piercings, you didn't pierce your nipples."

"I get in too many fights for a nipple piercing. Did you see what Killyama did with that poor bastard's ear?"

"Ouch," Diamond murmured, moving to his other

nipple. "I want you so bad, Knox."

His hands went to her waist, lifting her up to meet his eyes. "If I fuck you, it doesn't mean I care about you. It doesn't mean I'm ever going to care about you. You're just another pussy to me." His stern face didn't soften.

Tears filled Diamond's eyes at his harsh words. "Okay."

"Dammit to hell." Knox's face broke into a tortured mask that made her cry even harder, feeling his conflicting emotions. He dropped her onto the bed, jerking off his t-shirt before he lay down between her legs.

"You're too much, Diamond. You're too sweet, too beautiful and you mean too fucking much to me." When Knox's head nuzzled her neck, his body shuddered against her. "Quit crying."

"Okay."

His lips found hers, giving her everything she wanted and more. The passion they had always shared was still there except now it was heightened because they hadn't been together. The pain of neither one getting what they needed from the other tore at their emotions.

"I can't not love you, Knox. I know you need me to only have sex with you, though; to be just another in a long line. I don't need the words from you anymore, Knox. That's what I was calling to tell you. I simply need you." Her hands looped around his neck, cupping his head to her.

Knox's hand went to her breast, lifting it to his mouth. Finding her nipple, he sucked it into his mouth, making Diamond's hips arch upwards to rub her mound against his hard length behind his jeans. Her hands went to unsnap his jeans then to pull down his zipper at the same time that Knox's hand went between her thighs. Finding the wet warmth waiting for him, his finger plunged within her.

"I've missed you so much," Diamond whispered into his neck, her hands sliding upwards to his shaven head, stroking the smooth flesh as he teased her nipple with his tongue ring.

Knox raised his head to stare into her eyes. Lifting himself slightly away, he maneuvered his cock from his jeans then his hand moved to her thigh to spread her wider. When his cock brushed against her opening, the naked, silky skin had Diamond freezing in place as he pushed himself into her pussy. The unbelievably erotic feel of his flesh without the condom was something Diamond had never experienced before. The piercings on his cock rubbed against her, causing her to shudder.

Staring up at him, she opened her heart and soul to a man who'd had his ripped out time and time again until he had nothing left for her. Diamond took the only thing he had left to give, his body. In return, she gave him everything she was without regret or recriminations, letting her love surround them until she felt as if she'd touched his soul.

Knox's head dropped to her shoulder as his hips thrust into her, burying his cock over and over into her silky pussy that grasped him tightly.

"This is what I want from you, Diamond."

"It's yours, Knox. Take me." Her words lit a storm within him that had his strokes becoming rougher as his control began to loosen at the feel of her surrounding him.

"If I take you the way I want to, you'll be sore tomorrow," Knox warned.

"There's always the hot tub," Diamond tempted as her hand went to his back, scoring him with her fingernails.

At those words, Knox lost his restraint to the point that his strokes became hard enough to send the bed slamming against the wall. Diamond's hips thrust back against his, coming as his piercing found a spot that had her screaming. Knox's cock jerked within her as he climaxed at the same time, finally bringing both of them down from the torturous need that had been driving them.

When he moved to her side, pulling her onto him,

Diamond lay relaxed and drained on his chest. His hands stroked her hair, straightening the tangled mess. The calming movement made her drowsy since she hadn't slept well last night.

Diamond woke sometime later when Knox rolled her to the side, getting out of bed. Lifting her, he carried her into the bathroom before turning on the shower. Opening the shower door, he pulled her inside under the warm water where his hands picked up the soap and washed her slick body.

"Open your legs." Knox gently commanded.

When Knox rose, Diamond took the soap, putting a generous amount on the palm of her hand. She began washing him. The muscled smoothness had Diamond grinning up at him. "I think you've lost a little weight."

Knox looked disgruntled. "Maybe a few pounds."

"You need to eat more."

"My appetite may be coming back. Let's go raid the kitchen."

"Sounds good to me." The thought that she might have been the reason he had lost a few pounds had her stomach doing flips.

They dried off and Knox put on a pair of sweats before giving her a large t-shirt that fell to her knees. Searching through his drawers, he then managed to find a robe that fell to her feet.

"I didn't think you would own a robe," Diamond joked.

Knox grinned back. "It was a Christmas present last year from Beth. She gave all the brothers one." Diamond laughed.

She had expected the party to be over, but there were still several members and hanger-ons downstairs.

Heading towards the kitchen, Rider gave her a sideways grin when he saw how she was dressed. Blushing, she went into the kitchen to see Evie and Cash sitting at the table eating a sandwich.

"Take a seat, I'll fix us something," Knox said.

As Diamond took a seat next to Evie, the silence at the table was uncomfortable. "I'm sorry, Evie. I lost my temper when I went in the bedroom and thought Knox was there, which is no excuse, but I'm sorry."

"Your sister is a bitch," Evie retorted, not ready to accept her apology.

"I know, but to be fair, she was going to walk away. I'm the one that egged it on." Diamond accepted full responsibility for the fiasco upstairs.

"You did?"

Diamond nodded. "I didn't know I could get that angry," she confessed.

"That kind of happens when you care about someone, don't you think?" Evie probed.

"Yes, but I still had no right. Knox hasn't made any promises and I was wrong to take it out on the women. I should have just kicked *his* ass."

Cash and Evie both shared a glance. Evie started to say something, but was cut off by Knox setting a sandwich down in front of Diamond then sitting down with a plate for himself.

They obviously didn't want to continue the conversation with Knox there, so the topic switched to a big order The Last Riders had going out next week and how much the new employees hired from Treepoint helped with the grueling schedule.

"When did the Blue Horsemen start caring about what Sex Piston and her crazy assed friends did?" Cash asked, changing the subject again.

"The Destructors became a charter of the Blue Horsemen. I think Sex Piston and her crew are going to be in trouble for helping me get in to see Knox. Stud didn't look too happy with them."

"They broke a big rule going into another clubhouse," Cash explained.

"They weren't inside ten minutes," Diamond took up

for her sister and friends.

"I don't think it's going to matter to Stud," Cash said with a grin, as if the thought of Sex Piston getting in trouble was a good thing.

Diamond didn't say anything else, she merely gave Cash a dirty look, which he ignored. Picking up her sandwich, she was about to take a bite when the basement door opened and Jewell and Raci walked out, both flushed with red faces, wearing t-shirts that made it obvious they had nothing on underneath. Shade followed behind them, his hair also wet, and he was wearing nothing other than jeans. His whole upper body—to his neck and dipping below his waistband—was covered with tats.

His eyes met Diamond's open-mouthed stare with the sandwich halfway to her mouth as he closed the door behind him.

The silence in the room was tangible as the two women went towards the refrigerator to make their own snacks and Shade walked to the liquor sitting on the counter. He grabbed one of the bottles then went to the cabinet to get a glass, coming to take a seat across from Diamond who had managed to take a bite of her sandwich. Chewing it slowly, she felt the startlingly blue gaze on her and Knox. She could almost feel his mind at work while she barely managed to swallow the bite of sandwich.

"You going to need my vote?" Shade asked, his gaze on Knox.

Knox stared back. "Yes."

"Then handle it," he said, getting up from the table, taking the whiskey and glass with him. Looking back at Evie, he asked, "Coming?"

Evie grinned, standing up to take her dishes to the sink before going to Shade who was waiting. She went down the stairs, giving Knox a final stare.

"I'll take care of it." Knox must have said what Shade wanted to hear because Shade left the room, closing the door behind him.

Diamond took another bite of her sandwich.

Raci and Jewell both sat down at the table with their plates of food. "I guess we all have the late night munchies," Raci said, picking up her peanut butter and jelly sandwich.

Diamond took a drink of her water, unable to take the chance of strangling on her food. She had already managed to make an ass of herself once today and having the Heimlich performed on her at two in the morning would have been more than her pride could take.

"Finished?" Knox asked.

"Yes. I couldn't eat another bite." Diamond got up, taking their plates to the sink before they said goodnight to everyone and returned to Knox's room.

"Tired?" Knox asked.

"Yes."

"Get in bed. I'll take you by your house for some clothes when we wake up."

Diamond turned and climbed into bed, not wanting him to see her expression. She had been worried he would take her home now, and she hadn't wanted to leave him yet. Knox turned off the light, getting in bed beside her with his hand on her stomach as he pressed her back against his naked body.

Diamond sighed, relaxing against him.

"What?" Knox asked, half-asleep by the sound of his voice.

"Can I ask you a question?"

"Go ahead." From the tone of his voice, Diamond knew he was aware of what question she wanted answered.

"I thought Shade had a thing for Lily."

"He does."

"Then why all the women?"

"Do you think Lily has a thing for Shade?"

Diamond knew that Shade was Knox's friend, but she wanted to be honest. "No."

"That's why all the women. He knows Beth and Lily

both want her to finish school."

"So he's waiting?"

"Yeah, he's waiting."

"What was he talking about when we were at the table?"

"He wants you to keep your mouth shut about seeing him with the other women. If you do, he's willing to give you his marker if you decide to become a Last Rider."

"What does that mean?"

"That you'll get his vote without having to fuck him."

Diamond mumbled under her breath.

"What did you say?"

"Tell him I'll keep my mouth shut." Diamond's fingers laced through his on her stomach. "This feels good."

She wouldn't have said anything anyway, she had learnt from her father's club that certain things weren't to be talked about. Inevitably, sticking your nose where it didn't belong could get you in trouble, and Diamond didn't want trouble with Shade. She had seen how he had looked at Lily and was smart enough to know Lily was going to have to fight that battle on her own.

CHAPTER TWENTY-TWO

"Can I have one of these?" Diamond asked, picking up the tiny flashlight no bigger than her forefinger with a beam which was remarkably strong.

"No." Knox put one in the package they were putting together for a customer.

"Why not?" Diamond asked, clenching and unclenching the flashlight in her hand.

"Because you already have two other flashlights," Knox said, checking for the next item on the packing list.

"But this one charges when I squeeze it," Diamond said. "The other one is solar powered and the other one takes batteries. What if we lose power and there's no sunlight and I don't have batteries?"

"I'll get you one," Knox relented.

"Cool." Diamond helped him fill two more orders. Then, collecting the items for another order, she sat down on the stool at the table looking through the items.

"Can I have one of these?"

Knox didn't bother to look at what she had in her hand. "No."

"Why not?" Diamond asked. "I really need one of

these." Knox looked sideways at the backpack in her hand.

"No, you don't. I already bought you one last week. Why do you need another one?"

"I already made my bug-out bag, but I have to make yours now."

"You can have it. Now let's finish getting these orders out." Knox gave her an exasperated look, which she ignored. The Last Riders' survival business was more than successful, it was booming. He had volunteered for a couple of extra shifts while Viper and Winter interviewed new employees. Diamond had begun sitting with him while he filled the orders over the last month, but she often was more of a distraction than help.

"I have everything we need now except, Knox, I think we need to buy a small island," she said, picking up a pocketknife.

"A small island?" Knox turned toward her, taking the knife out of her hand.

"Yes." Diamond nodded enthusiastically. "Did you know that you can buy small islands? They're kind of expensive, but if we save, we could buy one in a few years."

"Diamond…" Knox started to say something, but closed his mouth. "Why an island?"

"Because zombies can't swim," she answered, placing another item in the box.

Knox just stared at her. "They can't?" Knox tried his hardest not to laugh when he saw she was serious.

"Can they?" she asked, looking at him with a quizzical expression.

"I don't know, but no more zombie movies for you for a while." Knox checked the list before taping the packaging closed and then taping the address onto the large box.

"Can I have…?" Diamond began.

Knox took the small tube tent from her hand. His hand going to her hair and tugging her head back for a soft kiss.

"Diamond," Knox growled.

"What?" she asked, returning his kiss.

"I think Sex Piston isn't the only nut in your family."

* * *

Diamond rolled over in the bed, kissing Knox's shoulder before getting ready for work. He was lying on his stomach, naked among the rumpled covers while her lips traced the tat on the back of his shoulder. She could recall it from memory; he had the Navy Seal insignia of an anchor wrapped along its length by a snake with the head at the top of the tat, giving an unnerving stare. A variety of objects surrounded the insignia; two revolvers pointed at each other with a metal chain linking the two together, a hand of cards, a razor knife and brass knuckles. The whole tat had a dark overlay, giving it a shadowed appearance.

Her lips went over each one, counting the objects. She had already figured out it was the club tattoo and had guessed who most of the symbols belonged to. Razer was the easiest; the razor Knife. Knox and Rider were obviously the Revolvers; Knox kept his near at all times. The lawyer in her was concerned until he had opened his wallet showing the concealed-carry permit. Rider also made no attempt to hide that he carried. Diamond didn't have to ask to see his; he had volunteered to show her. The chain, and playing cards were still mysteries to her. The snake was obviously Viper and the shading Shade. The Brass knuckles was the last one she had figured out when Cash had gotten in a fight with a drunk at Rosie's when they had stopped for a beer.

"You want to fuck?" Knox asked sleepily.

"We just did twenty minutes ago." Diamond laughed against his shoulder, rubbing her cheek against him.

"Keep doing that and you'll be doing it again in five," Knox mumbled into the pillow.

Diamond pulled away, laughing as she climbed reluctantly out of bed. "I can't. I have to go to work. I'm already late. Holly needs to talk to me before court. I think she's going to ask for a raise. I'm going to give it to her, she's certainly worth it."

Diamond showered and dressed, going back into her bedroom and smiling when she saw that Knox was sound asleep. Picking up her briefcase, she left, not wanting to wake him. Going down the short flight of steps, she pushed the unlock button on her new SUV. She still felt weird climbing into the expensive vehicle, but Knox had convinced her to spend the extra money to drive a safer vehicle.

* * *

Diamond smiled when she looked out her window and saw the buds on the trees; the pretty weather had tricked the trees into blooming early. Straightening up, she stretched, yawning. Holly had gone to lunch earlier. When she had opened her mouth to ask for the raise, Diamond had cut her off, giving her a nice raise and benefits, too. The surprised woman hadn't known what to say, so Diamond had given her a hug and told her to go to lunch.

She heard her front office door open and then saw Knox walking into her office, coming to a stop when he saw her behind her desk. She could tell from his face that he was going to try to walk away again. He didn't say anything, just stood there and stared at her. Diamonds eyes watered as she stood up from her desk, going to him. Sliding her hands tightly around his waist, she placed tiny kisses along his taut jaw.

"Please don't, please don't, please, baby, please..." Diamond pleaded.

"Dammit to hell!"

Diamond found herself backed across the room until her desk was at her back. Pressing her backwards onto her desk, her briefcase and cell phone fell to the floor as Knox swept them out of the way with his hand before going to her knee, bringing it up to his hip.

His fingers slid underneath her panties, finding her warm and ready for him. Tugging her skirt to her hips, he yanked at the material of her panties, tearing them apart. Diamond watched as he unzipped his jeans, bracing herself on the desk as he pulled out his cock.

"Knox?"

"What?" His disgruntled voice brought a tender smile to her lips.

"Could you close the blinds?"

* * *

Knox's boots crunched on the late spring frost as he got off his bike, parking it near the old fireplace on Cash's homestead property. He started the walk up the mountain path that had been made through generations of Cash's relatives. The steep path was kept clear by either him or Cash.

At the top of the mountain, he paused a second, looking down at the huge trees, seeing Treepoint in the distant valley below. Taking a deep breath, he released it, seeing the vapor in the cold morning air. He was glad he had made Diamond put on her coat as she left the clubhouse to go to church with Beth, Winter and Evie. The sunny day was deceptively cold and she would have frozen her ass off before she would have been able to get inside the SUV.

Knox turned, walking forward into Cash's family cemetery. The older tombstones mixed with the newer ones and told the amount of time the cemetery had been in existence. He stopped in front of a pink marble headstone, staring down.

Cash had offered a final resting place for his young wife. Like him, she had no family, so he had accepted Cash's offer.

"Sunshine." His aching voice filled the silence of the cemetery.

He dropped to his knees beside her grave, not feeling the coldness of the frozen grass through his clothes. Knox's voice broke as he talked to her.

"I promised I'd love you forever, that no one would

217

ever take your place. Sunshine, I tried not to love her. I tried to stay away and break it off, but I couldn't. When I realized that I loved her, I tried not to let her have my soul. To keep a part for you; to keep a part of me with you. Always, Sunshine, that's what I promised you on our wedding day and the day I buried you here on this mountain.

"But I have to give someone else those promises now. I love her, Sunshine. She's become a part of my life, and when I look into her eyes, I see the same promises I gave you. Promises I need to give her now. I'm not leaving you behind me; you'll always be with me, a part of mine and Diamond's life."

Knox felt a warm touch on his shoulder; the warmth flowed through his body as he turned to see who was behind him.

"I'm sorry, I didn't want to startle you." Rachel Porter stared down at him, her hand still on his shoulder. Her gaze went to the tombstone before coming back to his. "My parents are buried over there. I like to bring Mom flowers every Sunday after Church, catch her up on what's going on in our lives. She wouldn't be very happy with my brothers carrying on the family business. She never cared about how much money it provided, she always said 'God may not give you what you want, but He will provide for your needs'." Rachel removed her hand, stepping back. Without another word she walked to the end of the cemetery to stand in front of two graves, laying the flowers down on one.

Knox sat there with the sunshine on him, feeling the guilt he had felt for the last months melt away like the frost on the grass, removing the final barrier from giving Diamond his love.

CHAPTER TWENTY-THREE

Diamond came out of church with Evie, Beth and Winter and each of them took their turns complimenting Pastor Dean on his service as they left.

"You're becoming a regular at my services and I haven't heard any Adele lately. I take it you're doing well?"

Diamond blushed with the other women listening. "Yes."

Pastor Dean laughed at her reaction, however Diamond managed to evade further questions when another parishioner came up behind her.

They walked to Beth's SUV in the church parking lot, each of them climbing inside except Diamond.

"I'm going to go to my office to do some paperwork I need to get done before court tomorrow. I'll call Knox when I need a ride home."

"You sure?" Beth asked.

"Yes, I'd rather get it done in an hour instead of having to do it tonight."

"Want us to give you a lift?"

"I think I can manage the walk," Diamond said, smiling.

"See you later then," Beth said, closing the door as the

other two women waved.

Diamond walked across the parking lot, crossing the empty street to go inside the quiet office building. As she went to unlock the building, she found it already unlocked. She wasn't terribly surprised because there was usually someone always was in the building that had four offices; two on the bottom and two on the top. Her office faced the street and the insurance office that shared the top floor with her had the part that faced the back. Someone had probably had an accident, which was why someone was ordinarily in the insurance office.

Diamond went up the steps to her office only to find the insurance office's lights were off. Frowning, she went to her office door starting to unlock it, when the door suddenly opened and she stood facing her secretary.

"Holly, what are you doing—" A sudden push against her back cut her off and had her falling forward into her office. Holly tried to catch her, but a hand pushed her back out of the way. Diamond heard her office door slammed shut as she landed on her hands and knees.

"Stop it, Mitch!" Holly screamed as Diamond was lifted off her feet and dragged from the front to her private office.

"Shut up, Holly." The man Holly called Mitch flung her forward. Diamond fell against her desk which looked like it had been ransacked.

"I don't understand," Diamond said, looking at Holly who was staring at her with frightened eyes.

"I'm so sorry, Diamond. I didn't mean for this to get so out of control."

"Get what you need, Holly, so we can get out of here."

Holly ignored Mitch. "I've tried talking to you several times, but either you were too busy or I got scared and chickened out. I didn't know what to do," Holly began.

"Holly?" A small child's voice from the couch drew Diamond's attention.

"It's okay, Logan. Just sit there, we're going to leave in

a few minutes," Holly said.

Diamond looked at the little boy and recognition dawned. "Oh, God, is that…?"

Holly nodded, her eyes pleading for understanding. "Vincent Bedford hired me to be Logan's nanny. He rented a house for us in Jamestown, but when he was arrested, Samantha moved us here to Treepoint to be closer to her. She ran out of money when her father went to jail, so I quit taking a salary from her and got a job supporting us. Mitch, my boyfriend, watched him while I was at work. We were going to go somewhere else. Sam wanted a fresh start. The day Samantha died she called and said she had enough to get us out of town.

"Then after she died, I didn't know what to do. That day you handed me those notes about Samantha's grandmother, I didn't know she even had any relatives. I was afraid that, with Samantha dead, everyone would think I did it or had kidnapped Logan. I didn't know what to do." Holly took a deep breath.

"We need to go, Holly," Mitch said.

"Holly, there's no need to run. You haven't done anything wrong. Why did you come to the office today?"

"I saved enough so that we could leave Treepoint, but I wanted to see Sam's autopsy report. Logan gets sick a lot and we couldn't get insurance since Sam is dead. I thought, if I could see her autopsy report, I could find out what's wrong with him. I've looked everywhere for it and couldn't find it, so I figured you kept it in your locked drawer which I didn't have a key for. Mitch was going to break it for me then we were going to leave town tonight."

Diamond took a closer look at the dark, curly haired boy who looked exactly like his father. His skin was pale and he had dark circles under his eyes. He was a beautiful little boy, but he didn't have the healthy glow to his cheeks as he should have.

"We're still leaving," Mitch snapped at Holly.

Diamond ignored Holly's boyfriend, trying to make

Holly understand the seriousness of Logan's possible condition.

"Samantha died of a genetic kidney disease, Holly. He needs to see a physician as soon as possible."

"Oh, God." Holly looked at Mitch. "What are we going to do? I don't have the kind of money that will cost." Tears came to her eyes as she went to the silent child, lifting him into her arms.

"You don't have to, Holly. His father will help. If not, there are programs that—"

"Mitch?" Holly looked at her boyfriend for guidance.

"Let's go, Holly. You found out what we needed to know. If we stay here, you'll lose the kid. Is that what you want?"

"No, but I don't want him sick, either."

"I'm not staying in this town. Make up your mind; either stay here or go with me."

"I don't give a damn what either of you do, but that kid isn't going anywhere," Pastor Dean said, coming into the room.

Relief flooded Diamond, knowing that Pastor Dean would be able to prevent them leaving with Logan until Mitch drew a gun from the pocket of his jacket.

"Mitch, no!"

"I'm leaving, Holly. Let's go; either take the kid or leave him, but you're going with me."

"I can't leave Logan," Holly said, crying. "Put the gun away, Mitch."

"Then I guess we're taking him." Mitch turned the gun on Pastor Dean.

Diamond watched in stunned amazement as the Pastor moved forward, jerking Mitch's gun hand upwards. Mitch struggled, trying to regain control when Pastor Dean's other hand snapped out, hitting Mitch's nose with enough force to snap the man's head back, sending him crumpling to the floor.

As soon as Mitch was down, Diamond went to her

desk where she picked up the phone to call the sheriff. Holly stood, crying and holding Logan close as she rocked him. Diamond talked briefly to the dispatcher before hanging up while Pastor Dean stood over Mitch, holding the gun while the groggy man began to regain consciousness.

"Don't move." Pastor Dean cocked the gun, pointing it at Mitch's head as he lay back down, not moving.

"Diamond?" Holly screamed as the sheriff barreled into the room.

"Holly?" Logan cried, twining his arms around her neck.

"It's okay, Logan. Holly, calm down. I'll help you get this straightened out."

Holly stared at her in hope. "I'm sorry I handled this so badly, I don't deserve your help."

"Holly, you might be my secretary, but you're also my friend."

"You're going to let me keep my job?" Holly wasn't alone in her surprise. Pastor Dean and the sheriff were taken aback by Diamond's gesture as well.

"Of course, you didn't commit any crime. Samantha hired you to take care of her child. That's not against the law, and I gave you access to my office. You got in with the key I gave you, didn't you?"

"Yes." Holly's lips trembled.

"Holly, you were only trying to do what you thought was in the best interest of Logan. I can't fault you with that, neither can the law. Everything is going to be all right."

Holly finally breathed a sigh of relief, loosening her hold on Logan who gradually quieted.

"Well, now that it's settled that she didn't commit a crime, how about that man lying on the floor with a gun pointed at his head?" The sheriff gestured toward Mitch.

"Him, you can arrest for attempted murder," Pastor Dean spoke before Diamond could. *He shouldn't worry,*

Diamond thought, *I'm going to make sure Mitch stays in prison for a long time.*

Her eyes lifted to Pastor Dean. "You saw them through the window, didn't you?

"Yes."

Damn, he had seen Knox and her that afternoon that Knox had ignored her request to close the blinds. His amused expression didn't try to hide the fact that he had gotten quite a show. She was buying curtains for the window the first chance she got. The man had gotten his last show of her and Knox.

* * *

Diamond answered Mrs. Langley's door when the knock sounded. The Porters stood on the porch, white faced and nervous. The law didn't faze them, but the prospect of a child frightened them to death.

"Come in." Diamond opened the door wider, letting the family of four enter then closed the door behind them, motioning the Porters into the living room.

Holly sat on the couch with Logan as Mrs. Langley sat on his other side. Diamond had not been able to hold back her tears when Mrs. Langley had seen her great-grandson for the first time. Diamond again received all the reassurance she needed that she was doing the right thing when she saw the Porters' reaction. Dustin took a hesitant step forward as his sister and brothers hung back, letting Dustin meet his son without their overwhelming the small boy.

"Are you sure he's mine." Dustin was trying not to embarrass himself, but unable to keep his eyes from watering.

"Pending a DNA test, we're pretty sure," Diamond reassured him. "I think the curly hair and the eyes are pretty good clues, but I think what she named him confirms it."

"What did she name him?"

"She named him Logan. That was your father's name,

wasn't it?" Mrs. Langley asked Dustin. Diamond could tell Dustin almost lost it at the name of his son.

"I told Sam when we married and had kids I was going to name my son after my dad." His hoarse voice had Rachel bursting into tears. Greer put his arm around his sister's shoulder.

Dustin carefully walked closer to the little boy sitting silently by Holly's side. Slowly he dropped to his knees.

"Hello, Logan. Welcome home."

CHAPTER TWENTY-FOUR

Diamond came out of her office, running late again. She hated being late when Knox was with her; he always used it as an excuse to punish her with one of his diabolical tortures. Driving home, she saw him already sitting in the parking lot as she pulled in.

"Damn," Diamond said.

She saw the smile on his mouth as she went inside to grab her overnight bag. She came back down, handing him the overnight case, which he tied onto the back of his bike.

"It would be easier if you just left a few extra outfits at the clubhouse," Knox said, getting onto the bike before handing her his helmet.

"I would if they would still be there when I needed them. The women can swipe clothes from you while you're still wearing them." Knox laughed, starting the motor. His easy grin sent her heart soaring as much as the ride to the clubhouse.

The last month since Dustin had found his son had been good. The DNA results had come back proving without a doubt Dustin was the father and Holly had worked out an arrangement with Dustin so that she could remain in Logan's life. Holly had remained Diamond's secretary as well without the constant fear of someone finding out her secret. It had given the woman a boost of confidence that Diamond hadn't seen in her before.

Knox had changed in the last month also; more easygoing and affectionate with her. When she left him in the morning, she no longer worried that it would be the last. Holly wasn't the only one who had gained some confidence.

As his bike pulled into the clubhouse parking lot, the club was already busy for a Friday night. Knox packed her suitcase up the steps. When they entered, the crowd was already making it hard to fit inside the room.

"There a lot of people here tonight," Diamond said.

"We're making one of the women a member tonight," Knox replied.

"Oh." Diamond's heart plunged. Sex Piston had told her that they had to have six votes out of the eight original members' votes to become a Last Rider. They had to have sex with the men or cause them to have an orgasm to get the vote.

As she went upstairs to get changed, her eyes studied the new faces of the women.

She tried not to think about the night ahead as she took a quick shower and dressed in Knox's room while he waited patiently for her. She had attended several Friday parties over the last months, but they had always ended up in his room alone after dinner. She didn't know who or how often he was with the other women because she had adopted 'the don't ask' attitude and buried the worry as deep as she could.

Never, Never Land was good. She didn't want to leave and was afraid that, if she asked and he told the truth, she would have to leave her make believe land and lose Knox. It was messed up the way she was thinking, but like any gambler that was going for the big money, she was all in.

She merely hoped when he was finished with her that she had enough money to pay the mortgage on her soul because that was her collateral.

Knox's eyes watched her dress in her new blue jean skirt that hugged her butt. The black camy she put on instead of her bra had his eyes lighting up, although when she picked up a sheer, black top that tied at her breasts, he was instantly getting off the bed.

Diamond hastily backed up against the door, her hands going to his chest.

"When did you get that outfit?"

"I went shopping with Jewell and Raci."

Knox's hand slid up the inside of her thighs, tugging the baby blue underwear off. "Knox, give my panties back."

"Nope, that's what you get for being late."

"I'm not going downstairs without my underwear," Diamond protested as he tossed her underwear onto the dresser.

"No one will even notice," he said as he propelled her out of the room.

Going down the steps, Diamond saw that the party had heated up since she had been upstairs. Jewell was between Rider's legs, sucking on his cock, and Ember was dancing with Cash and Train.

They went to the bar where Evie was talking to Shade and Bliss and Evie handed her a beer.

"Thanks, Evie."

"Did you eat dinner?" Knox asked, taking a drink of his own beer.

"Yes, I picked something up at the diner," Diamond said, not looking at Shade.

She had gotten to know him a little better over the last few months. Better than Winter or Beth did, that was for sure. He made no attempt to hide the women from her that shared his bed. Knox was a dominant lover, but Diamond had a feeling that Shade was the real deal. She was honestly unable to imagine the fragile Lily with a man that was as hard as Shade.

"Let's dance." Knox broke into her thoughts, took her hand, and led her onto the dance floor.

As they danced a couple of fast songs, their bodies sliding against each other, Diamond began feeling her body heat in desire. With no underwear on, she was self-conscious, yet the movement of her dancing brought constant friction against her uncovered pussy. When the lights went off and the side lamps were turned on, the music slowed. Knox turned her until her butt was against his crotch as they moved suggestively to the music, proving that he was as affected as she was with his hardened length tightening against her ass.

Afterward, they went back to the bar to finish their drinks. He grabbed each of them a bottled water before finding an empty couch to pull her down on. Sitting her down on his lap, he played with her knee while he nuzzled her cleavage.

"Knox." Diamond wiggled on his cock.

"You ready to go upstairs?"

"Yes." Diamond circled his neck as he rose to his feet, lifting her and carrying her up the steps. At the top of the steps, Diamond noticed Viper's door had remained open.

"That's only the second time since Viper's been with pretty girl that he's allowed anyone in." Diamond had learned the hard way that an opened bedroom door meant that whoever was inside was inviting the members to watch or participate. One night she had gone into Jewell's room to borrow shampoo and had been embarrassed to see her with Rider and Train.

Instead of turning into his bedroom, Knox continued down to Viper's room.

Diamond stiffened, not actually believing that he would seriously take her inside Viper's and Winter's room. She should not have underestimated him because he went inside without pausing.

Diamond's eyes widened in shock to see Winter completely naked, lying on the bed, her face a tortured mask of desire as Viper pumped his cock inside her pussy. Her lashes lifted, seeing Knox carrying Diamond into the room.

Knox sat down on the couch, turning Diamond as she sat so her back was to Winter and Viper. Her knees straddled his hips, his hand sliding up her thighs, pulling her tight skirt up until it was at her waist, baring her ass to the room.

"Knox…" Diamond started to protest.

"Give it a try. If you don't like it, we'll leave."

His hand went to the back of her neck, tugging her down so that his lips could take her in a passionate kiss that momentarily distracted her. His tongue licked her lips, sucking the bottom one into his mouth before releasing it to thrust his tongue into her mouth. He explored the moist warmth as his fingers glided across her clit, massaging the tender flesh until Diamond began to move her hand against his own hand. Moisture coated his fingers as one spread the fleshy lips to target the bundle of nerves that had Diamond ready to climax. Knox then pulled his finger away to thrust it inside her pussy.

Diamond couldn't prevent the low moan of pleasure that escaped her as he continued to escalate her passion until all feelings of self-consciousness disappeared and all that mattered was getting to have the orgasm he was steadily building.

"Bed or Couch?"

A male voice coming into the bedroom didn't register even when Viper answered, "Couch."

Train sat down next to Knox on the couch. His shirt was off, showing the muscular chest and his lean hips with his jean unsnapped and partially open.

Train didn't say anything and made no attempt to touch Diamond as he sat there, though.

Knox pulled off Diamond's sheer top then pulled off

her camy, letting Train see her breasts. Still, Train made no attempt to touch Diamond.

Diamond was almost able to come when she heard another male voice.

"Couch or bed?" Cash asked.

"Couch." Diamond heard Cash take a seat in the chair beside the couch. Diamond glanced sideways to see Bliss with nothing on her bottom and a white lace top that had nothing on underneath.

Diamond tried to tell herself to get out and run away back to Knox's bedroom. She knew it would make no difference to him. He would spend the night fucking her, but there was just that extra bit of spice, having him play with her in front of so many men.

She saw Cash unbutton his jeans and pull out his cock. Putting on a condom, he lifted Bliss then lowered her onto himself. Diamond's head fell onto Knox's shoulder.

"Watch him fuck her; it's hot as hell." Diamond turned her head, watching as Bliss moved herself up and down on Cash.

Knox lifted Diamond, setting her on Train's lap while he undid his jeans, pulling out his cock. He looked up at her, staring at her mouth. Diamond couldn't believe what she did next, going down on Knox, sucking his cock into her mouth. She drew him in deep, giving him her mouth the way he wanted it.

"That's it, Diamond," Knox growled. His hands went to her hair, holding her to him as he thrust within her mouth.

She played with his piercing around the head of his cock until Knox's dick hardened as he began to come. Diamond sat up when she was done, proud of herself that he hadn't been able to last long.

Knox stood up, looking down at Diamond, leaving her on Train's lap. He turned her to face Viper's bed so she could get a better view of Cash and Bliss. Going to his knees, he spread her legs before his hand went to his mouth.

"Diamond, you're going to enjoy this."

Knox's face dropped to her pussy, licking her clit, almost making her come with one stroke. As his tongue ring rubbed against her silken flesh, Diamond felt a tingling and couldn't understand the sensation, too overwhelmed with desire to realize what was going on.

"What?" Diamond asked.

Train's naked back laughed at her reaction. "He must have in his mini vibrator." Train's mouth went to her neck, whispering against the tender flesh. "He never do you with it before?" He then moved his hands to Diamond's breasts, squeezing her nipples tight until Diamond whimpered. He held them for several seconds before releasing them. The slight sting of painful pleasure had Diamond's hips thrusting against Knox's vibrating tongue. Diamond thought for a second she was going to lose consciousness it felt so good. When Diamond stiffened, her climax brought a relief because she hadn't been sure she could have taken much more.

Knox pulled her away from Train, taking a seat on the couch and reseating her on his lap. Diamond was shaking and breathing hard. Knox soothed her body, rubbing his hand up and down her thigh. Winter's moans could be heard from the bed, but Diamond didn't have the energy to watch.

Train went over to Bliss who was still on Cash's lap. When she leaned to the side, taking his cock into her mouth, Trains hiss of pleasure left no doubt that he wasn't going to last long. Knox stood with Diamond's limp body pliant against his chest. Her face was buried in his neck as he carried her back to his bedroom, shutting the door with his foot. He carried her to the bed, laying her down on the comforter.

"Are you okay?" Knox asked as he pulled off her skirt and shoes.

"Mmm-hmm," Diamond mumbled. Knox smiled and

lay down next to her, lifting her to his chest. As Diamond lay across him, her thigh lifted to rest across his hips.

"You going to knee me in the nuts for doing that?"

"No; I should, but I feel too good to bother doing it right now."

Knox's hand smoothed out the tangled curls. "Diamond?"

"Knox, I'm not pissed, but if you keep bugging me, I might become pissed. You're messing with my afterglow."

Knox's chest shook against her cheek. "I wouldn't want to do that, go to sleep. We need to talk tomorrow." Diamond pretended to go to sleep, feeling Knox relax under her. She worried until dawn lit the sky that the talk he wanted involved her return to reality.

Much later, Diamond rolled over, half-asleep. Looking over at the clock, she saw that it was afternoon. Turning to wake Knox, Diamond wasn't surprised to find him gone.

Wendy and Peter Pan had never had their happy ending and neither would she.

CHAPTER TWENTY-FIVE

Diamond had just gotten out of the shower and dressed when her cell phone rang. Her stomach sank when she saw it was Knox calling.

"Hello"

"You finally awake, sleepyhead?" Knox's cheerful voice had her sagging spirits lifting.

"Yes, I just got out of the shower."

"Good." His voice turned serious. "I want you to meet me at this address in an hour." Diamond's spirits dropped again. "Beth said you can borrow her SUV, the keys are already in the ignition.

"What's the address?" Diamond knew that there was no use in putting off the inevitable.

She repeated the address back to him before hanging up. Diamond sat down on the side of the bed, looking at the clock as she watched the minutes click past, one after another. She had become fairly familiar with Treepoint and with Knox's instructions was sure she would have no trouble finding the house.

When she had no choice other than to leave or be late, which she was tempted to do, but she couldn't bring herself to keep Knox deliberately waiting. She got to her feet, straightened her shoulders, and gathered her pride, determined this time to accept his decision without breaking down and pleading with him not to stop seeing her. As she went out of his room and down the stairs, she missed the concerned looks everyone she passed gave her when they saw her white face.

She managed to keep her resolve all the way to Beth's SUV. Climbing in, she drove to town, and with each mile, her resolve weakened. She would only ask for more time once. When she was a couple miles away, she would only cry a little bit. By the time she pulled into the driveway of the big house she was unfamiliar with, she got out of the car and walked to the front door. Her resolve completely disappeared, knowing she would go down on her knees and beg if she had to. She wasn't going to let the big jerk go. Whatever he said, he was hers.

Diamond started to knock on the door, but the note taped to the door stopped her.

"Diamond the door is unlocked. Come in, I'm waiting."

Diamond read the short note twice before she gathered enough courage to open the door.

She stepped into the average-sized living room, which was completely unfurnished. Diamond took a hesitant step forward, seeing a suitcase sitting at the bottom of the steps. As she drew closer, she heard music from the upstairs. She slowly went up the steps until she reached the top where she saw a door opened and could hear the music pouring out from the room behind it. Diamond walked into the room and came to a stop.

"Knox." Her hand reached out, bracing herself in the doorway.

The bedroom was completely decorated with her bedroom furniture; her dresser, her chest of drawers, her chair with her nightgown on it. It was all exactly as she'd left it. Everything perfectly like it had been in her apartment except for the bed. It was a king size bed with a beautiful comforter on it.

"I don't understand," Diamond said.

"If you don't like it, we can pick out something else. I thought this wouldn't be too far from your office and would still be convenient for me to make a quick stop every now and then when we're not busy at the office."

Diamond didn't take her eyes off Knox.

"Are you wearing a... is that a..." Knox walked forward, moving to stand in front of her.

"A deputy's uniform," Knox said. "The sheriff wants to retire in a few months. He's tired, Diamond. He wants to leave the town in someone's hands he can trust. I'll be a deputy for a few months while he trains me before I take over as sheriff. The mayor has already okayed it and doesn't think the city council will cause any opposition."

"You're going to be the sheriff?" Diamond asked in disbelief.

"Yes. I'll have a regular job. I want you to move in here with me."

"Knox, are you sure?"

"Diamond, I'm sure. I love you." Knox went to his knees in front of her then, looking up at her, he said. "I need you. I don't expect you to believe me, but I can be the man you need. I can be reliable, faithful and there for you and our children. I love you, Diamond. I'll always love you. I haven't touched another woman since that first time with you."

"Even when we were apart those months?" Diamond asked in shock.

"Even then, that's why I gave my bed up," Knox told her.

"Knox, I love you, too." Diamond smiled down into his face. The shadows that were so much a part of him were gone. His beautiful eyes were clear, making no effort to hide his emotions from her.

At her words, he stood, picked her up, and laid her down on the bed. Knox then began pulling off his clothes, and Diamond sat up to take off her own.

She smiled as she crawled to the end of the bed. "What would you have done if I wasn't such a sure thing?"

"Diamond, you were never a sure thing. Even when you gave me everything you had, I thought you would give up and leave before I could straighten out my shit. I wanted you to stay at the same time that I was afraid you *would* stay. You were becoming more precious to me than the air I breathed. You showed your strength and love for me every day. I'm going to prove my love to you for the rest of my life."

"We don't have to live here. We could do like Razer and Shade; build our house near the clubhouse if you want," Diamond made the offer, leaving the choice to him.

"They'll always be my family, and now you're a member we'll for damn sure be going to some parties, but only on the nights that there's no one from town there."

"I was the new member voted in last night?" Diamond teased his nipple with her tongue.

"Yes. But we're going to be busy with my new job, getting married, fixing up our island."

Diamond's head moved away from his nipple. Not sure which one surprised her more.

"You bought us an island?"

"A tiny one in Florida."

Knox spread her thighs, placing his cock at her opening and thrusting deep, his piercing sliding across her vulnerable flesh. Diamond arched at the pleasure in her sheathe as he started to torture her nipple.

"I have a question," she said, holding onto him as he raised over her, reaching down to her pussy to spread her legs so that his piercings would rub against her clit every time his cock thrust inside her.

"What?"

"Do they make those vibrating rings for your cock, too?"

"Oh yeah," Knox groaned.

"Can I have one?"

Also by Jamie Begley

The Last Riders Series:

Razer's Ride

Viper's Run

Knox's Stand

The VIP Room Series:

Teased

The Dark Souls Series:

Soul Of A Man

ABOUT THE AUTHOR

"I was born in a small town in Kentucky. My family began poor, but worked their way to owning a restaurant. My mother was one of the best cooks I have ever known, and she instilled in all her children the value of hard work, and education.

Taking after my mother, I've always love to cook, and became pretty good if I do say so myself. I love to experiment and my unfortunate family has suffered through many. They now have learned to steer clear of those dishes. I absolutely love the holidays and my family put up with my zany decorations.

For now, my days are spent at work and I write during the nights and weekends. I have two children who both graduate next year from college. My daughter does my book covers, and my son just tries not to blush when someone asks him about my books.

Currently I am writing three series of books- The Last Riders that is fairly popular, The Dark Souls series, which is not, and The VIP Room, which we will soon see. My favorite book I have written is Soul Of A Woman, which I am hoping to release during the summer of 2014. It took me two years to write, during which I lost my mother, and brother. It's a book that I truly feel captures the true depths of love a woman can hold for a man. In case you haven't figured it out yet, I am an emotional writer who wants the readers to feel the emotion of the characters they are reading. Because of this, Teased is probably the hardest thing I have written.

All my books are written for one purpose- the enjoyment others find in them, and the expectations of my fans that inspire me to give it my best. In the near future I hope to take a weekend break and visit Vegas that will hopefully be next summer. Right now I am typing away on Knox's story and looking forward to the coming holidays. Did I mention I love the holidays?"

Jamie loves receiving emails from her fans,
JamieBegley@ymail.com

Find Jamie here,
https://www.facebook.com/AuthorJamieBegley

Get the latest scoop at Jamie's official website,
JamieBegley.net

Printed in Great
Britain
by Amazon